ATLANTIS RISING

Amy Cip

ATLANTIS RISING

Warning: Not intended for persons under the age of 18. May contain coarse language and mature content that may disturb some readers. Reader discretion advised.

Cover Art Design by: Kelly Moran/Rowan Prose Publishing
Photo Credit: Adobe Images/Deposit Photos
First Edition
ISBN: 9781961967465
Rowan Prose Publishing, LLC
www.RowanProsePublishing.com
Published in the United States of America

Prologue

All this time, the wise folk of the world were looking for Atlantis in the wrong places. The great city of old wasn't flooded under a vast body of water, as the stories told, nor was it buried under sand in the desert. The sorcerers and the witches saw to it that the city was never in any place one would look. Unless, of course, one looked *up*, and only under the right set of circumstances. It was a shadow passing across the sky during the full moon, a billowy cloud with angles that jutted out in odd directions. It was a sharp gust of wind, meant to make you look the other way.

The king of Atlantis was many things, but a fool was not one of them. His kingdom was under attack. The time of magic was over, at least the type of magic found in Atlantis: magic built on love and goodness, could move mountains, change hearts, heal. The people of Atlantis were hunted, surrounded by enemies on all sides.

"Love has lost." Queen Aura squeezed the polished marble banister that overlooked the city. The view was once a joy, but beyond the great walls, dark clouds gathered. Lightning flashed. She felt the rumble of the city, a heartbeat of unease. They sensed what was coming.

"Perhaps for now." The king gently unclenched her pale fingers from the banister and lifted her hand for a brief kiss. A wolf howled in the distance. Lightning illuminated peaks of far-off mountains and highlighted concern in the queen's light blue eyes, but only for a moment before darkness again hid her features. "Love will not lose the final battle." He paused. "But perhaps it must retreat. The world is not ready yet. But it will be one day."

His breath fogged in the evening chill, and he coughed. The queen shuddered but not from the weather. The great sun had set in the western sky and the evening brought ill tidings. Where the citizens of Atlantis once danced in the streets, most now holed up in their homes afraid.

"How will we know when the time comes to return?" she asked. A tear had formed in the corner of her eye. It reflected the full moon as it slid down her cheek.

King Corin wiped it with his thumb. "The mages have foreseen there will be one strong enough to break the spell and bring the world back together, someday... when the world is ready." He looked up, his face pale in the low light. The wind whipped the blue and white flag at the top of the tallest spire.

She followed his gaze, but the moon slipped behind a cloud and left the flag in shadow. "And you trust them?" she asked, though she knew better. Several members of her own family were his advisors. Tasked with seeing the future, they saw only death unless Atlantis fled. The spell was the only chance they stood, and even then – the future was hazy. It was left to a girl with great magic and love, sometime far in the future.

His shoulders slumped. She'd forgotten what a heavy burden it was that he carried. "I must," he said simply. "Come." He offered his arm, and she took it, sparing a last look at the city streets at night. "Send word," he instructed his closest guard as they walked inside the great double doors. "Tomorrow it is to be done."

Casius nodded, sweeping the cloak off his shoulders as he opened the door. "Shall I alert the city?" he asked.

The king looked back. His face paled and the lines there deepened. "Let them rest," he said, running a hand over his chin. He was past his prime but not yet in old age. Too young to make such important calls, but too old to be impetuous. "They will need it."

His wife squeezed his arm. Casius was the last to follow them through the door. He looked over the city in the moonlight. His home. If he doubted the king, he could never let it show. But there was a certain tilt to his head, a certain squint of his eyes, that if you looked close enough, would betray sadness. Casius was younger than the king, and while he loved Atlantis, he longed to explore the world beyond its walls, and without warning, there were sure to be Atlanteans left behind. Friends. Family even. And someday, a girl who could break the spell. How would she ever know? A plan formed in Casius' mind. Was it treason to flee the city and wait to assist its return? Or could he be content to simply wait in the prison the king was planning?

In the morning, the city would be cursed to the skies, until the one came who would set them free. Until the time where love and magic were again welcome in the world. Until the time an unknown woman rose into her power.

Chapter 1

Devil's Island, Maine might be a rich folk's vacation playground in the short summer season, but to Ember Weathers, there was no worse, more dead-end spot to be stuck living out her twenties. While the state in its whole was known as vacationland, the three hundred or so full-time residents suffered the long winters only to kowtow to demanding tourists in the summer season. Those tourists made the town rich in creativity and crafters, not to mention a development of huge mansions on the north shore, but to Ember it had always felt like the island had sold its soul. It *was* named Devil's Island, after all. Perhaps the devil wasn't a little forked man at all, but instead a feeling of apathy.

Her folks hadn't felt that way. She remembered fondly how her dad used to say there were worse ways to put food on the table, but she only heard his voice in her memory now. He'd been gone three years, and her mom with him. The accident had put her older sister in long term care on the mainland and put an end to Ember's brief two years of college, as well as any dreams of leaving the island. Overnight she'd become an orphan and full-time proprietor of the island's only book shop, the Third Chapter. An inside joke, her dad always used to say the third chapter was when things started getting good.

She never did have the heart to clean out their place, though she'd moved into the apartment over the shop and sold the old house on the bluff to a developer who never developed it. The fact that it stood empty broke her heart, but at the same time saved her a headache in storage. Her folks' old stuff, including her mom's paintings, were safely stored in the attic. Ember couldn't bear to look at them, not without remembering her mother's stories of faraway lands and important fates and destiny. Fairy tales and nothing more. Just because her mom made them up and illustrated them beautifully didn't make them any more real. Destiny was dying in a crash on I95 on the way to an appointment in the city. Fate was a bitch.

Owning the shop gave her leeway with work hours, at least in the off season, and at the moment the season was as off as it came. Frost crept in from the corners of the door's oval window as she turned the old sign to open, mostly for show, no one would come by mid-January. The bay window behind the register gave her a view of the hilly main street which had been dusted with snow overnight. Across the street, Rudy was shoveling the walk to the town's pharmacy as an icy mist came down, a harsh scraping mixed with his occasional smoker's cough.

Aside from the market and post office just visible down the hill, the other boutiques, restaurants, and stores were closed up tightly. A little farther down, the waves peaked in the storm's early gusts and Ember figured the ferry would cancel for the day. The shop's forced hot air shuddered on, only barely covering the faint noise of ripping mixed with a low growl. *Not again*, Ember thought.

"Draco!" she scolded, as she frowned and pulled the curtain closed. Best Rudy not think she was talking to herself again. She already had a reputation as the girl who lost her marbles when her folks died. Little did they know she'd lost her marbles long before that.

The faint smell of smoke led the way to the reading nook at the back of the store, and it wasn't from the fireplace that had just about died overnight. Ember was in no hurry to chase down the source. It had been scourging her all week, and when she reached the back, the situation was exactly as she suspected.

"I keep telling you, they're not magic." She nudged the little dragon with the toe of her boot. Draco had been sure the delivery of placemats the week before were actually magic carpets and insisted on taking each one out and unraveling it. Perhaps because she'd named him during her Harry Potter phase, or perhaps because he was, after all—an invisible dragon—he loved the idea of magic. The small purple and white beast sat curled on an actual carpet (also not magic) by the fireplace at the back of the store, dutifully ripping it apart one strand at a time with his tiny fangs.

He huffed and looked at her with big, golden eyes – eyes only she could see. She rolled her own in response. It was too late to fix the placemat. Might as well let him destroy it. She ruffled the soft fur on top of his head, and he let out a contented puff of smoke from his little nostrils. Funny enough, the smoke was the only thing other people could see, and he'd set off many false alarms. The residents of Devil's Island might have thought the store was haunted, if they believed in such things. Most of them just thought the Weathers' were plain weird, and that's saying a lot in an artistic community.

She stepped on a singed thread and opened the door of the wood stove where the ash from the day before still smoldered. "Go to it," she told the little dragon as she placed a log inside. Draco abandoned the "magic" carpet and puffed out his chest to waddle to the stove. Taking a big puff of air, he blew the smallest stream of fire. She'd have to stoke it, but it was more than he could do the year before.

She had no idea how long imaginary dragons lived or when he would reach maturity, but she'd taken to teaching him tricks. One of which was managing not to burn down the building now that he could breathe fire. It was especially dangerous for him to be in the reading nook, surrounded by all the warm shelves and soft chairs and rugs overlaid with rugs, but she couldn't keep him from the fire. As if on cue, he happily curled up in front of it as she stoked the flames until they took.

She plopped down next to him, content to spend the next few hours with one of the classics from the shelf behind her. Inventory could wait—and bills? Well, they could wait longer. She'd been able to see the dragon since she was a girl, but a few forced hospitalizations taught her to keep her mouth shut. Now that her folks were gone and the island was quiet, they had the whole world to themselves. She took down an old copy of the *Canterbury Tales*. Draco soaked up stories of any kind. As far as she knew, the dragon couldn't speak in return, but sometimes she saw images she knew he projected. Some made sense—like the placemats and the magic carpets. Some were visions of far-off lands in the clouds, a man, seeking… a crimson cloak. The scene was so close to her mom's paintings Ember wondered if she weren't just making it all up. Her mom had never been able to see the dragon, and her tales were only bedtime stores.

Ember hoped she'd learn more as the dragon grew. There were more things she didn't know about Draco than what she did, starting with where he came from.

"*When good King Arthur ruled in ancient days,*" she began, then paused. Draco lifted his neck and narrowed his eyes, letting out a low growl. "Was that the door?" she asked, imagining she heard the tiny bell hanging from its corner. Indeed, she heard deep bootsteps and scrambled up. Draco rose to his feet and raised his hackles.

"Back off," she hissed. Though they couldn't see him, she didn't need Draco attacking the customers, or even worse, the locals.

"I'm afraid it *is* a customer." The man stood in the doorway of the nook, hat in hand and water dripping from his hair and beard, both a shade of amber brown that looked like it had drunk in the summer sunshine. Both were neat, if a little overgrown, and his hair started to show the slightest curl. He wasn't a local, that much she knew. She climbed to her feet.

"I'm sorry, I wasn't expecting anyone this time of year," she said, trying not to look back at Draco who'd begun huffing smoke which was quickly filling the room.

The man flashed a smile and waved his hat. "It's awful smokey in here." He coughed and looked over her shoulder at the fireplace. "Would you like me to take a look at that?"

Ember shot a look at Draco. "No, it's fine. The ventilation isn't good in this room. Let's head up front."

She slipped past him, smelling something that distinctly didn't belong on the island, but she couldn't quite express what. "We don't get many customers in the off season," she said, looking back to make sure he was following. He took a last look around the nook, his gaze lingering on Draco long enough to make Ember wonder, but then he shook his head again and turned.

"Yes, I'm sorry I'm afraid it was a bit of an emergency. Couldn't wait until spring." She couldn't place his accent, but it was musical. They had their share of foreign tourists, but in February? She opened the curtain and turned on the coffee maker which hummed. Rudy was gone, the main street empty. It should have made her nervous, but there hadn't been any crime on Devil's Island in forever, and if he were on the island for ill intent, he sure wasn't making a good start of it.

"Can I interest you in coffee or tea?" she asked.

"Tea would be lovely." His dark gaze darted around the store, and he smiled warmly. "It's a lovely place here, Mrs. Weathers."

Ember felt a flush crawl up her cheek as she fussed with the tea bag. "You can call me Ember," she corrected, handing him a ceramic mug from one of their local crafters.

"Oh. I thought this place was owned by a couple…" he trailed off, a question in his eyes she did not wish to answer.

"I'm afraid they passed away. I'm their daughter. Proprietor."

Emotion flashed in his eyes. "I'm terribly sorry," he said, though she read more than sympathy there.

"What brings you here?" She turned to escape the intensity of his gaze, making herself a cup of coffee. Draco took up a position at the end of the nonfiction aisle and watched this newcomer with narrowed eyes. She prayed there would be no fire.

"I'm an art collector," he explained. "Among other things." He placed the mug down on the weathered counter to fish out a business card from his coat pocket. It displayed a simple phone number. White writing on stark black with no additional information.

"There are plenty of galleries and artists here in season." She moved a quilt and sat on the stool behind the counter. "I'm afraid you'll have to chase them down one by one if that's what you're interested in, but I can offer you a souvenir on the way out." She gestured vaguely to the assortment of earrings and plastic animals next to the counter, along with a collection of *The History of Devil's Island* in paperback, which she'd never gotten around to reading.

He sipped his tea and looked at the walls of the store, covered with shelves and books. *What was he thinking*? she wondered. She sipped her own black coffee.

"I was looking for a particular piece by Maeve Weathers." He met her eyes as if studying her reaction to her mother's name. She blew on her coffee and played it cool. "And I'm prepared to pay greatly for it," he added.

Chapter 2

Ember eyed the newcomer who'd blown into the store like the storm they were expecting later, but she couldn't figure out if he'd be a passing shower or a category 5. When she hadn't replied to his offer right away, he took his mug and walked to the door, wiping a circle in the frost on the window to observe the empty downtown street. His face reflected in the dampness, but she couldn't tell if it were seriousness or humor reflected in his dark eyes. Light snowflakes drifted down, but that wasn't the reason Ember's pulse picked up.

With such a small population, it wasn't hard to tell when someone didn't belong on the island, but he didn't fit the profile of a tourist. It wasn't just the accent that gave him away, but his khakis and lined jacket were out of place, too fitted for the in-season crowd, a little too beat up, even paired with the sturdy boots. And where had the cap come from? Somewhere Ember couldn't afford, she guessed.

She considered his offer to buy her mother's art. After the sale of her folk's house, Ember had enough money to live comfortably, but there were still outstanding student loans for a degree she'd never finished and a life she'd never live, not after the accident at least, not to mention the store's inventory and day to day expenses. Living on an island wasn't cheap, and the last couple of years the bookstore had barely broken even. Ember squeaked by, and that was putting it mildly. That degree in English lit was a long lost dream now. She'd shelved it, along with any other dreams of traveling off the island. This was her life now. Whatever was left she sent for her sister's care, and Sierra needed a lot of care.

But what was he doing here? As far as Ember knew, her mother had never shared her artwork with anyone on the island or off. The tales she told were only bedtime stories, their little secret. Ember thought they'd died with her mom, the paintings of the city in the sky long forgotten. He held his cap in one hand, and she noticed the way the light played on his dark hair. He was a category 5 for sure. He drew a smiley face in the frost then turned with a grin, one Ember didn't fall for.

"What do you know about my mother's art?" she asked. It was too late to sound casual. He'd seen her reaction, but she'd also seen his. He hadn't known her mother died, and he wanted that artwork. Badly.

The grin slipped from his face. The smiley face began to melt and streak in drops. Wind shook the door and gently rang the bell, a whimsical charm that didn't match the feeling inside. Ember kept one eye on her dragon as Draco circled around to check the newcomer from the back. The dragon's hackles were still raised. Ember's were too.

"If this is some kind of joke…" she started. She knew what they said about her on the island. Just because her graduating class was all of twenty students didn't mean there weren't mean girls on the island, some of them middle-aged and owning the same stores Ember now worked alongside. She felt a flush rise in her cheeks and tried to hide behind her long bangs, but her hair was too short. Damn that last cut that she'd done herself.

"It's not a joke," he interrupted. He looked back and frowned as he wiped the face off the door, but a shadow of it stayed behind. He tucked his sleeve down and turned back, crossing the space between them to replace the still steaming mug on the counter.

"I'm sorry, I'm afraid I thought I'd be having a different conversation." He rubbed his forehead. "It's difficult to know where to start. Did she tell you at all about…" He tipped his head. She noticed a dark ring around his irises, a rare trait they shared. He struggled for his next words. "About her artwork?"

Draco nudged his way closer, sniffing the man's pantleg. The dragon communicated in images he sent, and the images he sent now were confusing to say the least, ones of her mother's stories of a city in the clouds and a man in a crimson cloak. Ember realized her mistake when she looked over his shoulder and smiled gently at Draco's aggravated huff. The man looked down directly at the dragon. His eyes widened, looking from one to the other. "You can…"

"… see him?" she finished.

They waited a beat, each hoping the other would explain first. Ember caught her breath. Was this man a figment of her imagination? Another delusion? Over the years, her doctors had thrown diagnoses about mental health, at least until Ember pretended to stop seeing the dragon and play along. Was this another hallucination? She measured her breath and opened her mouth to speak when she inhaled smoke and heard Draco's low growl.

"Oh, shit," was the only thing that came out. The stranger's eyes widened. He turned just in time to see the dragon lift his head and take aim at the red curtain around the bay window on the other side of the door. The window currently held a promo for the latest mystery that Ember thought would be a big seller in season, but not if it was burned to a crisp. Draco might be invisible to other people, but his flames could burn the place down.

She grabbed the fire extinguisher, which had seen good use the last few months, but suddenly everything seemed to go in slow motion. A wave hit her when she passed the visitor. His eyes were trained on the dragon, but not in fear or shock. The ring around his irises glowed. Slowly, he held a hand out and mumbled words in a language Ember didn't know, but Draco seemed to. It cut off the stream mid-roar, if that's what you could call it. Draco slowly turned to him. The flames licked the bottom of the curtain and petered out.

Time picked up again. Ember tripped, going headfirst into the display and knocking the novels all over the floor, but not, at least, catching herself on fire. The first thing she did when she got her bearings was search for the flame, but the curtains were out, only a singe mark remaining.

"How did you do that?" She rubbed her shoulder, which had caught the corner of the closest bookshelf. Draco didn't just breathe fire, but some special really hard to extinguish fire. She didn't want to use the word magic, but what else would you call it? She'd taken to ordering boxloads of extinguishers online, and sometimes it took a whole canister.

His eyes no longer gleamed, and she wondered if she imagined it. Now, they only looked tired. She hadn't noticed the bags under them before, or the lines on his face.

"It's complicated," he said, offering his hand. She got up as gracefully as she could and brushed off her pants. It was only her pride that was wounded, but at the moment she was more worried about her mental health than physical. He held her hand a beat longer than he needed to and stared directly into her eyes. Ember had always thought they were nothing special, she'd inherited her mom's simple hazel irises that were sometimes gray, sometimes green, but mostly muddy brown with that same circle her mom used to call magic. "You are her daughter, indeed." Finally, a smile crossed on his face. She pulled her hand back. "I'm known as Shepherd. It's as good of a name as any, but you can call me Shep. Your mother and I conversed for a long time. Oh, here. Her last letter."

He placed his cap on the counter and dug an envelope out of his inside jacket pocket. Ember waved the smoke out of the store and righted a few of the books. Across the street, Rudy sat on his stoop smoking, but one of the locals walking by caught his attention. Thank goodness, she thought, how would she explain this? She still wasn't sure it was real.

Shepherd showed her an envelope, small and the palest of blue. Ember's hand shook as she looked at it. The writing was her mother's familiar, loopy script. She came across it still on old invoices or recipes or scraps of paper that refused to be lost. The envelope had his name and an address in Boston.

"You're from Boston?" she asked, the silliest question, really, but one that would take up the space she needed to form her real question. It was swimming around her head, refusing to make itself into words. Because once she put it into words, she'd have to utter them, and the things she was going to ask were impossible.

He smiled, a warm, genuine look on his face. "I reside there currently, yes," he answered. "But as to where I'm from? Well, that's a little more complicated." He gestured to the envelope that she was clutching. "You'll find some answers in there but not all. Perhaps you should read it, and then I can fill you in."

She pursed her lips. "Aren't you in a hurry?" she asked. She glanced out the window. Rudy's customer was gone, and it looked like he was closing up. The snow was coming down harder. Hollywood flakes, as her dad would have said. "If you need to catch the ferry…" she said, but then she looked back.

"I don't travel by ferry," he answered, only the ghost of a smile on his face this time.

Draco fluffed his purple feathers and waddled his way to the nook in the back of the store. He'd taken to Shepherd quickly. Some customers she had to hold the dragon back from incinerating. It wasn't a great marketing plan.

"I have more of her letters," he said, averting his gaze to the snow outside, but somehow it seemed he was looking beyond it. "Not on me, though. You'd have to give me time to get them."

She turned the sign on the door to closed and turned the flimsy lock as he placed the letter back in his pocket. "How many letters?" she asked, her voice catching as the lock turned into place.

"A lifetime," he said simply, "and more than that, even. Please." He gestured to the counter, but Ember turned to follow Draco. A conversation like this needed to be had somewhere more private. She still wasn't sure if the neighbors would look in and see her talking to herself. She turned to follow Draco, and cleared her throat for lack of something to do.

"Follow me," she told him.

Chapter 3

A chill blew through the store as Ember passed the biography and history books. The section had been her father's favorite, although she'd let the collection dwindle a little, herself preferring far away tales of fantasy and outer space. Since she'd been able to see a dragon since she was twelve, she'd been more likely to believe those stories. Especially the ones her mother told.

She ran her hand over the spines to steady herself until she heard Shepherd hesitantly following her. Her hand shook slightly, and she balled her fist. She'd buried her mother's stories so deeply that she thought it would be a problem to remember them, but they came up in her mind almost unbidden.

The great city of Atlantis, filled with joy and magic and merriment. A blue and white flag. Tall spires. Great parties. Magicians, mages, sorcerers, and witches. All with their own form of power. The far-away countries that sought to topple them. The king's brother who was jealous of their magic. The king himself, grave and stone-faced, a

great weight that was slowly changing him. The queen…
lonely and sad.

Draco scurried in front of her to reach the nook first and she misjudged a step, tripping over him and into a display. But she didn't fall, not completely. Halfway down, her ascent slowed. Time itself slowed. Enough so she could see the corner of the bookcase coming straight for her cheek. She tried to raise her hands to stop it, but it was as if she were under water. Draco turned and slowly cocked his head in confusion. Ember opened her mouth to curse, but a hand grabbed her upper arm, and time came back into motion.

Shep pulled her to the side so that her fall wasn't as dramatic as it could have been, but not graceful, either. She landed in a crouch, his hand on her arm. He'd somehow crossed the space between them before she could fall. That's what she told herself, anyway.

"I meant to do that." She cleared her throat again, and he let go carefully as if she might topple again. "I thought you might enjoy the latest…" She turned. The display she had crashed into was self-help. Of course it was. "Doctor Mike?" She gestured vaguely. The summer residents would eat up the book about hormones in menopause, but she suspected Shep was not a big Doctor Mike fan. He smiled and backed up a step, seemingly content she wouldn't go toppling into an even more embarrassing stack of books. Perhaps one on puberty?

"No, thank you," he responded with a twinkle in his eye. Draco saved her from more embarrassment by attempting his little roar at the fireplace, but since it was already going and the grate was closed, Ember rushed to make sure nothing else caught.

"I told you, wait for me." She tweaked the dragon's nose. His scales were still soft, almost like fur. Shep knelt next to him as she stoked the flames. Ember watched from the corner of her eye as he studied the dragon. She'd done the same when the dragon had appeared at her window when she was just a child. Then, he'd been not much more than a ball of purple fluff. He'd been growing into his long neck, great golden irises, and a deeper purple with spots of white. His scales were becoming coarser, and then, of course, there was the roar.

"May I?" Shep asked. She wasn't sure if the question was directed to her or Draco. She put the poker down next to the fire and closed the grate. The sound of the fire crackling carried. Draco narrowed his eyes. He huffed, then dipped his head.

"He's never officially met anyone." Ember watched carefully. If Shep could see Draco, it was possible the dragon could hurt him, though Draco looked plenty submissive at the moment.

Shep touched the dragon's neck, then turned his attention to Ember. She was surprised to see flecks of the same gold in his dark eyes. "He's met *you*," he countered.

"I thought he was a hallucination," she admitted. Even her mother, with all her stories of fantasy and make-believe, had never believed her.

Shep closed his eyes but kept his hand on the dragon's head. Draco leaned into him as if the dragon, finally, had met a long-lost friend. Was he *purring*? Ember had never heard the dragon purr. She kicked her shoes off and dug her feet into the deep carpet, a trick she'd used to ground herself that wasn't working now. Time seemed to stand still, but not in the magical way. In the way her breath stilled before something big was going to happen. In the way that this morning was a lifetime away from this afternoon. In the way that everything, from here on in, would change. She could feel it in the very air, weighted with expectation. This stranger had brought more than an offer to buy her mother's art. He brought change and possibility. Adventure maybe. Excitement for sure. And she could use that.

"Is there anything else you think you're hallucinating?" His words were soft, but the intent jarring. Not even the scratchy fibers of the carpet could save her from the memory of seeing the great floating city. That had been the first time she was sent to the doctors on the mainland, but not the last. She'd only seen the city one other time, but she'd convinced herself it was a figment of her imagination. Her mother's stories and paintings come to life, and she was not ready to relive that.

"What did my mother write you?" she countered. She was scared to realize how close she'd been to confiding in this man, and how happy the dragon already was. Shep sat cross legged on the floor, and Draco had made himself comfortable on his lap. He'd probably get purple fur on his pants, not that anyone would see it.

Shep sighed, not in the way that he was trying to put her off, but rather that it was a long, sad tale to tell. Ember could read things and people, and she was usually right, even if she didn't always want to be. His story would be sad and long, and it involved her mother and certainly herself in ways he didn't want to tell. Sad ways. Lonely ones. Ones she should have known long ago.

He shifted enough that Draco let out a low growl. Shep absently patted the dragon on the head as he reached in the inside pocket of his coat and produced the letter. It had been closed with a blue and white wax seal, one she'd seen on her mother's desk when she'd packed up her things, but the symbol itself was something she couldn't identify. Her hand trembled as she took the envelope and turned it over in her hand.

The fire took nicely, crackling and burning enough so Draco didn't feel obliged to burn the shop down, but then, he was clearly content. She lifted the two handwritten pages, feeling a pull from the loopy letters inside. Her mother's penmanship was so unique, he couldn't have faked this if he tried. And he couldn't have faked seeing the dragon. Things were happening that she didn't understand and wasn't sure she wanted to see through. She could kick him out, go back to her hibernated life, but things had gone too far already. The letter pulled her like a string through a maze, around corners she couldn't see, and dangers hidden in the open.

He rubbed his chin, and the corner of his lip turned down. "Your mother and I conversed for a long time," he said. She followed his gaze down to the carpet, where he pulled at a loose string. She'd never noticed the pattern on it before, one that matched the seal, though more elegantly hidden. "Though we never had the chance to meet in person. This was her last letter." He gestured to the papers in her hand. "It has been years."

Her curiosity piqued, she unfolded the pages. With the first sentence, she could hear her mother's voice in her head. She covered her mouth to try to keep her emotions in, but emotions didn't work that way. They immediately popped back up as a tear in the corner of her eye.

Shep–

No.

The answer is no.

Your arguments hold merit, even the ones about past lifetimes. I can't deny your research is solid, or that my daughter has stories of lifetimes that seem eerily real. I have chalked it up to imagination, but there is no doubt she is special. Extraordinary. Both are in their own ways.

I've always known, but I will not put pressure on her at such a young age. She is just a girl, Shep. I know you worry for her safety, and I do, too, but you cannot get back a childhood spent in fear. I will give that to her, at least in this lifetime if what you say is correct. I will give her the freedom to know herself before I force this upon her. I will give her the freedom to learn, to love, to make mistakes. If I could not give it to her in other lifetimes, I promise it to her now. I promise her freedom, for how else could a city such as Atlantis be restored? Not through a child imprisoned, but through a girl, no, a woman, with a heart filled with great love. She will never fill that heart if she's chained. You know how Atlantis' magic works? Even if they are nothing more than rumor, what great thing ever came from a cage? It's freedom, Shepherd. Freedom and love.

Return when she is older. Perhaps then we can talk but know I will always protect her. In the meantime, my art grows more specific. More dire, but even within that, there is hope. Perhaps my daughter is the one who can return the great city, but if that's so, there is one who must call to her first. In my visions he is in shadow, but he grows clearer by the day. When it is time, I will show you what I see. Until then, leave us in peace. Help us stay hidden.

Ember let the papers fall, willing the letters to rearrange themselves. She squeezed her eyes closed but that stubborn tear was still there. "She knew it was true all along?" she said. "Her stories. The paintings. The city that I saw…"

He didn't reply right away. Draco snored. "She knew," he confirmed. "But she was trying to protect you."

She turned to him. "Who are you?" she asked, the questions forming one after another. She held up the pages. "What is all this?" She'd always sought an explanation for the dragon without the word delusional in it, but she'd come to accept that, even embrace it. But now something even more weird was going on. She might have blown the whole thing off except for the feeling of abject sorrow that emanated from Shep. He scooted back from the flames. His cheeks had taken on a flush.

"It's difficult to know where to begin," he said, leaning back on the bookshelf where the shelf of Dickens shifted slightly from his weight. Ember wouldn't be leaning anywhere. She was at attention, all directed at this stranger.

"How did you meet my mother?" She only choked slightly on the last word. She'd known Maeve Weathers as mom. As an artist, a bookshop owner. Someone who lived a small life on a boring island Ember couldn't wait to escape from. But she'd always suspected there was more.

He closed his eyes and tipped his head back, taking a deep breath. "It begins long ago." He waited a beat, then righted his head and looked at her. "Before you or I, I'm afraid, and generations before that. It begins when Atlantis was still on the ground, a vast, magical kingdom."

Chapter 4

The great city of Atlantis was the center of the old world. In commerce and trade. In culture and in sheer number. No, Shep couldn't guess how many, but more than the ancient world had ever seen and thriving.

"…and the city was filled with magic," he said, tipping his head back and closing his eyes. He smiled as if he'd been there. "Magicians and sorcerers, yes, but everyday magic too. Atlantian children were taught to harness the power of energy when they were quite young, and they could wield it."

"Wield it for what?" Ember asked when he paused a minute too long.

His smile widened. He opened his eyes and looked at her. "Anything," he answered. He picked up one of the placemats Draco had been pulling apart and played with the frayed edge of what was once a snowman. "Energy is the basis of their world, and this one too. Though the art has long been lost."

He frowned as the fireplace crackled and the wind picked up outside. "The rest of the world feared the power of Atlantis, and none more than the king's own brother, Zyah. It's impossible to know when his heart turned black, but the rumor is, it was borne of jealousy. He was raised in Atlantis but refused to use his magic for good. The king put up with his petty thievery, but when people began to get hurt, he made the difficult decision to send Zyah away. But Zyah was no fool. He raised a great army that threatened the survival of Atlantis itself. The king had no choice but to enchant the city to the sky."

Shep paused and looked out the window as the snow piled up. He absently patted Draco. "At least that's how the story has been handed down. Who's to know if a different decision could have had a different outcome? Perhaps, if the king had not sent Zyah away, Atlantis would still be on the ground. Or perhaps the city would have been razed and destroyed. I imagine it's something the king wondered too. *Wonders*," he corrected.

"They're still alive?" she asked. "After all this time?"

Shep offered a sad smile. "The story says the same folk were frozen in time in the sky, until…"

Ember waited, but he didn't continue. "Until what?"

He met her gaze. "Until one comes with great magic and love." Ember blew out of the corner of her mouth as he continued. "His brother has continued his campaign to hunt down Atlantian descendants here on the ground too, with no evidence he has aged or died. Atlantian magic, especially royal, is strong."

She cleared her throat. "How many descendants are there?" she asked.

Shep shook his head. "It's impossible to know, but there were many outside the gates that day. It's not hard to sense magic in one's blood."

Ember let the story sink in, but she found the words already there in her heart, and the magic too, if she looked deep enough. Draco was all the proof she needed. He purred contentedly on Shep's lap.

"How did my mother know?" she asked. Her mother's paintings depicted the city in the sky, but who else had seen them?

He shifted, but Draco wouldn't remove himself from Shep's lap and instead issued a low growl. "Your mother was a descendent of Atlantis, as am I. We found each other and conversed about the prophesy of the return…"

Ember had never been able to hide her emotions, and she was sure skepticism showed all over her expression, from her narrowed eyes to her pursed lips. Even outside this strange situation, her very vibe screamed lone wolf, from the ripped jeans to the dark eyeliner and dyed black hair. Why should she believe this man, who showed up in a storm validating everything she'd always dreamed? It was almost too good to be true, and if she knew anything from the books she'd read, it was that too good to be true always came with a caveat. What would it be this time? A sacrifice? A heroes' journey? Probably a long, difficult one involving a siren, or a kraken. Maybe a vampire, and not a hot one.

He interrupted her internal panic. "I can prove it." He shifted slightly to nudge the dragon onto the carpet and stood. He stepped up to her, close enough she could see the gold ring around his irises. The fire flared behind him as he held out his hand and opened his palm. He closed his eyes, and took a deep breath in, chanting something under his breath. Both fascinated and concerned, Ember backed into the doorway, but there was nowhere to go unless she were to kick him out, and she wasn't ready for that. She felt something in the air, a vibration that set her teeth on edge. And then, a flicker. The smallest flame sat cupped in his palm.

He opened his eyes and let out a breath. "It's been some time since I could call up that kind of energy, but with both of us together, it's stronger."

Ember watched the flame dance in his palm. She reached out her own hand and felt warmth, but not heat. "Open your hand," he said. She couldn't deny her own curiosity and opened her hand. He tipped his over it and turned his body so he was bracing her.

"Close your eyes," he instructed. Her hands were no longer trembling. "Feel the energy all around you. It's calling us home. Your mother thought it might be time. I think so too. Pull that energy into your hand. Wield it. You are a child of Atlantis."

She felt it all right. Her hand was becoming warm, and then something tickled her palm. She forgot to breathe, instead feeling the sensations crawl not just up her arm but all over her body. He held her, or she might have fallen again and not from clumsiness this time. "Open your eyes," he said.

His hand cupped her palm, and a flame danced on the inside. She gasped, tipping her hand to see it react almost as if the flames had a spirit itself. Almost as if what he was saying were true and this flame were made of energy. *Could she wield it,* she wondered? Their reflections flickered in the light of the flames. His, questioning and concerned. Hers? Her reflection spoke of power, a power she'd never felt in this lifetime or this place. She saw the tall spires of the Atlantian castle kissing the clouds as it slipped by. A man with a red cloak. Her standing next to him on a cliffside where an army had camped.

Before she knew it, the flame had grown almost to the ceiling. Shep yelled, trying to shake the flames off her hand, but for a brief moment, she didn't want to relinquish them. What power it was to be able to burn the world to ashes. Power she held in her palm. She shook the thought away.

"Shit," she muttered. "How do I shut it off?" But she knew, instinctively to cup her hand and cut off the energy. At that point, the curtain was on fire. Proper fire, not the kind Draco was capable of.

She balled her fist. "The extinguisher is in the corner," she told Shep, who scrambled to put it out. It hadn't been her first fire, though she'd have to replace the curtain for sure. Shep opened the window and let in a chill. A brisk sea breeze pulled the smoke out, but there was the hint of a foul smell in the air.

She looked up. The feeling of power and destiny hadn't gone away, instead it was as if the fire had burned something away, something that had covered her true purpose. But instead of feeling powerful, she felt afraid. She shook her hand, trying to rid herself of this fate. Of anything but this moment and the soggy mess on her floor that she couldn't even blame on her invisible dragon.

Shep was still waving smoke out. He'd rolled up his sleeves, presumably so he didn't catch fire. Draco sat on the carpet, still as can be. The dragon was never still. She tipped her head, and in response, Draco nodded.

Can you... hear me? she attempted. She'd felt things from the dragon before, but she always assumed she could read the dragon's expressions. This was different.

The fire had unlocked something inside her. Draco's eyes widened. Ember leaned back on the doorway.

"This is a complication I was not expecting today," she muttered.

She was used to things that were unusual, but she'd come to accept Draco's presence in her life as some kind of mental illness that she was dealing with—and as long as she never told anyone—it would be fine. Things were spiraling out of control. She held the wall and felt the old wallpaper, which had thankfully not burned.

"I'm sorry." Shep turned. He'd vented the room, but his face was flush from the cold. It made him seem real. Human. Would a figment of her imagination flush? She didn't think so. He wiped extinguisher foam off his forearm. "This is not going the way I intended at all." He tipped his head down, then looked up. "*You* are not what I intended."

She swallowed, thinking perhaps they could go back to the register and drink a shot of some of that whiskey she stored in the third drawer before any more attempts at magic.

Chapter 5

Ember had barely reached the middle of the YA section when a gust a of wind shook the windows and doors of the bookshop so violently the panes shuddered in their frames, and a chill made its way through the aisles, leaving frost in its wake. Ember shivered, but Draco did more than that. He scampered around her, and Ember was almost sure she saw the dragon take flight for a moment, nearly knocking down a stack of the latest vampire romance.

"Easy," Ember told him. "It's just the storm." But when she looked out the window, it was the dark that caught her attention. "That's weird," she commented. She'd seen all kinds of snowstorms on the island but none as black as night. Frost crawled up the panes and branched out.

Shep caught her arm and whistled low. Her breath caught in her chest. Something was off, as if the world had gone off kilter. It was like the feeling of stopped time, but time was still ticking. At the end of the aisle, Draco raised onto his haunches and growled as the bell over the door jingled wildly. Shep whistled again and the dragon whimpered and backed up in time for the door to blow open.

In one fell swoop, Shep had one arm around her shoulder and swept up Draco in the other arm. He covered them with a translucent bubble, a trick that was sure not to work. She would have told him so, but her voice seemed not to be working. He frowned when she let out a small squeak.

Draco seemed to have no such qualms. The dragon nuzzled under Shep's arm and stared out through the bubble, which was reddish on the inside and felt like being underwater. Ember wanted to touch it to see if it felt as thin as it looked, but she didn't dare move. Heavy steps shook the front of the store. Shep pressed them back behind the vampire display as a deep roar shook the stacks. It was so loud and so deep and so foul Ember wanted to cover her ears, but instead she shrunk closer to Shep. Safety in numbers and all that.

Whatever the beast was outside their bubble moved so quickly it knocked books right off the shelves. The stack next to them shook but righted itself. All Ember could see were giant hairy legs, fangs, and yellow eyes. It ran past them, then paused. She could hear the rasp in its breath and held her own for several beats. Draco was as still as she'd ever seen him. She longed to take hold of the dragon for comfort, but she didn't dare. Shep risked squeezing her shoulder. The beast turned its head and sniffed the air, then let out another terrible roar. Another answered from outside, and it swiftly turned and burst back through the door, leaving a fowl stench in its wake.

Ember let out an unsteady breath. She balled her hands, but that didn't stop the shaking. Shep waited until the roars faded, then took a step away, putting Draco on the ground as he removed the magic.

"What. Was. That?" she asked, surveying the damage to the store. Wherever the beast had stepped, it left black muck in its wake. It was all over the stacks and reeked of sulfur.

Shep ran a hand through his hair. "That..." he swallowed. "That was a hell hound. Blast that they found us this quickly. Things are moving fast now." He turned in a circle, but what he was looking for, she couldn't guess.

"A *hell hound*?" Her voice became steadier. Anger replaced fear. She'd read about hell hounds in books. They were supposed to be imaginary, but so were dragons and cities in the sky. What else could be out there beyond the bounds of her imagination? She attempted to peer out the front window at the same time as shrinking away from it. It resulted in a tiptoe back and forth that had her unsteady on her already unsteady feet.

Nothing seemed amiss outside. Lights glowed inside the pharmacy, and there were no tracks in the fresh snow. She leaned forward until she heard the bray of a hound – to the west, if she could guess. Shepherd took her arm and pulled her gently back.

"No one else can see them," he said softly, but his explanation wasn't enough.

"Then why am I seeing them?" she asked through gritted teeth. A blob of the black goo fell from the desk onto the floor where it sizzled. Draco growled.

"There is a prophecy," he said, but he was cut off by the bray again, closer this time. He cocked his head, but only the howling wind carried. "There's more than one hell hound. We need to get out of here. Is there anywhere we can go?"

He looked at her as if he hadn't just asked the most absurd question. *Why yes, complete stranger who is a party to my delusions,* she thought, *let me just find us an isolated spot where I can complete my nervous breakdown. Perhaps somewhere near the water?*

But then, he seemed pretty solid. She hedged her bets. If there were an off chance that those hellhounds were real, he was right. They needed to move. And if this was a delusion? Perhaps it would be better had somewhere isolated as well.

She looked at the ceiling, where there was a water mark in the shape of a rabbit where her sink had leaked last year. Her apartment was on the second floor. She'd read enough horror books to know that wouldn't do. And they were on an island, so the choices were limited.

"Perhaps you could take me where your mother's art is?" he asked.

"What is your obsession with that?" she mumbled. Out of instinct, she rounded the desk to shut off the register and grab the keys as if a hell hound wouldn't just burst through the door and steal her petty cash. At least it would keep anyone else away. She noticed her hands were shaking when she grabbed her coat. He noticed too. His eyes narrowed as he took her in, perhaps deciding if she were on the verge of losing it. She pressed her lips together in a semblance of normalcy, then she forced them into a smile. "Her art?" she prodded.

He exhaled. "She left messages in them," he said, simply. "Ones only I can interpret."

"Seems pretty easy to interpret," she answered. "A city in the sky." She followed him to the door.

"Yes, but *where* in the sky. And when." For a moment, his brown eyes glistened as if they were on the verge of a grand adventure. And for that second, she wanted to be on an adventure with him. She wanted to be more than the crazy orphan who ran a barely profitable bookstore, her days, weeks, and years all the same until they rolled out to an end. Shep cautiously opened the door, looking up and down the street. She noticed a black jeep parked next to her Corolla. How had he got that on the island?

She closed the door behind them. Through the frosted panes, she could see everything she considered normal. The bestsellers, all stacked up and ready for the seasonal guests. The coffee maker. Even the rabbit shaped water stain. She couldn't shake the feeling that she'd never again have the comfort of normalcy. It was something she was excited for and dreaded all the same.

From the outside, nothing appeared out of order. She closed in the winter all the time. Inventory, or just plain boredom. Even Rudy wasn't nosy enough to be looking. Snow fell lazily down. Clouds gathered and the day held a bitter chill that froze Ember to the bone. Draco followed on her heels as she climbed in the passenger's seat. The dragon didn't leave prints either, but he never had. She lifted him onto her lap.

"Atlantis is more than a city in the sky," Shep said, turning the key. The engine was louder than she anticipated. There was power under the hood. Magic, maybe. She hoped it was enough to outrun those hellhounds and gave an involuntary shiver.

"What is it, then?" She tucked her jacket around her. Suddenly she was aware of the danger that accompanied such an adventure. While all her heroes had made it through their journeys in the fantasies she loved to read, they were pretty severely tested along the way. And those were in books. Would she have the mettle to pass such a test, or would she even get the chance? As Shep backed up, she heard the faint bray of the hellhound in the distance by the docks and pointed the other way.

"The mansions are pretty empty this time of year," she said. Shep raised the heat, but the chill she felt had nothing to do with the weather, or even the hellhounds. She knew where she had to go. She'd left her mother's art there along with all the memories that went with them. In order to go forward, she'd have to revisit both, and she wondered if she wouldn't rather tangle with a hellhound than with her own heart.

Chapter 6

The storm had closed most of the shops on Main Street. The diner's regular customers were absent, the parking spaces all empty of their Buicks and Volvos, instead covered with a dusting of snow. The street hadn't seen a plow yet, and Ember wasn't surprised. There was only one plow on the island. He'd get to it when he got to it. She ducked down in her seat, but no one was out to see her.

It was quiet up to the rotary in the center of the island's downtown. The road was surrounded by the tiny post office, library, and town hall with a grassy common in the middle. A gazebo hosted concerts in the summer, and some statue to the founder of the island Ember had never really bothered to learn about. Shep had gone around the rotary twice before he cleared his throat.

"Oh." She wiped a circle in the frost on the window before Draco could fog it up again with his breath. "After the town hall, to the right."

He downshifted as he rounded the corner but still the tires slipped. She absently patted Draco's back. "I wouldn't expect much from the roads. They won't be cleared until tomorrow." They passed the town's small elementary, lights shone in the windows. Ember shivered. She'd never been one to fit in, even then, and had few good memories of the small building. The high school up the hill had been worse, but at least they wouldn't pass by it.

"I can handle it," Shep replied confidently, but his hands gripped the wheel, and he kept his eyes trained on the road. Draco let out a low growl and hunched on her lap. This route would take them past the shore to the mansions on the north side. Most were empty this time of year, but not all. Ember knew where to avoid. For extra money, she'd offered to look in on a few, so her presence wouldn't be unusual. Her presence in a jeep with a strange man might be. And technically she wasn't allowed in her old house, but she knew how to get in, and she knew it had been abandoned since the day they swapped keys.

She didn't say much except for directions. The snow continued in small bursts, but Shep was right. The jeep could take the weather, or maybe the driver could. She knew he had more questions. It was written on the tilt of his head and besides, Ember could always read people that way. She also had more questions.

"What do you expect to find in her paintings?" she asked quietly. The only other sound was that of the heat, pushing out musty air. Ember wiped her hands on her pants, the memory of the hellhound haunted her mind though she couldn't hear it now, and in this bubble, she felt almost safe. They crested a hill, and the ocean appeared off to the side, whitecapped and angry. No, the ferry wouldn't be running today. They were stuck.

Shep put a hand over the wheel casually, but she could see right through the gesture. "Your mother had great magic," he said, "perhaps not enough to return Atlantis, but enough to see its fate. Moreover, she was kind. Although I don't suppose I have to tell you."

The car slipped a little, and he over corrected as he made the turn. They wouldn't have been the first to go off the side of the hill. Even the guardrail didn't seem to stop one or two accidents in the tourist season, never mind in the snow.

"Careful." The word came out automatically as she thought of all the rides home from school with her sister, who tended to take the corner too aggressively in her little Miata. She could almost hear Sierra's bubbly voice tell her to relax. Her sister's laugh still echoed in the breeze, especially here. It was as if she haunted the whole island, which was impossible and dumb because Sierra was still alive. If you could call that a life.

"You can tell me," Ember said, "about her. How you knew her, and whatever this is about her magic." Ember had known her mother to be kind, and she missed that. She missed talking about her mom. Talking *to* her mom.

Shep kept his eyes on the road but smiled as he turned and headed up the hill that led to the summer residences. "I met her online when she was selling a book on Atlantian fantasy. We conversed for a couple years through the mail, and I started to suspect how strong her magic was. She knew things before they happened. She knew facts about Atlantis that weren't in books. She told me a little of the things she saw. She wanted me to come here to see her paintings myself, but she was concerned." He looked at her out of the corner of his eye. "For her children. Whatever she saw in her dreams didn't convince her that she would return Atlantis, but that someone in her line would. Her daughter, perhaps." He paused. "And that it would be difficult."

Difficult, Ember thought. More difficult than seeing an imaginary dragon and everyone thinking she was crazy? Probably. At least Draco hadn't threatened her life. But still, what she wouldn't give to ask her mother all this herself. They passed thick woods where Ember still went on long walks, dreaming of the city in the sky. She absently chewed her fingernail, a habit she couldn't seem to break despite the black nail polish. There were things she couldn't tell Shep, like the fact that sometimes, those woods talked back. The fact there were deeper and darker things on their island than her little dragon.

"Hey?" Shep's voice came like an echo, and she pulled her gaze from those soft, snow-covered trees that seemed innocent in the light snow.

"I'm sorry. Left," she said. To their right was a power station, and coming up were some smaller, more spread-out developments. Shep slowed down. "It's not any of these," she gestured to the cookie-cutter houses, wiping a circle in the window where Draco had again fogged it up. "I promise, you'll know when you see it."

Shep slowed to let a feral cat dart across the street. The island was full of them. "You know, I never pictured your mother as someone with money," he commented. The mansions came into sight on the hill.

"What's that supposed to mean?" She'd been teased for her status before she was teased for her lack of one. That's the thing with bullies, they target your insecurities and Ember had plenty of those.

"Nothing, really." He shook his head. "I'm sorry if you took offense. She was just very… pardon the expression but down to Earth."

Ember couldn't help but smile. She tried to place his accent but there was more of a lilt than English, and she was no expert. All she knew about language she'd learned from subtitled movies. "It was my father who had the money." She pointed left again. The mansions were spread out from each other to make each one a spectacle unto itself. There were dozens. He eased off the gas as they passed a four-story Tudor, boarded up for winter. She tried to read his gaze. It wasn't envy, but if she had to guess, sadness.

She cleared her throat. "He lived here on the island," she said, watching the reflection of the jeep pass in the windows. "She came for vacation. And never left. At least that's how they told it."

He eased the jeep up the hill. Her father's house was at the crest and stood alone past a long driveway. "What do you know about where your mother came from?" He spoke guardedly, but there was an urgency to his question that raised her hackles. She hugged the dragon, who didn't seem to notice. Draco always liked car rides. He jumped his front paws up and pressed his nose on the window.

She wanted to snap back that it was none of his business. She'd been telling nosy tourists that all her life, but they'd gone past that. Once she'd gotten in the Jeep, she'd sealed her fate. "Not much," she admitted, chewing the nail again. Shep hit a bump and Draco jostled on her lap. Her leg bounced. Being this close to the old house always did that. She didn't want to admit how little "not much" was. All she knew was that her mom was from off island. She raised an eyebrow. "What do *you* know about her?" she asked, her voice a mixture of accusation and burning curiosity.

He looked at her with concern, but perhaps that was because Draco was digging his claws into her jeans. "Cut it out." She pulled them out one by one. They passed another mansion but barely slowed this time. Its blue turrets were covered in snow.

"They were travelers, her family," he responded slowly. "At least that's what she told me. Moved around constantly, always looking for... something. Her father was, well... those of us from Atlantis know something is wrong. There's a deep burning in our hearts. A knowledge that we're not of this world. A curiosity." He paused. "A pain."

"That's very poetic." She swallowed a lump in her throat. In only a few lines, Shep had covered how she'd felt her whole life. "The turn is ahead."

"Your grandfather didn't deal with that well," he said, turning onto a side road that wasn't much more than a dirt road covered in snow. "The things he sought, well..." He took his hand off the wheel and ran it through his hair. "They were not the right things. He chased every conspiracy, until he drove himself mad, and threw himself off a bridge. Your grandmother was convinced someone was chasing them and that he was murdered. She gave your mom money to go away, and she ended up here. Do you mind if I ask again how she died?"

"An accident," Ember said. The information he'd given her made sense, but she was resentful it came in such a way. He wasn't without emotion, but there wasn't time to grieve either. "There," she pointed. The drive had grown in since Ember had last been here. She sometimes walked past, but not since late summer. Bare branches scraped the sides of the vehicle as he turned and passed a decrepit mailbox.

She held Draco tightly as they rounded the curve, and the old house came into sight.

Chapter 7

The jeep skid on the gravel drive before coming to a stop. "This isn't what I was expecting at all." Shep leaned forward to take in the house, and Ember couldn't help but smile. Though it was a shadow of its former self, the structure set an imposing profile just the same. Not the way the other houses on the street did. No, there was a reason the estate known as Weatherstorm was set off on its own road.

"It's unique." Ember didn't wait for him to put the car in park before she pulled the handle and jumped out. For a moment, she remembered playing with her sister on the estate's wide front lawn before it became overgrown with weeds, now topped with snow. Sierra had always been embarrassed about the old house and had never invited anyone over. Ember didn't have any friends, so it left them plenty of time to linger in the shadow of the old Victorian. It had gone through phases where her mother painted it all shades, but in the end, it had settled on a deep blue that had faded mostly to gray, like the horizon at the end of a cloudy day.

Draco ran around her ankles then up to the steps as if he remembered he was going, though it had been many years. Ember wiped her palms on her pants. "We have to get the key," she told him. She'd come back a few times, so she was relatively sure there were no cameras, but she always looked anyway. Nothing was disturbed. Shep had parked and walked up to her.

"She has character," he said, admiration in his eyes and snowflakes melting on his lashes. Ember pointed to one of the house's turrets.

"My old room," she said, suddenly shy. She'd never fully moved out. *Were her old things still in there?* The posters she'd abandoned in her haste to leave that life? "It faces the ocean," she went on. "You can just see a swath of blue over the trees."

He followed her gaze, and a cautious smile broke out on his face. "I'd expect nothing less." He cocked his head, listening for a sound she couldn't hear. On the steps, Draco whined and the hair on the back of Ember's neck stood. She didn't have to be told they needed to hurry. She approached a loose board on the lower side of the stairs under the porch and swept the snow off. The massive brass key was only half hidden. Though once covered by a rock, any thief worth their salt would've had no problem finding it, but none had. The house had always had a way of protecting itself. Even though they were, technically speaking, trespassing, the house welcomed her back. Others had commented on how out of place the architecture was, how off-putting in a neighborhood full of pricey mansions. The home had been in her father's family a long time, at least so the story went. She'd never known any of his family, though. Her father was the last surviving Weathers.

"Sierra hated this place," Ember commented, taking the steps as slowly as she dared to the top where the porch had blocked the snow, revealing the weathered wood. The third step still sunk. Once, there was a hanging swing, but all the outdoor furniture had been removed. She assumed someone had snagged up the land hoping to demolish the house and rebuild something that looked exactly like one of the neighbors. That's how people with money were, she'd never understood it. Why would you want to live like everyone else? But years had passed, and still it stood. Ember peered in the window next to the door.

Shep ran a hand along the railing. "I can't imagine why anyone would hate this." Like everything else, it was unique and intricately carved. Her mom had done much of the detail work. It was one reason Ember couldn't wait to leave. The memories were too much. She traced a finger on a curve.

"Are you making fun?" she asked softly. She'd heard it all before but never so kindly. Somehow that was worse.

His brow furrowed as if he hadn't even considered the possibility. "Do people here make fun of such beauty?" he asked. He tipped his head as if he weren't talking about the house specifically. Ember turned and put the key in the lock before she could blush. It squeaked and caught. The door popped open.

"They make fun of anything they don't understand." Ember paused in the doorway. "Which is a lot." She took in the dark foyer as she waited for her sight to adjust. "What do you mean by 'people from here?'" She raised an eyebrow. A cold wind shook snow off the nearby treetops and threatened to close the door, but Shep had it wedged until Draco slipped through his legs and inside.

"A conversation for later," he said, pulling the door closed slowly. Though the light was low, she knew her way past the study on the left where her father had collected his books, down the hall which seemed empty without the table they'd put their school things on. The carpet was the same, and even in the low light Ember saw the wallpaper had faded. Her mother had always joked the wallpaper would outlive them. She'd been right.

They reached the kitchen. The room had always been the most modern part of the house, but now the appliances looked dated, the counters and floor cracked and filthy. It hurt more than Ember wanted to admit. She pushed the daisy curtains to the side to let more light in and a mouse skittered out from the island and into the dining room.

"She could have owned a bakery," Ember said, and the kitchen seemed to sigh in agreement. They'd always got along well, this house and her mom. It had personality, her mother had said.

Shep looked out the sliding doors, covered in so much grime they could barely see out. He frowned as the wind picked up and snow crept up. Draco hopped on the island and Ember patted him as she considered what to say next. They were under a time crunch, that was for sure. But did she trust him? More than the hellhounds, she guessed.

"Your mother was a member of one of the surviving families of Atlantis," Shep said without turning. "And high up too. Higher than ours. Her ancestor was a King's Guard. Sent out on a mission to gather intel when the city just disappeared on him." He turned, finally, but didn't meet Ember's eyes, instead pushing dust around on the floor with the toe of his boot. "At least that's how the story goes.

Some of the refugees died off. Some were hunted. Still are hunted." Finally, he looked up, pain evident behind his dark eyes. "But her family held magic that got stronger over the decades instead of fading. It presents in different ways. Seeing the future. Affecting the elements. Raising a dragon is a new one though, I must admit."

He watched Draco jump down to follow the mouse into the kitchen. She crossed the room to look directly in his eyes. *Could you look into the eyes of a delusion?* No, she decided. Not with this sincerity and emotion and pain. He was telling what he thought was the truth. And he was real, she was sure of it. As real as her and Draco.

"And *your* ancestors?" she asked.

He smiled. "It's complicated," he replied.

She blew her long bangs out of her face. "I'll say," she said.

He shrugged, a moment between them had passed, but a moment of what? "I am here of my own choice," he said. "A sacrifice had to be made…" He stopped abruptly and looked out the window where a bray echoed over the wind. A dog, perhaps, or a coyote? The island had them. That didn't stop the shiver that went down her spine.

"That was a dog, right?" she asked, taking a step back from the doors. She'd never known a dog to sound like that.

"Of a sort." He frowned. "We must see her artwork. I must decipher the prophecy."

She wanted to make a smart remark back about patience and holding his horses, but she couldn't seem to find the words. The bray had settled in her very bones, turning her as cold as ice from the inside out. Her hands shook as she pointed the way to the staircase.

"They're in the attic." She cleared her throat. "At least that's where I left them when I moved. I didn't want…" She couldn't continue. A tear escaped her eye, and she wiped it with her thumb. Was that grief, still? After all these years? How strange how it popped back up.

His expression softened. He reached out and she took his hand and accepted his unsaid condolences. It was only a moment, but from it she knew he had felt pain in his life. She reluctantly let go. "This way." She avoided the other rooms, but she felt them as she passed. One functioned as an office, one as a library. Though most of the books had made their way to the store, the shadows of those she left cut across the hallway. They had been her father's personal collection. Not worth anything, she'd assumed, except to the most unusual of collectors.

The stairs were crowded into the corner, as if the second and third floors had been an afterthought. Shep had to duck as they turned and climbed. Quite accidentally, Ember had a memory of racing her sister up these stairs. Sierra was taller and had longer legs. She'd always won. Ember rubbed a spot on her arm Sierra would have grabbed to pull her back all those years ago. She passed the rooms without much note, entering a cubby that held a built-in staircase to their third floor.

She yanked the door open. It still stuck. "They started remodeling the upstairs the year before they died, but they didn't have a chance to do much." She tried the light switch, which, to her surprise illuminated a small bulb at the top of the stairs. "It's still pretty much an attic."

Shep made a noncommittal grunt that suggested he wondered who was paying the electric bill as well. For a moment, Ember thought of the corporation that bought the house. It was under a trust. She held the rail tightly as she made her way up and stopped so abruptly Shep almost ran into her.

It wasn't the musty, ill-used smell that she was expecting. The last time Ember had seen this place, the room was covered with white sheets, her mother's art and collectables left to collect dust, but this… she put a hand on her forehead. Was she hallucinating?

"Someone lives here?" he asked. "I thought you said it was abandoned?"

The upstairs had been set up as an apartment, with what can only be described as a sitting area on one side and a futon on the other. "They don't." Ember took a step in. "They shouldn't," she corrected herself. But why shouldn't they? Someone owned this place. Someone that neglected the whole house and cooped up in the attic? She looked around shelves and displays of her mother's old things. Shep made a beeline to the slanted walls, where her mother's artwork was propped up at odd angles as if on display at a private show. Ember remembered the paintings, but she'd never seen them laid out like this. Together they seemed like they told a story. She picked up an old telescope that had never worked and twirled the dials as Shep took a notebook out of his shirt pocket and started scribbling furiously.

"Oh, you've made it, I see," a voice called out. "About time!"

Ember startled so hard she dropped the telescope, and it clattered on the floor. The woman stepped right out of the fireplace. While it wasn't currently on, there should have been no access behind it. Shep raised an eyebrow but looked less than startled. "I'm so sorry," Ember breathed.

Were they trespassing? Could she go to jail? Was that worse than getting eaten by a hellhound?

Chapter 8

The woman shot Ember a stern look as she brushed ash off her long skirt, but her expression quickly turned into a warm grin. "You were supposed to get my mail," she said.

Her gray hair fell in waves past her shoulders, and the wrinkles on her face told of a long life. Her eyes were a dreamy cerulean Ember had only seen in the sky. Draco rounded her legs and sniffed at the bottom of her skirt. She reached down but Draco backed away with a low growl.

"I…" Ember remembered part of the deal with selling the house was she picked up the mail for a few months, but she could never bring herself to do it. There were probably catalogues spilling over.

The woman tipped her head. "I've been waiting for you, Ember Weathers. It would have been much easier if we'd met a long time ago. But we can only move forward now. Come, you like your tea with honey, is that correct?" The bracelets on her arm jingled as she waved her hand over a small coffee table. A tea set appeared, porcelain and delicate, decorated with scenes of an island in the sky moving across the delicate surface. The teapot let loose curls of steam which obscured the destination of the city, but perhaps it was doomed to circle the teacup forever. Small bowls of sugar and honey rounded out the setup. Ember grabbed the back of the closest chair as her vision swam.

"Magic?" she asked Shep, but there was a bigger question in her eyes. *Is this possible? Is this real?*

"Oh, much more than that," the woman answered for him. "There's a chill today, don't you think?" She waved her hand again and the fireplace she'd stepped out of roared to life. *That would have been useful at the store*, Ember thought, as Draco backed toward it. The dragon couldn't resist the warmth of the flames, which flickered as if they were images impossible to interpret.

Shep cocked his head. "The hellhounds have arrived," he announced. "Whoever you are, talk fast." The woman shook her head. Her hand was steady as she poured two cups.

"You're safe enough here, for the moment anyway," she said. She sat down on a round cushion, one used for meditation. Ember fell ungracefully on her own, spilling some of the tea. "I suppose you don't want tea, Mr. Shepherd. I've had the art you've been looking for all this time."

Shep narrowed his eyes. "What do you know of this art?"

"More than you," Ember guessed. He frowned at her. "She did step out of the fireplace. You came through the front door." She shrugged and lifted the mug, watching the ship disappear in a cloud.

The woman smiled. "Like your father, I see. Practical. Your mother was the dreamer. Comes with her heritage, I suppose." She dropped a dollop of honey in her tea. She was in no hurry, despite the brays becoming louder.

"How did you know my family?" Ember asked. Shep divided his attention between the paintings and the conversation. The woman spoke lower.

"I've been watching you for some time, Ember. There are so few of us remaining, and fewer still with your type of power." She eyed Shep out of the corner of her eye. He returned the suspicious gesture, and Ember was glad they were several paces apart. "Your friend, though. I've heard of this mysterious art collector, but his magic was harder to track. Weaker."

Shep stepped back as if the canvases themselves were pulling him. His grin was calculated. "Perhaps you're mistaking ingenuity for weakness," he said. "And I noticed you haven't told us who you are yet, and why you occupy a space with these important works?" Draco seemed to agree, growling by Ember's side. "What business do you have here?" he asked. "What do you know of Atlantis?"

The woman grinned in return, and if there were a contest for who was more calculating, Ember couldn't tell who would win. Only that she could usually see through people much more easily, but magic seemed to muddy people's intentions. *What a clever little trick*, she thought. It was one she'd pay dearly to have. Her own emotions tended to play out on her face, and at the moment she was sure she reflected confusion, and possibly exhaustion. More and more by the minute. She sank down into the pillow.

"I go by Maryse. They call me an oracle." The woman rose. She walked to Shep, who stood in front of a painting showing an army gathered on a bridge to Atlantis. Ember took a breath in. She'd seen this view, from the top of a hill. She'd been standing with a man in a red cloak in a dream, but was it a memory or warning? The woman continued.

"I'm an ancestor, like you I suppose" she continued. "Or are you?" Shep paled, but she continued. "Like Maeve Weathers, I have seen visions of things to come. I've seen a woman in them, but her face is covered. I seek her, like you. I seek to return Atlantis home, but our magic is too weak still. Its' king has become unstable, and he will never return on his own. Shame on him for thinking he could remove all the good magic from the world and pay no price. He has paid a price, indeed. And so have his people. Balance must be restored."

Ember realized the woman looked like an old depiction of a witch, and suddenly found it all so funny. The more she drank of the tea, the more her thirst grew. Shep kept an eye on the old woman as he walked from canvas to canvas. The scenes were so familiar to her, but never had she seen them so set up, as if they told a story. An old story, one still playing out.

"How could you know if I have power if I don't even know it?" Ember asked, but as if in response, she felt magic welling up inside her. Once it had been unleashed, it was difficult to pull back. It would also be difficult to wield, she supposed, so she worked hard to keep herself under control. Her instincts screamed that something was wrong, though that was to be expected when you saw someone walk out of a fireplace.

Maryse shook her head and blew on her tea which was still hot. Ember noticed details she hadn't seen before, the sparkling strands of silver in her hair. The intensity of her gaze, which was almost hungry. The sigils on her dress and the pillow beneath her. The fear under her magic, welling up. The tingling in her arms and legs.

"Magic cannot be hidden just because it's not taught," the woman admonished. "Those of us who are attuned can feel you miles away, but you've been protected. Your mother made sure of that, at least on this island, but the spell grows weaker. I've been waiting, Ember. For you, I think." She smiled warmly, a gesture Ember could not return.

"Waiting?" Ember had taken to just repeating the last words someone said. It was a coping mechanism. Her hand shook as she put her teacup down. Draco lifted his head and narrowed his eyes, his golden irises only a suspicious slit.

She tipped her head, an expression of worry crossing her face. "Perhaps it will speed things along if I help your *friend* Shepherd through these paintings. They tell a story, indeed, though the ending is unclear." She emphasized the word friend enough that Ember knew she was suspect. Shep knelt beside one of her mother's paintings. The fire cracked and sparkled. Draco made his way back to her side.

Ember rose as the words settled in her soul. She'd called herself a lot of things in her life, most not very nice, but she'd never called herself powerful or destined. Instead of feeling a weight, though, she felt a loosening as if binds were being removed. She flexed a fist and moved away from the others to think, but the room was warm and the calls of the hellhounds so close. The house protected them. It always had. She felt her mother's magic like wings surrounding them, but how long would those wings hold?

Long enough to solve the mystery of the prophecy, she hoped. Learning to use her own magic would take much longer. She could hardly lasso an island and pull it down, but she felt it there, and something between. She wiped a bead of sweat off her brow and turned.

The paintings were set up in such a way that a story was laid out. One of a land of magic and creativity and love. The next paintings panned out and showed a darkness in the distance, an army gathering. A mad king at the front.

"The king's brother?" Ember guessed. She didn't remember this painting. It showed a man looking out a dark window at Atlantis in the distance as it raised off the ground. His face was shadowed but she could see it screwed up in rage. He held a ruby crusted sword so tightly his hands were white. Words formed on his lips, the utterance of the curse, perhaps? His face was strangely familiar.

Maryse seemed to read her thoughts. "Yes. Zyah. His lasting curse was that any Atlantians left the ground would never live in peace, and their children as well." She placed a hand on Ember's shoulder. "He spent lifetimes chasing the remaining survivors."

"A barbarian." Shep cursed.

"Perhaps that." Maryse maintained an unreadable expression. "But he had his reasons, as well. Not all believed Atlantis was wholly good. In fact, some, like Zyah, thought they hid a great evil."

Shep's face flushed. "Evil enough to curse an entire city?" he spat.

Maryse stared at the evil king. For a moment, the attic was silent of all but the crackling of the fire. That same shadow over Zyah's face seemed to pass over

Maryse, giving Ember a moment to see the woman behind the veiled expression and the view gave her a chill. She hadn't always believed her intuition, but this time it was strong. And it told her to run, but the thought and motion seemed strangely disconnected.

"Good. Evil. All based on interpretation, aren't they?" Maryse asked.

"Not really," Shep argued, but their time was growing shorter. The wings of her mother's protection were fading. "What happens after this painting?" he asked.

"It's the last," Maryse said, but there was a hint of hesitation in her voice.

"No." Ember shook her head, and her mind continued spinning after her head stopped moving. She turned to Shep but couldn't focus. "I've seen it. This hill. Does it look familiar to you? I've never left this island, but I've seen this place, and not in a book." She took a breath. She wasn't prepared to reveal her vision, but she knew this place from something more concrete. "It's the hospital my sister is at."

Shep squinted at the painting and inhaled a long breath. "Sierra?" He knelt before it, running his fingers along the painted shoreline. He turned to Ember. "Are you sure?"

She closed her eyes. The world swam. "I've never been more sure," she said, but what she didn't tell him was that she'd seen this place often in her dreams.

She felt a wave of nausea as Shep and Maryse argued something about the hospital and the route there. Her knees buckled.

"I'm sorry about this," Maryse said as Shep caught her. Ember felt a wave of magic hit Shep, then pain, and then she fell.

Chapter 9

Ember dreamed.

She knew it was a dream, but she was helpless to stop the visions that swam in front of her face. Old visions, ones that had been inside her all this time but bound by deep magic. They fought past her binds to the surface of her consciousness.

She cursed. Words floated out of her mouth like a soft breath. Her mouth? No. She didn't have one. She was only spirit. She *thought* the curse. Handy.

She floated in a space outside of time. Before she existed. Before Atlantis. Before even the universe was formed, or maybe far after. It was a place of eternity, as frightening as it was calming. Stars and colors and bursts of light fought for her attention. The space was full of possibility and hope and destruction and built around the warm feeling of love that settled inside her. It was the force of creation in action, but what had been created? She was pulled along, past worlds created and destroyed in the space of just a second. Far away in both space and time and perception. Too strange to understand, so she only took it in until they came close enough for her to recognize her own world, just one little globe in a sea of darkness.

Time played games, like it did when Shep had manipulated it, so Ember didn't know if time sped or slowed, but she slowly tumbled into a time and space where magic reigned free. A village, filled with tents and music and revelries and joy. While she should have been frightened, or angry (and she was those things), for the moment, intrigue took over her senses. And she did have senses. When was the last time she'd smelled roasted chestnuts in a dream, or felt a warm breeze across her cheek? The chestnuts came from a stall in a market along a gravel main street. They floated over flames that turned different colors, popping and dancing, and smelled of the most delicious sweetness that Ember wished she did have a mouth in which to taste them.

"Daisy for the pretty lady?" Ember turned. A tall man in a robe and pointed hat wasn't talking to her but a small girl behind her, who laughed with joy as the flower he handed her turned into smoke, and the smoke turned into a dragon that took flight on the wind slipping through the crowded street before disappearing. He clapped his hands and produced another bloom which he put behind her ear. She was so tickled she ran off into the crowd in search of the smoke dragon.

He stood and tipped his head up, testing the wind. "Curious," he said in a deep, musical voice. She'd heard his voice before, in a dream perhaps. One long forgotten. He looked not at Ember, but through her. *What would happen if he could see her*, she wondered? Would she warn him that Atlantis would be cursed? Could she change the course of time? Not from here, though the way he looked through her made her wonder.

Magic was all around. It vibrated the particles in the very air surrounding them. But something else was in the air too—joy. Atlantis, if that's where she was, was a place of joy. Ember had never considered magic before, not any more than she read in books, but she'd heard warnings of curses and ill spells and spite. There was none of that here. Was it a feast day, or was this how they lived every day?

Far past the merry main streets, a tall white castle rose. Its spires were decorated with blue and white flags that fluttered in the breeze. Clouds passed lazily overhead, so Atlantis was still on the ground. This was before, and it was magic. She passed by side streets where vendors sold wares such as orbs and wands and spells, as well as the more mundane fruits and fabric and jewelry. Every turn she made was a new place to explore, but she felt herself fading. *There is still something here to find*, she thought as the day grew long and shadows filled the streets. Still, she was not scared. Lanterns hovering over the street bobbed and danced as they burned, and music carried in the wind. She followed a crowd of people to the steps of the castle, where she was able to hover over all of them to see the king himself with the queen by his side.

"It is a night of great merriment," the queen commented. Her voice was as light as the air, and her hair too, as if she were woven together from the stars themselves.

"Indeed." The king's voice was deeper, as was his countenance. Wrinkles already lined his forehead. "But in the distance…"

She placed a hand over his. "The distance can wait," she replied softly, though a shadow passed across her features too.

But there was, indeed, a shadow in the distance. Ember could see it rolling like a dust storm from far over the gates and past the bridge. Should she warn them? What could she say? She floated closer to the king, and the guard closest to him turned with a start. His hair was close cropped and his eyes a mix of gold and brown. His face was so familiar. He unsheathed his sword.

"You," he said, his voice a mix of amazement and scorn.

Ember startled. "Can you see me?" she asked, but alas, she had no voice, and when he waved his sword, it only cut through clear air. She was pulled back before she could see the king's reaction and she reached out to grasp a piece of his red cloak which ripped off in her hand. She was pulled back through the fabric of reality and time, landing with a start in her own body.

And she was pissed.

"What was that?" She woke with a start, in control of all her faculties again. She opened and closed her mouth to be sure, but it seemed to be working, and she was going to use it.

"A test, so to speak." Maryse rose from the chair opposite hers, while Shep was spread out on the floor, snoring lightly. Draco was curled up next to them. Maryse had cursed them both to sleep. Ember frowned as the woman put a hand on her shoulder and she shrugged it off.

"Before I went any further, I just had to know," Maryse said.

Ember stood, waking Draco with a nudge of her foot. Shep startled and put an arm around the dragon.

"Wake up," she told him. "She's crazy." They were getting out of there, hellhounds or no. "You needed to know what?" she asked to keep Maryse talking as she stepped slowly backward toward the steps. Shep sat and shook it off while Draco yawned, then growled. She didn't need her powers of instinct to see the anger rising in Shep's expression.

"If you were the one," Maryse responded sadly. She doused the fire with a single look and a chill filled the room. "You're not," she finished.

"Excuse me?" Ember stopped. She didn't particularly want to be "the one" but it felt like quite an insult.

"I tested your magic," Maryse said simply, as if it were the most ordinary thing to do and not a total invasion of privacy and personal space. Ember crossed her arms in front of her as Maryse continued. "If you were the one, you should have told me how Atlantis will be returned. Instead, you stared blankly ahead… and drooled."

Ember looked down. There was, indeed, a drool spot on her shirt. She wiped it angrily. Shep wavered as he got to his feet. He looked between the two. "What happened?" he slurred. Clearly, she wasn't the only one drooling. What the heck had Maryse hexed them with?

"If she were fated to be the one to return Atlantis, she'd have told me under the spell." She shook her head, shooting an entirely inappropriate look of anger at Ember.

Shep's voice cleared quickly. "That's not how Atlantian magic works." He pinned her with a look. "You don't hex someone and pull it out. But you know that, don't you?" He tipped his head. "Who are you?"

"I'm a survivor, as are you," she responded, the look of anger replaced by one of contemplation. She tied her long hair back. "Perhaps you're right." She retreated to the table where the tea had disappeared, and a dark bowl appeared filled to the brim with a shimmering liquid. Maryse reached in a pocket and sprinkled herbs on the surface, which bobbed and dipped. Shapes filled the ripples and despite her reservations, Ember craned her neck to see. Draco whined.

"There's more than one way to test her. Come, child. Look in the waters and tell me what you see."

She didn't have to come closer to see. She felt the same man from her vision. She ungripped her hand and she was still holding a piece of his crimson cloak that she hastily threw in her pocket, Maryse's eyes widened. Shep grabbed her arm to hold her back.

"Don't," he warned, but she was pulled by a magic older than her. By the man with the crimson cloak. He needed her help. Atlantis needed her help. The king? The king was... not well. She put her hands on her temples and fell to her knees.

"Make it stop!" she said, but it wouldn't. The visions came faster and harder, burrowing into her head. Decades passed by as if they were nothing. Decades of boredom as the king grew more and more unwell, and the queen watched for her in the same bowl Maryse had now. It wasn't water, Ember realized. It was tears. She saw the queen at the same time the queen saw her, and they both let out a gasp. And still, the man watched. The man who was so familiar.

Maryse pushed the bowl off the table and the liquid spilled in slow motion and evaporated before it hit the floor, then the bowl itself smashed like a million teardrops. Draco issued one of his little roars and flew up as far as he could, before his wings gave out and he raised his haunches by Ember's side. She patted him absently. "It's all right, Draco, they won't hurt us. They can't."

She stood.

"I am the one you're looking for, but that doesn't mean I'll help you."

The attic was as silent as Ember's old house had ever been. In it, she heard the shadows of herself as a child. Of all the secrets her mother had carried and tried to bury in her art. They breathed through the very woodwork in the walls. *Help them*, it said, but still, Ember wasn't sure. Some help they'd given her mother, or her grandmother before her. How long had this been going on? Her mother's art, which had always only been a fantastical story, made sense in the most tragic, epic, personal way. The house shivered as snow piled up outside, and somewhere, the hellhounds sent by Zyah hunted her. She could feel them just outside the safety of the house, their frustration mounting. They were out for blood, but so was she.

Maryse cleared her throat. She waved a hand, and the shards of the bowl disappeared. Ember flexed a fist. Maryse was powerful, yes, but so was she. "Perhaps..." Maryse began.

Ember waved her off, headed to the back pile of her mother's works. They told the story of Atlantis, mostly it's rise and downfall, but there was one, somewhere that Ember remembered. The prophecy was in front of them all this time, but they'd filed it away. Typical. No one ever saw what was right in front of them. She started digging through a stack in the corner when Shep touched her shoulder gently.

"Be cautious of whatever it is you're about to tell us." He tipped his head to indicate Maryse standing just over his shoulder, hungry for information. The look on her face was almost worse than that of the hellhounds. Ember didn't know what the woman wanted, but she knew once Maryse got it, she and Shep were expendable, and perhaps Draco too. It was Ember's magic she was after, her actual life just an afterthought. And she did not want to die in this attack, or anywhere else for that matter.

"Hmm," she said, by way of agreement. She didn't tell him that the only person in that attic she trusted was four-legged and winged, and he couldn't talk. Draco snuggled up to her leg as if he'd felt her loyalty.

Maryse stepped next to her, almost tripping over Draco who glared at her and growled. "These paintings aren't part of the series." Maryse waved off the discarded paintings. "Half finished, or irrelevant."

"Irrelevant. Hmm." Ember came upon a painting of the backs of herself and Sierra, holding hands and with their feet in the ocean, which was a combination of the most delicious blue and whites on a windy day. The sea met the sky on a far-off horizon, and the sky was clear. Atlantis wasn't always on her mother's mind.

"I'd hardly say my life is irrelevant," she said, but she said it too low to hear because even now, she wasn't sure. Her life had surely felt irrelevant, even taking the dragon into account. She was no one of note. She held down a humble job that didn't exactly change the course of the world. Perhaps she'd given a few smiles in her life, perhaps she'd even made some people's lives easier when she shoveled the neighbors drive or made meals for an ill friend. Those things didn't exactly scream importance. Still, there was something important in the care her mother had taken with this picture. There was something important in love.

"They're not irrelevant," she said louder, finding the painting she was looking for behind the one of the girls. From love to … what? Possibility? Intrigue. Magic, for sure. This painting had hung in their dining room for so long that Ember had forgotten to ask who he was. The man in the red coat, looking over what she'd always thought was a cliff. The man in her vision. The man who was going to help them save Atlantis. This was a vision of the future. She'd seen it.

"You." She turned and met Shep's eyes. The same dark eyes from the painting. The same ones she'd seen in her dreams and visions. He wasn't an ancestor. He'd been there, somehow, and he was here now. The corner of his eyes turned up as he smiled sadly.

"Yes," he answered. "It's a long story, for later." His eyes flickered to the woman.

"I'll take that raincheck," she said, but she was cut off by the bray of a hellhound at the very door. More joined that. They were trapped.

Chapter 10

The alarm sounded on Shep's jeep, a strangely familiar beep, but it was cut off by a giant ripping, then a howl of frustration. The hellhounds beat at the walls of the house. How they'd not breached them sooner was a mystery to Ember, but old magic cloaked her home. Of course, she'd only been able to see that magic when the veil was lifted from her eyes, and after that she saw many things she hadn't seen before. So many things that she hadn't yet had time to adjust. Visions of the past and future swam before her eyes. Lightness and dark battled. She hoped she had time to change their fate.

Magic surrounded the whole island. It was apparent not just in the dragon, though now she felt his thoughts and feelings much deeper and sharper. He was currently hunched by the glazed windows overlooking the weedy backyard, growling below where the hellhounds (there were more than three, she was sure) howled in annoyance as they tested the perimeter.

"Other people really can't hear them?" She cringed. The howls were so grating she wanted to put her hands over her ears, but it wouldn't have helped. The noise shot right through her chest. There would be no blocking it, not if you felt magic. Fortunately, the winter residents who remained on the island were cooped up in their own homes to ride out the storm, blissfully unaware of the danger unfolding in their midst.

"Magic is a special frequency," Maryse muttered as she knelt by the fireplace concocting a spell. "Most magic is still simply herbs and words and intentions, but at the moment, those don't seem to be working." She looked like she was trying to create a portal like the one she'd stepped out of, but the hellhounds were siphoning off her magic.

"They'll call more," Shep had positioned himself by the stairs, not that his presence would help if they were overrun, but it was calming just the same. He gestured for her to follow him, but she was intrigued by the way the flames changed colors as Maryse blew gently on them.

"How are we going to escape through a fire?" Ember wondered.

"Oh." Maryse turned to watch the flames take quickly. "You're not. You're going to die here, but you might as well be warm."

These words might have rattled Ember only a day before. Now, she shared a look of annoyance with Draco, who raised his haunches and attempted a growl at Maryse's indifferent acceptance of their fate, his purple feathers prickling. *Those hellhounds would eat him alive*, Ember thought.

"Several centuries I've been at this," Maryse muttered and started pacing. "Kings I've trained, men and women with power. I've wielded magic stronger than anything you can imagine. And this. Here. With you..."

She sighed. "I was sure you'd be the one, but the timeline seems to have diverged…"

Ember had never held much sway with prophecies, not in the books she read and not in her heart, however – if this prophecy said they were supposed to die here then she was more than okay with changing it. And she was too intrigued by Shep's mysterious past to give up now. He was the man from her mother's visions. She knew that now. She felt his magic, but more… she felt a pull toward him. He was Atlantis, personified. He was the man in her dreams from the red cloak. The protector. More than just the bulk of his arms, his chest. The tilt of his head at any sound. It was his heart. His mission. He was sent to guide her to… what? Return Atlantis? Talk about a weight on their shoulders. How long had he been alive? How long had he wandered the ground, looking for magic and love?

Maryse muttered a spell under her breath, but nothing took. "The hellhounds will fall back at my signal." She looked Ember up and down. "Though I don't know why I should call them off. You're useless to me. Let them eat you."

Shep balled his fists, but Ember returned Maryse's stare. Useless, hm? Perhaps now, but not forever. This would not be the end, not here in this attic.

Shep pulled her by the arm. "We have to get out of here," he whispered. "Our only chance is a portal, but I cannot find one. Was there something in the house? Something… unusual?" He pulled Ember to the stairs while Maryse stoked the fire. "A place that was, perhaps, off limits? Somewhere they disappeared to, quite literally."

Ember shook her head as wind rattled the windows. "What do they look like?" she asked, praying for anything that would avoid an altercation with the beasts outside. Their cries increased in number. Shep had been right. They were calling more. Massing.

"Big enough to step through," Shep answered, a hint of desperation in his voice. She didn't blame him.

"Like a doorway?" she asked. There were plenty of those, but she'd stepped through them all when she'd lived here. They only led to the various rooms in the house, which Ember ticked off in her thoughts. Bedrooms… bathrooms… closets. None led anywhere special.

"Like a doorway, but… not." Shep frowned.

"Helpful." Draco followed close behind as she made her way past him and to the stairs, taking a breath at the top. The downstairs rooms were just as protected as the attic, but the hellhounds snarls seemed to be louder down there. She felt more vulnerable, as if by taking a step, she was admitting she was in something that was far bigger than her, far more vast, and far more frightening, and it was up to her to get them out. She took the first step. In fact, she'd taken the first step long ago, she just hadn't known it. She bent to pick Draco up, but he'd flown past her as if he were leading the way. His magic was growing too. She felt it waft past.

"You'll not outrun them, but you can try." Maryse called after her, but Shep kept them moving. Perhaps they could outrun her, at least, though Ember wanted to turn back and punch the woman in the face.

"A window, perhaps? Anything reflective," Shep added. "Somewhere you weren't allowed to go." Ember turned the corner before she could hear any more bullshit from Maryse, but no doubt the woman had magic enough to find them if she wanted. The wallpaper was peeling in places, but otherwise the corridors were the same as they were during her whole childhood. She passed her room, which she'd covered every inch. Sierra's. Their bathroom. Her parents room. Draco led them to her parent's room, where she stopped short.

"Maybe in here?" she said. She'd rarely gone in their bedroom before, and she was surprised to find herself so emotional now. The bed and furniture were covered in sheets, giving the room an otherworldly feel. Even the hellhounds increasing brays felt muted inside. Shep managed to close the door behind them and lock it, while Ember shivered. Draco whinnied by the bathroom door. Did he have to pee?

"There is a strange magic here," Shep commented. Even new to magic, Ember couldn't disagree. She pulled the curtain from the bureau revealing an ornate mirror. Some of her mother's things were still on top, and Ember caught a whiff of her rose perfume.

How did you activate a portal? She looked at herself. Her dark, scissored bangs that she liked to hide behind. Her dark eyes. The coal eyeliner and shadow she'd put on that morning that she thought was for her own benefit. Would she have worn something different than an old concert T-shirt and ripped jeans if she knew she was going to die? Probably not. She stared intently. Nothing changed but Shep desperately pulled sheets off the rest of the furniture, then dug through the closet, but it wasn't the closet that Ember saw when she backed up. The bath. Of course. She was never allowed in there. The faucet had always been broken, almost as if it had been made that way. She walked slowly past him and cracked the door.

The white bath was the same as she remembered. No sheets covering anything. No dust, even. And strangely, the lights worked. She heard someone calling her name from far away and stepped back. Almost as if she were pulled. Shep yanked her arm.

"We almost lost you!" he cried. The lights seemed to have gotten lower. Had time passed?

"What happened?" she asked.

Now it seemed as if the hellhounds were at the very door, scratching and screaming. "We have to go together," he said. "Hurry now." He took Ember's hand with Draco tucked under his arm.

"The bathroom is the portal?" she asked. She barely had time to register how weird it all was before he stepped into the bathtub. There was still a drain with a hose where her parents had claimed it was broken, but she'd never noticed the bath was so white she could see her own reflection, or that there was an ever-present couple inches of water at the bottom.

"The portal is the bathroom?" she asked over Draco's increasing whines.

"That would be silly," Shep said, stepping his boots into the water as the window buckled from the hellhounds constant pressure. "The bathtub is. Get in."

Ember stepped gingerly but quickened when the window buckled, and she could see the teeth through the hole they made. They growled and scratched, but the scene before them seemed to fall into a thousand sparkles, and she fell.

"Where are we going?" she asked, but the world folded, and again, she fell.

Chapter 11

At least the portal wasn't the toilet, Ember thought as she tumbled through space and time briefly enough to catch a view of the entire universe before Shep yanked her wrist and pulled her out the other side. The next thing she knew, she was flat on her back with Shep peeling her eye open.

"You can't lose focus when portalling," Shep said with aggravation as Draco flapped his wings wildly.

Ember attempted to sit, but her head swam. "Pardon me, but I've never portalled before," she grumbled. Draco rubbed up next to her and she put her face in his feathers for a moment. He smelled familiar, like the ink and woodsmoke of the bookstore. She chanced opening an eyelid to see the pulled string of a placemat. "Are we…?"

Shep laughed. "Of course we're at the shop," he said. "Where else would your parents portal to, I suppose," he said.

"I can think of a few places that might have been more helpful," she answered. Shep sat back on his heels, apparently confident she wasn't going to pass out. It was cooler in the reading nook now. The fire had burned down only to embers, sending shadows across the bookshelves that looked like monsters. The lingering smell of sulfur hung in the air, and it didn't help Ember's headache, which had settled into a low throb.

"Who was that woman Maryse?" she asked. She fought nausea to sit up, squeezing her eyes closed until it passed. Draco put his two paws on the window and patted it. He was trying to say something, but her head wasn't clear enough to get it. "Easy." She patted him down, but the dragon became more insistent, growling and crying to go outside.

"Someone who wants Atlantis returned, but not for the right purposes," Shep said by way of answer. He eyed the dragon. "Does he have to, umm… go out?"

Ember frowned. She wanted to maintain Draco's dignity, but Shep might have a point. "I'll take him," Shep said. He squatted down and Draco jumped right into his arms so aggressively he lost a purple feather on the way. It floated to the floor.

"Traitor," Ember mumbled, leaning back against the shelves. Poetry, if she could remember correctly. The bell over the door jingled and let a draft in the store. Ember pulled down a faded copy of Bukowski, but the words blurred. She waited until they passed, and Draco came bounding back.

"Was I supposed to…" He made some kind of hand gesture that Ember guessed was supposed to mean pick up Draco's waste. She laughed.

"I think it's okay. No one can see it." She sat up, and Shep picked up the Bukowski and leafed through it. "Who was that woman?" she asked, the first of many questions.

He tossed the book. "She considers herself an oracle, but I'd not trust her prophecies." He frowned. "The descendants of Atlantis are as different as they are magical. You can't trust them all. In fact, there are some that would sell out Atlantis to Zyah…"

She scoffed. "No way he's still alive," she countered.

Shep shook his head. "Perhaps not, but his magic remains. Someone hunts the ancestors of Atlantis. Some of them have banded together, but I'd caution you to be selective with your trust."

She climbed to her feet, only a hint of dizziness remaining. "Why should I trust you?" she asked.

The answer was that she didn't have a choice, but he wasn't someone to throw out an easy response. Instead, he shifted his gaze from the dragon, who was daintily licking himself in the corner, to the discarded book which had landed open to a short poem about life and death, to the fire. The flames danced in his irises, pulling out the magic in them. It was all around them—how had she not seen it before?

"I'm not unaware, that given the circumstances, it is a big ask." He finally shifted his deep brown gaze back to her, pinning her with its intensity. "And I'm sorry I was the one to have to drag you, Ember Weathers, into this. But trust, like magic, is intuitive. What do you feel, truly, in your heart?"

Ember closed her eyes. She'd always been different. When she was young, it was in ways she couldn't explain. And when she was older? Well, she could see a dragon, but that was the least of it. She saw things, sometimes, before they happened. She knew what people were thinking. She could read their moods and emotions. She could close her eyes and see scenes from far away in time and space. She'd convinced herself it was nothing more than her strong imagination. That those things that made her special also made her mental. A freak. She hid them, and in doing so, bound her own power. It was so clear, now. If she so chose, she could wield a flame that could burn the whole island.

If she so chose, she could bring Atlantis back home.

Ember perched on her favorite easy chair, moving Draco's green blanket. "What is it like there?" she asked, ignoring his question about instinct.

"Atlantis?" Shep asked. He looked up, far past the ceiling and it's water marks. "To say it was magic wouldn't do it justice, would it? And the city needs justice, after all this time." He paused, holding his palms together until a blue orb grew between them. "Once, I could have shown you from the memories passed down, but that magic grows weak without its source. One day it will disappear altogether. But words? I suppose they are magic of their own kind, aren't they?" The blue orb fell into a thousand glittering pieces of dust, reflected in the low light. Ember thought she saw a thousand faces reflected within, the pulse of true magic. Happiness. Joy. Merriment.

The glitter faded.

"Magic is not an otherworldly force, as this world would lead you to believe." One small blue orb remained. Shep rolled it back and forth between his fingers. The orb revealed nothing more than light, but Ember thought she could see the spires of a tall, white castle inside. "Magic is nothing more than love, of the purest, most wholesome form." The orb faded until it was little more than a translucent blue bubble. Ember watched her reflection in it.

She shifted on the seat. "Then what about those who seek to do harm?" she asked. "Why would anyone turn on love?"

Shep let his hands fall and a shadow crossed his face. "Love can do all kinds of cruel things," he said, simply.

Ember closed her eyes, only belatedly realizing how long it had been since they'd returned when she heard the bell and a commotion up front. She could usually tell how many people entered, but the shouts and the footfalls carried over each other. Shep beat her to the front of the store, and she took a place beside him. Two men and a woman who looked like they belonged in the children's section by the pirate books spread out in front, checking out the bestsellers.

"Is this a joke?" she asked, but it surely wasn't. The closest walked up to her with a long, curved sword and her heart caught in her throat. Slaughtered by pirates. Was that in the prophecy? His blond hair was held back by a tie, and he had a dirty blond mustache and goatee that was struggling to grow in. It was the puffy white shirts that made the costumes, but Ember was starting to fear they weren't costumes at all.

"You're lucky we found you before the hellhounds," was all he said.

The ginger haired girl smirked. "Yes, this way the hellhounds can kill us all at once. Makes it much easier." She rubbed her chin and gave Ember a wicked grin that made Ember like her. They didn't look like the pirates from the books or movies, unless you were talking *Peter Pan*. They couldn't be much older than her. Their faces still spoke of youth.

The one who approached her elbowed the girl. "Not today, eh? Take them to the ship."

The girl raised her eyebrows and winked at Ember as if they shared a secret. "That begs the issue if *we* can escape, Captain. At the moment, that might be a problem."

The one they called Captain had already started making his way out. He paused by the biographies, the cover of Dr. Mike a stark contrast to his profile. "We shall fly," he said simply. He turned and looked over his shoulder at Draco, who was nestled under Shep's arm. "After all, we have a dragon now. And some strong magic."

Draco seemed more than comfortable with the entire situation, resting comfortably in the nook in Shep's arm. Shep leaned over. "Am I supposed to do something to activate him or something?" he whispered to Ember.

"Activate him? He's not an antacid!" She took slow steps on purpose, though the place still smelled of sulfur.

"How else do you suggest getting out of this?" he asked.

I don't know, she wanted to say. None of this makes any sense and until this morning, I was a nice, normal orphan. But the truth was, like Shep had said, she'd always known. That power she'd felt earlier seemed to have receded though. And through her fear, she couldn't even manage to light a cigarette.

The pirates led them through the blowing snow and down the deserted main street. The sun was setting now, leaving the snow in silhouette and the main street empty. Several inches had fallen, and they had to trudge through. Good thing the pirates were wearing those ridiculous boots. Ember wasn't though. Shep paled when they saw the harbor. She followed his gaze to a ship moored where the ferry usually was, only it was hovering about a foot off the water. Of course it was.

"Bounty hunters," Shep whispered. He'd lost his hat and coat, and his shirtsleeves were rolled up. He was entirely unprepared for this little adventure.

"Bounty hunters?" The pirate closest to him laughed. "The only person after you, mate, would kill the both of us. Naw, we're here to save you. Someone has to protect the children of Atlantis." They were casual, as if this kind of thing happened all the time for them. And maybe it did. Ember searched her memory for books with space pirates, but the ones she remembered all involved war or other unpleasant situations.

"How exactly are you going to save us?" Ember asked, but they'd reached the end of the street where a genuine wooden plank let up to the ship. Under it, waves crashed and struggled to reach the hull. Magic, she thought. The ship hummed with it, but it hummed weakly.

"Hurry now," the young Captain said, ushering them on. He watched the skies, and he watched the grounds. There was danger all over. Ember didn't know where to look. Draco hopped twice, then flapped his wings. He hovered for a moment then flew on the ship himself, landing on the rail.

"Huh," she said. "I guess he can fly." *Maybe all he needed was motivation all along*, she thought. She wished he could fly them all out of there, but then what? She looked over her shoulder at Shep, grimacing in his now ruined jacket. Gods help her, these space pirates might be her best option.

Chapter 12

Though the gangplank was split and broken in places, the ship was surprisingly modern on the inside. In fact, impossibly modern. Even the weather was warmer on board, the sun peeking out of the high clouds and snow circling lazily until it melted on the deck.

"Is this a yacht?" Ember asked, eyeing the hot tub. She took a step back and almost lost her balance on the slick floor. From the gangplank, it looked like a wooden pirate ship from an old movie. One step on the ship though, and they were in an entirely different world.

"Of course," the captain replied. His puffy shirt was replaced by a smoking jacket, and his long hair was pulled back in a leather band. "We might be low on magic, but we're not barbarians."

"Of course," Ember muttered. The captain eyed Draco warily. Even the dragon looked more majestic on the bow of an expensive ship. His purple stood out against the white walls and railings. She was almost sure he'd gotten bigger in the last day.

The orange haired girl that had joined them at the bookstore tapped the captain on the shoulder. She'd also transformed, though less dramatically. Her green slacks and khakis were more staff looking, and more comfortable. With a weary look she said, "Captain Hawk, some of the crew wants to cage the dragon so we don't lose its magic." She eyed Ember then looked down. "Begging your pardon," she mumbled.

Captain Hawk pinned Ember with a gaze before she could open her mouth. "I don't think that will be necessary, do you?" He spoke in a way that was both reassuring and threatening at the same time. A nifty trick.

"What about it?" Ember turned to Draco, puffing his wings on the rail. "Are you going to fly off and leave us?"

She felt a message back that had more to do with the fact he'd never leave her, and she distinctly heard a low *no* that caused a shiver. "He'll stick with me," she replied with confidence, not mentioning that they were hostages at best. She picked at a string from her old concert t-shirt, wishing the ship's magic had changed her own looks too. She tapped snow off her boots, and it made a puddle on the pristine deck, which the captain frowned at.

"What about that one?" the captain inclined his head to Shep, who was conferring with another of the pirates, this one in a red shirt that said "entertainment" on the back. His lips pressed thin, Shep watched Ember out of the corner of his eye.

"I've no idea about him." She frowned. All she really knew was he was the man from her mother's visions, and hers to. He'd saved her from the hellhounds, and from Maryse, for whatever that was worth. As to what he was doing here, she had no idea how it was possible.

The staff began to unhook the ship from the dock, and it rose another foot in the air, listing perilously to the left and right. Draco was the only one who didn't seem to have a problem with it, lifting himself to flap his wings in midair. Showoff. The captain clung to the handrails so hard his knuckles turned white, and if Ember wasn't mistaken, his face took on a green hue.

"Are you seasick?" she asked incredulously. Once the ship was unmoored, the listing subsided. Shep came back and clapped his hands.

"Good news. Dinner is at 7 and there's a show following."

She clenched her jaw. "I'm not here for a show," she countered. "Where are you taking us?"

"Wherever it is it's better than here," Shep responded. "Someone very strong is after you, Ember. My magic would be no match." The hellhounds had reached the main street and were gaining. She sure hoped they couldn't fly. Shep leaned in. "I can read them, Ember. We can trust them. More than those hellhounds, anyway."

She eyed the situation wearily. Weird magical pirates or vicious hellhounds? She'd have to take her chances.

"Take flight," the captain directed, and the staff who weren't in red shirts scrambled about. Ember tried to avoid the red shirted ones, they looked like they wanted to break into song. She followed this captain across a large promenade and up a set of stairs to what looked like a bridge. She took the door behind him before it could slam. Draco stayed back with Shep, and she was right, someone was breaking into what sounded like a showtune. She let the door close behind them, and the silence in the bridge was deafening.

The captain leaned over a large steering wheel, looking exhausted. The sun had already set, leaving a pink streak in the clouds. Ember stifled a yawn. She couldn't rest until she knew they wouldn't be killed in their sleep.

"I'm afraid we're not going where I intended, at least not in the way I intended." He closed his eyes for a moment, then tipped his head up before opening them. "Captain Hawkins Shallow. My friends call me Hawk."

She eyed him. The smoking jacket wasn't a good look on him. He looked better in pirate gear. Here, he looked like a boy playing dress up. "I'd hardly call us friends," she said, but he went on.

"And you are Ember Weathers. Welcome to my ship, the Utopia. We're here to save you."

"Thanks." Her voice dripped sarcasm. She ran her finger along the line of strange instruments with funny gears and dials, taking care not to press any buttons. Through the main windows, she could see the sea below them and land fading away. "We were doing okay, though."

He tilted his head, a measure of amusement in his eyes. "Were you? Those hellhounds would have found you in mere minutes. You're lucky we arrived when we did. We were tracking them."

Ember let out a breath. "Who sent them?" she asked. "Why me? Why now?"

He laughed, and she immediately warmed to him. It wasn't a laugh that was forced, but a laugh that said she'd regret asking that question when she knew the answer. "I imagine I can't convince you to have a rest, is that true?" She shook her head. "Or catch the show?" That smile again.

"No thank you," she responded.

"Ahh, I think they are working on a musical. They have little to do. We are what's left of the people of Atlantis here on the ground," he explained. "At least those we can find. We've banded together because—as you can see_there are forces against us. Yet somehow your family slipped through the cracks all these years." He stared her down with eyes of intense brown, but she had no answer for him.

"As for who hunts us?" he continued. "Rumors say it's Zyah. He was so angry at the raising of Atlantis he vowed to hunt every last ancestor, but that was centuries ago. I'd hardly think he's alive, but his curse lives on – as does his queen who had a reputation even bloodier than his. Dark magic can be…" He looked out as the last rays of light turned the sky a deep purple. "…stubborn and vexing, not to mention deadly. It continues through the energy of anger, of which there is plenty."

There was something in his countenance that was personal. "Were you there on Atlantis?" she asked quietly. It seemed like such a dumb question. How could he be hundreds of years old? Yet, so many things she didn't think were possible had happened already.

This time he only smiled and shouldered his way out of the jacket, under which he seemed just a regular young man. "I am older than I seem, but not that old. My grandfather was a trader. Off in a foreign city when the raising happened. Left behind, as so many others. We have cobbled together a brotherhood with our remaining magic, but we don't have the magic to counter such evil as the hellhounds. We risked much to get you, but our hope is your dragon will help us remain in flight. I've never seen a dragon. I'd thought they ceased existing." Ember fell into a chair and rubbed her eyes.

"How well do you know Shepherd?" he asked as he took a seat next to her. The ship steered itself.

"As well as I know you," she said with a yawn. "Which is to say, not at all. I am entirely friendless, unless you count my dragon." She reached out for Draco in her mind, wanting to be assured by his presence, but instead felt he was listening to show tunes. Traitor.

Hawk took a breath and pulled his shoulders back. "Well, we can't have that." He held out his right hand. "Captain Hawkins Shallow, but you can call me Hawk." She was touched by the gesture but didn't quite trust him completely. Still, she had to sleep, or she'd fall over.

"Ember Weathers. Thoroughly confused."

"Well, Miss Weathers, we take care of guests on my ship. Let me see you to your quarters."

"Where are we flying to?" she asked, as she got up to follow him out the door.

He wound her down several staircases and down long corridors, clean and clear but with evidence of people. Scuff marks. Faded music. Half drank coffee left on tables. "Circling your island, for now," he answered. "We don't have the magic of Atlantis to escape detection. We'll settle down in the water when we're far enough from the hellhounds." He paused at a white door and waved his hand over a sensor. A sea of sparkles fell from the top to the bottom. Enchanted, Ember guessed. He opened it and gestured her into a suite larger than she'd ever seen.

She walked through a sitting room with a couch and a desk complete with stationary and ink quill reading *The Utopia.* She ran her hand over the feather. Who would she be writing to, and about what? She looked over the ocean, where the moon was rising in the sky. Full, of course it was. This was probably all some kind of fever dream. They were so close to the water she could see the whitecaps.

"The hellhounds?" she asked.

"Cannot swim," he answered with flourish, then frowned and looked out over her shoulder. "At least not to our knowledge. Certainly, they can't leap out of the water. I hope, anyway." He rubbed his goatee. It somehow managed to make him look younger.

His gaze was dreamy as he looked over the ocean. Did he dream of returning to Atlantis, a place he'd never been? Or did he, like Ember, simply seek a place to belong? She started with the realization of her own loneliness, but she should have known it all along. Her heart didn't need adventure as much as it needed loyalty and comradery. Could they exist together? No one had ever been on her side, not since her parents died.

"We've spent years on the ocean, and still, I do not tire of it," he said, breaking out of his reverie. "Do you suppose that's how they feel in the sky?"

Ember looked out the window. She remembered the city from her mother's paintings – the reverie before the city was cursed. The sadness after. She shook her head sadly. "I think they wish to come home," she answered softly.

He looked away. "I believe that as well, but all we can do is be ready for them."

"Perhaps we can do more than that," she said, thinking of the magic Shep had called up in her. "Why did you ask me if I knew Shep well?" she asked. "And where have you brought him?"

Captain Hawk retreated back through the sitting room. "I've been at this more years than I can tell you, Ember Weathers," he said. "I've tracked down magic.

Strong magic, not as strong as yours and never with a dragon, but still… I've not heard of him, nor felt his presence. Something is… off. I can't tell you exactly what. Take caution with him."

She followed him to the door, intending to lock it however he'd done it. He reached it first and took her hand, holding it halfway between a shake and a kiss, as if he were lost in time and the customs of this world were foreign even though he was born here. She smiled, and he kissed her hand briefly. She felt a breath of Atlantis in his touch that sent a shiver down her arm.

"As to where he is, I believe he is watching a musical. He will not bother you here." He released her hand and patted the doorjamb. "We do not have much magic, but we've made some modifications. You'll be safe." He turned to leave, then looked over his shoulder. "Oh, and don't be startled when we land in the ocean. It can get a little… bumpy." She knew she wasn't mistaken when she saw a look of mischief cross his face.

"Oh dear." She smiled. Perhaps she was in for both adventure and camaraderie. She almost missed the pirate outfits he'd first appeared in, but she was going to have to tell him something about dressing for the 21st century. Shame, though, she'd look good in a corset and puffy shirt.

"I'll hold on," she said.

"See that you do. Good night." He turned and walked down the hall. When the door closed, it released a shower of sparks, and she knew she was safe for as long as she stayed hidden.

Chapter 13

The man now known as Shepherd walked the deck of the ship, steering clear of other Atlantian descendants. It wasn't hard. Shep's senses were sharper than normal, even more so at night. And lucky for him, he didn't need sleep the way the rest of them did. He'd let them take him to a fancy room, then skirted their magic to duck out and seek the stars.

He found himself on the front rail of the ship, next to a bubbling jacuzzi that made him grimace. Leave it to these amateurs to use their magic for such indulgences instead of a ship that actually flew. Magic should have risen them above the clouds, but instead the ship was so close to the water he could feel its spray if he put his hand over the rail. The wind was brisk and chill, but the snow had passed. They were far enough from the island to barely see the peaks of the north side.

She was correct. He'd once been known as Casius, long ago. Walking away from Atlantis, well… it had not been pretty, but he had the blessing of the queen, and her hopes, as well. His hands gripped the rails as he watched the dark ocean collide with the stars – always on the lookout for danger. He'd searched for her in this lifetime, yes, but in other lifetimes as well. She didn't remember, but her lives had stretched from a village in Romania in the early 1900's all the way back to the dark ages, and before. Always, he was too late. By rights, Atlantis should have returned centuries ago. But in his fever to keep Atlantis away, Zyah had always gotten to her first. He sent hellhounds, soldiers, and mercenaries. But never came himself. He was resourceful, and he desperately did not want Atlantis returned.

Shep searched the stars for the place he once called home. He'd lived longer than most. A gift, or a curse. One he willingly sought. He had unfinished business on Atlantis, business he was unable to let go of throughout several lifetimes. A woman? No. The shadow of a smile crossed his face. There was one, that's true, that he'd loved and lost. She left this world bearing his child, and not even the magic of Atlantis could bring her back. Shep knew that, and he'd done his mourning. Years of it. But leaving his daughter had been a sacrifice he almost couldn't make. But if he did not go, no one would. And Atlantis would be cursed forever. Aurelia would be cursed forever. No, it is the bane of a father to do the right thing, no matter how hard, and this? Atlantis had asked almost more than he could bear, but he bore it. For Aurelia and for the city. Someday they would be reunited.

He kicked the rail, but the ship was sturdier than she looked, and he cursed the pain in his toe. It had been centuries. Of course, his daughter had grown, but yet the stories were vague. Vaguer, even, than the hope in his heart. Some said they were frozen in time, his child still only six months old with the most beautiful smile.

He'd devoted his life to finding her.

"Rough night?"

Shepherd turned. Rarely was anyone able to sneak up on him. Captain Hawk was there, the dragon padded midway between them as if brokering a match. Shep knew of this captain by reputation. Older than he looked with his blond hair and baby face, yet much younger than Shep in years. What would Captain Hawk think if Shep told him he'd once played ball with Hawk's grandfather in an alley in Atlantis? He'd want to know Shep's secret, but he'd never told another soul. He'd sold more than his soul for his longevity.

Shep plastered on his best fake smile and gestured to the view over the rail. "It's the best place on the ship to think," he told Hawk. "At least that I've found, though admittedly I'm new here."

Draco flew off to investigate a pipe trailing out steam. Hawk approached the railing, then turned and leaned on it. He looked older in the low light. His face pale, his eyes restless. He tapped his toe. "I've spent lifetimes searching out bloodlines. Survivors." He turned his gaze to Shep, and it hardened. "Sometimes we're just in time. Sometimes we're too late. But you..." He pushed off the rail and paced. "You I've never felt or heard of, yet you have magic of a kind I've never felt. It's restless. Old."

Shepherd brushed him off. "Surely you don't know every ancestor from Atlantis."

Hawk shrugged, looking down the pipe Draco had disappeared into. "Perhaps not, but we've done extensive research. Exhaustive." The dragon popped out of the pipe and shook dust off its purple mane before testing his wings, hovering a few feet in the air.

"What is it you're accusing me of, Captain? Shall I prepare myself for the brig?" Shep asked it in jest, but he prepared himself just in case. He would not let himself be taken. Ember wasn't safe enough under these juvenile's care.

"Nothing." The captain waved a hand as if they were just talking about the weather, cool and windy. It rustled Hawk's long ponytail, but Shep's own hair was too closely shorn to rustle with something as insignificant as wind. "It's just curious, is all. Have you known all along? Where did you come from? What line?"

Shep waited a beat for a gusty wind to pass. Should he tell this boy, and make him an ally or potentially an enemy? The things he had to do to remain immortal were ethically challenging at best, but the ends justified the means, or so he'd told himself for the last century, and that end was finally within his grasp. The boy would have questions. A man that lives for thousands of years, even one from Atlantis, is and should be appropriately suspect.

He opened his mouth, but he hadn't decided how to respond when a horn sounded deep within the ship and echoed over the air. Hawk tilted his head when the noise ceased and inhaled a sharp breath when it sounded again. He looked over the bow, grabbing the rail with his hands.

"What…" Shep asked. Hawk held up a finger to silence him.

"Two…" he mumbled, then cursed when it sounded a third time.

Shep waited a moment, but the air was charged. Even the stars seemed brighter, pointed directly at them like a million tiny spotlights. The wind picked up and buffered the ship from side to side.

"He's found us again." Hawk nailed Shepherd with a look. "And we've no magic to escape. Do you have any suggestions?"

Shep didn't have to ask who. Zyah's ire at Atlantis was legendary. Shep had managed to stay out of his orbit, but in every lifetime, he sought Ember, and in every lifetime the king had slain her. He paled. "We must protect her," he said.

"We are on the same side of that, at least," Captain Hawk answered. "But how?" Shep had no answer to that. His magic would not lift a ship, and where would they go?

"Come with me to the bridge," Hawk continued. "You may be of help yet."

Chapter 14

Ember didn't wake when the horn sounded three times in warning. She was deep in a recurring dream she'd had as far back as she could remember. One where she was running, both away and toward, but she seemed to go in circles. She never reached her destination, not in all the years she'd been dreaming it, but she saw glimpses of lives that were both familiar and foreign. Of loves, death—so much death. So much fear, and above all that, an island she could never reach.

She woke with a start. The ship was listing so hard water lapped the window on the side. Water? She thought they were above it.

"Draco!" she called, but the dragon was nowhere to be found. She felt him nearby and got up quickly to search him out, stumbling when the ship righted itself to the sound of, if she weren't mistaken, cannons.

She scrambled to dress in the clothes that had been left, a long sleeve shirt and jeans close enough to her size. Out the window, the sun was high enough for her to wonder how long she'd been out. It felt like more time had passed than a simple day. Another lifetime, perhaps.

She stumbled into the hallway using the walls to right herself. Her guards were nowhere to be found, but the ship seemed to react to her magic, flickering when she touched it. She felt the same tingling in her hand as when she held the fireball, and wondered, briefly if that same magic could launch the ship up and over whatever enemies they were facing. She climbed the stairs and ended up in the kitchen, where a couple of the crew were preparing a meal. She raised an eyebrow, but her stomach grumbled at the spread they'd laid out.

The girl that had been with Hawk at the bookstore was behind an island, baking as if they didn't seem to be in some dire situation. Ember stopped short. "Happens all the time," the girl told Ember with a shrug, tucking a wayward lock of ginger hair behind her ear and putting on an oven mitt to check muffins. She turned back. "They need a few more minutes." She closed the oven door. "It's dangerous business, rescuing Atlantians. But what else are we going to do? Hide?" She held a hand out for Ember to shake but looked down and realized she was still wearing an oven mitt printed with lobsters.

"Sorry." She laughed. "They call me Paine. Like the bread, not the feeling. Hang on." She held the counter and Ember followed suit as the cannon blasted and the ship shuddered. Paine let go and wiped her hands on her apron, already covered with flower. Her hair was tied back in a long braid, and freckles splashed across her face.

"What is that?" Ember asked, still gripping the counter, but eyeing the pastries.

Paine shrugged, a curl escaped it's confines. "The sound or the pastries?" she asked with a smile.

"The gunfire," Ember responded, though Paine had put her at ease.

The girl shrugged. "Sometimes a warning," she said. "Sometimes someone chasing us. If it gets bad enough, we'll pool our magic to get out of here, but it takes a lot and there's not much left." She eyed Ember. "'Least not until you showed up. What can you do?"

Ember rubbed her eyes, still not focused from sleep. "I have no idea," she admitted, her hand making its way to the pastry.

"Oooh, you're one of those." Paine's green eyes widened. "What's it like to never have known?" She rested her elbows on the table and leaned in. "Most of us grew up on the run. We don't know any other life. Or lives." She sniffed the air then cursed, turning quickly to put the oven mitt back on and rescue the muffins which were only slightly burned.

"It's… confusing," Ember admitted. The ship shuddered, and Paine spoke with her back turned.

"You better get up there. They might need you," she said, shedding the oven mitt to gently take a bite of muffin.

"Need me for what?" Ember asked. She'd already stuffed one of the pastries down when Paine wasn't looking and tried to talk through the mouthful.

Paine smiled. "Defense, I guess. You're chock full of magic, I can tell."

Before Ember could ask, the other crew member who'd taken them from the bookstore strolled down the stairs, not at all looking like he was in a hurry. His face screwed up in annoyance. Dark stubble covered his chin, and a t-shirt covered his wide frame. Ember was thankful it read "I'm with the band" and not "entertainment," though maybe they were one in the same. He grabbed one of the muffins then cursed when he burned his hand. Didn't stop him from eating it, though. Paine swatted him lightly.

"Hey Nate," Paine said to him.

He nodded to Paine then turned to Ember. "Been looking all over for you," he said. "You weren't in your room." He paused. "I was supposed to be guarding, but…" He trailed off and shrugged. Ember frowned. Good thing she didn't need protecting. She nabbed another pastry from the counter.

"Take me to my dragon," she told him with as much authority as she could muster with crumbs all over her shirt.

"That little bugger's yours, is he?" Nate asked. Ember bristled but he said it with a spark in his eye. "Been nipping at the crew."

"I wonder why?" Paine laughed.

"Anyway, there's some emergency," Nate said leading her out.

"Oh, the three whistles," Paine called as they left the kitchen. "They'll have to zap us out, maybe. Always fun. I'll wait to hear."

Zap us, Ember wondered. She hoped that was a phrase and not an actual description. She pushed her sleeves up. The shirt they'd given her was a size too big. They passed a dining hall, an open deck, and…

"Is that a casino?" Ember asked. Most of the crew areas were empty.

Nate smiled. "Small wagers only," he said, as if that explained everything.

"Huh," she said. She'd missed out on a lot not being part of this merry band, though if Paine were to be believed, at least she'd had the benefit of a childhood. She wouldn't have traded those years for anything.

They emerged on the sunny deck, and it was as Ember feared. They were low enough she could see the sea lapping the sides of the ship over the low sun. And the sea was as angry as it appeared Captain Hawk was. He shouted orders to his assembled crew, but they didn't seem to know what to do. She walked off to stand next to Shep at the rail who seemed strangely put together, as if he were the eye of this storm.

"Evasive maneuvers!" Hawk cried to a chorus of yells and grumbles.

"Where are we?" she asked in a soft voice.

Shep looked her up and down. "Nice outfit," he said. He'd been given a new pair of khakis and shirt, only his shirt was a size too small instead of big and fitted over his wide chest and arms. Of course it did.

"Not exactly my choice," she responded. "Where are we?"

"It turns out those bastards can swim," Shep said. "Hawk pushed us out to sea to outrun them, but they're fast too. Look." He pointed to a spot on the horizon where a pillar of smoke came up. "At least we got them away from the island, but he doesn't have the magic to keep us going at this rate." He eyed her up and down.

"Here we go again," she mumbled, but she couldn't deny the feeling of giddiness as magic pooled in her fingers. She looked at Shep. "The last time I tried this I almost burned down my store."

"You're not in the store now," he pointed out. She eyed the ship around them. It was clearly flammable.

"And there are hellhounds," Hawk joined them, not looking like the pirate she'd first seen or the ridiculous showman she'd seen next, but just a boy who was afraid. He was sweating through his white shirt. "Close," he told her. "Really close."

Evasive maneuvers consisted of banking right. It was nothing but a fancy zigzag. There wasn't even any magic involved. The other members of the crew rushed back and forth on the ship, but what they were doing Ember couldn't tell.

Draco flew up and out from one of the pipes leading who knows where. His coat was covered in dust, and he dropped a rat at Ember's feet. He'd grown just in the time they were there and if she wasn't wrong, he was enjoying himself. He practically purred as he hovered in front of her.

"They need us," she said, ignoring the rat for the time being. It had always been easy to talk to Draco, probably because the dragon didn't talk back but projected comfort. It wasn't comfort that she felt now. The dragon was itching for a fight. He huffed smoke. The rest of the world fell away as she concentrated on the dragon.

"No," she told him. "Not that way." Draco against a hellhound in a fight? She wouldn't risk it. She lowered her voice. "Magic," she told him. She felt his excitement pick up. "Have you known all along?" she asked. But of course he did. Why else did dragons exist if not for magic?

She looked up to the clouded sky, still as far away as ever. Atlantis wasn't going to come down and save them. They'd have to do it themselves.

The crew was still shouting but Shep and Hawk had gone silent, watching this interaction with interest. She balled her fists. "Okay," she said. "Tell me what to do."

Chapter 15

Shep watched from the shadows as she summoned her magic, and it was every bit as amazing as he thought it would be. She didn't know how to wield it, that much he could tell, but it seemed to come as second nature to her. It had been many years, but he'd never even seen a sorcerer on Atlantis with this kind of power. Some could wield the elements—a dribble of water, a touch of wind—but none could call up a tower of flame as she could and use its energy for magic.

The flame spun in her hand and grew about a foot in the air before she stopped it. The flame reflected in her eyes, pulling out the gold which indicated magic she had no idea she was capable of. Her gaze was far away, connected to her dragon, if he had to guess. The small beast circled and gave out a roar, the first he'd heard in a long, long time. Hope grew in his heart. Perhaps this was the lifetime. Perhaps this was their chance. Perhaps he'd see his daughter again.

Ember was everything he'd seen in those other lifetimes but never held. Powerful, but cautious. Brave and beautiful, but not in the conventional way of Atlantis or these times. There was something special about a woman who had her own style, who walked away from the crowd. She thought it made her stand alone. Perhaps she thought she was pushing people away. If so, it was because there were none other like her. No wonder she'd felt lonely in this lifetime. In all of them.

She had no idea the power in her hands. He stood poised, ready to intervene if things went out of control, but she'd taken to it fast. Of course she had. She'd been born to this. And born and born and born. This time, she would not have to die for it. He'd see to it she didn't and protect her with his life.

The hellhounds fell back. He didn't hear it as much as feel the release of pressure, but at the same time, the flame in her palm began to grow and the skies grew dark. Draco howled. Clouds circled around her and wind whipped her hair up and around. Before Shep could step in Hawk reached Ember and broke her out of her trance. She balled her fists again and the flames were extinguished as quickly as they'd been formed. The clouds that had gathered around them fell like insignificant pieces of dust on the wind. The ship began to take flight ever so slowly, rocking the slightest bit as it emerged from the water. Even the water itself wanted to hold on, regretfully letting go of the ship with a splash as they ascended.

Ember shook her palms while Draco took flight and circled them, calling forth his own stream of flames. The beast was growing by the day, and his flames more dangerous. Not dangerous enough to take on the hellhounds though. For that, they had to retreat.

"Concentrate." Shep stepped by her side, bracing her again. Her small frame stiffened before leaning into him. In front of them, the ocean splayed out, the waves deep and treacherous. The wind had picked up, and clouds swirled above them, clouds that could be hiding Atlantis at this very minute, or any number of other dangers. Hellhounds weren't the worst of what he'd seen Zyah unleash on the Atlantis survivors. Indeed, if he were correct, hellhounds weren't the least of the tortures Zyah had given to her over the lifetimes.

"Block everything else out," he told her. It was easier said than done with the threat of hellhounds nipping at their heels, but Shep knew she could do it. He'd felt it the minute he stepped into her shop. Not just magic, though it was strong in her. Power. Stability. Stubbornness. Despite the fear on her face, there was strength in her heart. He held back a smile and placed his hand on her elbow as she pressed her palms together, heat rising between them. She bit her bottom lip, then her eyelids closed, and she exhaled a breath.

The very air around her shimmered and changed. The sea itself responded to her, even the hellhounds. Did this woman know the power she commanded? The power to save his very island, to return him to his daughter. To right the course of the world. Indeed, to broker peace between Atlantis and the rest of the world. He could feel that strength inside her, churning and seeking release. Like all magic and power, it was chaos waiting to be tamed in a way only she could subdue.

The dragon circled her. It was the size of a pig, and clearly bonded to her. It had been so long since he'd seen one, since he'd ridden such a magnificent beast. Draco's feathers had matured to a deep purple, with a white streak down his back. He'd be a force to be reckoned with someday if they could keep him safe until them.

Many lifetimes ago, Shep had been bonded with his own, until Zyah had destroyed them all. He wasn't there when Actuous had died, but he felt the blade in his dragon's heart as if it were his own. He still felt it, a hole that would never heal. He absently patted his chest as her magic swelled. The small dragon's purple scales shimmered in the light, and he let off a roar that lit the morning on fire.

Shep wrapped his palms around hers before she could set the whole ship on fire. Ember closed her hands on the growing flames, and they immediately extinguished, leaving a frost in their wake.

"Gently, with control," he told her. It wasn't exactly frustration in his voice, though she couldn't stop herself from feeling that. What was this power at her fingertips? How could she use it without destroying the world around her?

The sun cut through the clouds briefly to illuminate whitecaps on the ocean. She couldn't see the hellhounds, but she felt them hunting her. It was a dark pit in her soul. A feeling of something out of place. Anger. Evil. Roiling. Seeking them. Seeking her. And coming closer. They'd reached her once before. Maybe more than once. She felt the pull of those other lifetimes in her heart.

Shep had taken her as far as he could. She leaned on him, expecting nothing but a stable force to hold her up if her magic got out of control, but she was surprised to find he was more than that. He was a balance to her magic—calm to her chaos, safety net—but one she didn't know what to do with. She flexed her fingers before trying again. He still had a gentle hold on her wrists and rubbed a circle with his thumb. She'd never had safety before. She wanted both to embrace it and push it away, but the key to magic was balance. She knew this as she knew how to breathe. She'd have to embrace it, embrace him. She'd have to learn to trust.

Shep looked carefully into her eyes. She'd always been good at reading people, and she saw deep inside him to something that had hurt him greatly. A wound that hadn't healed, a loss. One that fueled not a desire for revenge, but one of understanding. He'd come from Atlantis, that much she knew. But how had he lived so long? And what price had he paid? Who was this man?

"People spend lifetimes studying this magic, but I'm afraid we don't have that kind of time." He held her wrists tightly and she saw both the past and future in his eyes.

"Who is she?" she asked, knowing instantly because why else would a man struggle against time? She tried to squelch the jealousy that threatened to grow in her heart. This man wasn't hers, and never would be. Talk about out of her league. Not in his looks, though a more perfect specimen of an Atlantian solider she'd be hard pressed to find. No, his strength. His vision. His kindness. His heart. And there had been something in his eyes when he looked at her. She was sure of it. More than recognition but less than love. Possibility. It was hard to let that go, but she felt enough for him already that she wanted to do right by him, however that was.

He tipped his head, but it wasn't a look of surprise on his face. Magic comes in many forms, this Ember knew.

And what she'd once thought was empathy, or perhaps deep intuition, was a form of magic just as strong as any she'd wield with the elements.

"Someone I love very much," he answered, curling his fingers around hers. She squeezed them back.

"Then we shall save her," she answered. "How?"

But before the words could come out of her mouth, she knew. She'd always known. It was deeper than intuition. Buried there before time began even, waiting for her to find the knowing inside. For her to acknowledge what had always been. Her power, seething under the surface. Draco again roared, eager to begin, but the noise settled to the back of her head as magic took over.

Shep narrowed his eyes as he gently released her hands. He held his palm up to show her how to lift the ship, but she only laughed. Lifting the ship would be so easy. She closed her eyes and felt the bulk of its weight like a feather in her hand. The souls on board glowed and hummed. Hawk, with a deep green confused aura. Paine, yellow and knowing. Shep, still unreadable behind his walls. All their lives in her hands. She gathered the magic to her, but she couldn't exactly say how. Only that it was a song her heart knew how to play, one that started so long ago and continued until it reached her stubborn heart, where it beat on the door until she finally had no choice but to answer.

She was vaguely aware Draco had merged their energy together. His wasn't just an aura, but pure, unadulterated magic. Purple, of course, the color of royalty. Of a new line of dragons. *Was he a king?* Ember thought with a smile. She remembered the times he'd burned down the biography section or torn apart all the postcards. Sometimes greatness comes from humble beginnings, she supposed. She knew to wave her hands in a circle as she called forth the ancient magic, but beyond that her senses seemed to have coalesced to a point. Even with her eyes closed, she could see the bubble of magic surround them.

The ship rose and she vaguely heard the roar of the crew. She would have taken them higher and higher, perhaps up to Atlantis itself if she could find it. But a panicked voice cut through. Magic was strong, but it was finnicky, and the moment she sensed fear, she faltered.

She opened her eyes, but the veil of magic remained, and to look through a veil of magic is to see the world as it really is. To see people for who they really are. To feel the energy that surrounds them. The love. The joy. The sadness and heartache. All of it, energy. She held on to it as long as she could, but the veil soon faded, disintegrating into a million sparkles all around them. Swallowed up again by the world around them, but now she knew, and it would never be the same.

He was still there, ready to hold out a hand, but she needed no such assistance now, and his face broke into a smile. She recognized the circle around his irises as the aura of magic. She had the same thing herself, though she wouldn't doubt hers was now a little brighter.

"Did it work?" she asked, but she no longer felt the weight of the hellhounds pressing against them. Instead, she felt a buoyancy. A lightness.

"You tell me." He gestured to the bow of the ship behind her. She knew from the cheering of the crew, from feeling their moods and emotions. She knew by the way the air was lighter, by the way their hearts were lighter. But the heart and mind are two separate things, and her mind needed to see, so she turned.

Her magic had chased the clouds away, so pure sunlight shone on… air? She had to step closer to the rail to see over the side. Her hands clutched the rail as she saw how high up they were. Higher than she'd ever been. She could see her island far to the side, and the mainland beyond that. If the clouds were near, she'd be able to touch them. All of a sudden, she felt very dizzy. She turned and closed her eyes.

"I forgot to tell you," she said as her knees buckled. "I'm afraid of heights."

Chapter 16

Ember leaned her head back on the wall while the dizziness passed. She's been in Hawk's study before, but it took a different meaning when magic was involved. It was everywhere. She could see it now. Not just in the words of the books that her mother had gifted him, though her mother's influence was clear. Ember recognized some of the titles, but others were entirely new. If she didn't know better, she'd think such titles as *The History of Atlantis* were fantasy, but her eyes were drawn to another title on Hawk's wide, oak desk.

"Why do you have the history of the Devil's Island?" she asked, risking lifting her head and feeling another dizzy spell. She tucked her feet under the sofa, which was built into the wall, and was tempted to lie back and rest for longer.

Hawk raised an eyebrow. "We've been looking for this island a very long time," he answered. He'd sunk down in the chair behind his desk, pouring a strong-smelling liquid from a decanter, then downing it all in one gulp.

Shep placed a hand on her forehead, and she batted it away. "I'm not sick," she told him, forcing herself to sit up. The nausea passed, but the knowledge they were so high up did not. Draco roared in the distance; he was clearly loving this new freedom.

"No." Shep had a vague smile on his face as he leaned back in his chair. "You're afraid of heights. Ironic, really."

"It's not funny." She clenched her teeth.

Hawk handed her a glass. "Try this," he offered. She sniffed it. Whiskey. It couldn't hurt. She couldn't down it like he did but sipped it. Quickly.

Shep took Hawk's place by her feet and placed a hand on her knee. She could barely contain her excitement, but Shep frowned, his dark eyes becoming seemingly darker as he searched something inside her, but if it was fear he was looking for, he'd find none.

"Isn't this what you wanted?" she asked, flexing her fingers to keep her magic in check. Atlantis called, and it didn't have much time. The sooner she returned the island, the sooner she would also be on solid ground. She tried not to think about the distance between the ship and the ground, but her magic was strong and sturdy. It would hold them up for as long as it needed to.

He tensed. She could feel it in his energy and the slight shift of his hand. "Not if it meant putting you in danger," he responded.

She raised an eyebrow. "Really?" she asked, the question weighted with subtext.

"Really," he answered, and there was no lying. It wasn't just in his eyes, but the beat of his heart. She placed a hand over his, feeling stronger every moment.

"We will bring them home," she said, feeling the weight of their lifetimes together. Lifetimes they just missed meeting. Lifetimes he'd chased her across the world only to find out she'd been killed, again. Lifetime upon lifetime upon lifetime. She wondered if somewhere, there was a lifetime they were lovers, but no…

She gently let go of his hand. There was someone waiting for him on Atlantis. He might not be able to ask Ember to do what was needed, but she'd do it anyway. She knew what she'd be risking. Atlantis would require a sacrifice to return. The magic demanded it. She looked out the small portal window where they were drifting through a wispy cloud. She had no tears for the life she might have lived. She'd shed those a long time ago. But she did have a certain wistfulness for the magic she'd never wield. For the secrets that Atlantis would keep from her. For her future, however dark or bright. For another lifetime cut short. Perhaps the last this time.

"Devil's Island is surrounded by the strongest of magic," Hawk interrupted, flipping through the book that contained the history of the island. "Magic so strong it's almost unlocatable. Your mother and I conversed, and she shipped these books to us from another location. All to keep you safe." He narrowed his eyes as if Ember were keeping a secret. "She knew. It's why she kept you here for as long as she could."

Shep helped her sit. "She was protective of you," he said. "I have letters and letters, begging her to let you help us. She wanted to wait until you were of age."

Ember rubbed her forehead. "And then she died," she said, softly.

Shep frowned. "About that," he began, but Hawk cut him off. He tossed the book on the island on the desk. It fell open to the town square, looking like it was shining in the sunlight. Was this place, the spot she'd been to so many community gatherings, really one of magic? Had the island kept her and her family safe, until it couldn't anymore?

"The real magic is in the history of Atlantis itself," Hawk continued, pulling out the book of Atlantian history. It was large and thick, with a dark binding that looked like one of the math books Ember had dreaded in school. But when he flipped it open, she spied the most beautiful moving illustrations. He paced closer to her, and she touched a page, feeling a zip of magic in its pages.

Hawk frowned. "What do you know of Atlantian history?"

"Besides my mother's paintings?" she asked. "Nothing, really." She looked to Shep for confirmation, but he only shook his head. What could have been done if she knew longer ago?

"Then we shall start at the beginning." Hawk sat in an armchair next to the desk. Shep folded his arms and leaned on the door. Ember sat back, her vertigo forgotten for a moment as Hawk dove into the history of the island of Atlantis, first filling his glass and downing it again.

Atlantis was a city built on love, and from that love, magic sprang forth. For what bigger magic is there than love? Wild. Unknown. Untamable. Every Atlantian was born with the power to manipulate the world around them, and each had their own gift. Some could speak to animals. Some could move the presence of objects. Some could affect

116

weather, or emotion, or elements. And the most powerful of all could read minds or tell the future. Those who could do so were often conscripted to the King's Guard to serve as sorcerers or soldiers. Serving the king was an honor, but one which came at a great cost. The King's Guard served at his leisure, never to return home or have families of their own. It was said that families often hid those with the greatest gifts, but those were nothing more than rumors.

"The King's Guard? Was that you?" Ember raised an eyebrow and looked at Shep. He pressed his lips together as Hawk continued without answering.

Atlantis, on the ground at least, was a magical, open, welcoming place to live for centuries. Though set on an island, and in need of nothing, the city often traded, and word of its uniqueness traveled far and wide across the land. Eventually, jealousy stirred. For the rest of the world was mired in strife, unhappiness, and war. It does not take magic to cure such things, but it does take love. And those without love often seek to steal the very hearts of those who do have it, either to claim as their own or to snuff out entirely and leave the world in darkness.

There are other kinds of magic that grow in those dark places. That dark magic took root in the heart of the king's own brother. He'd been born on Atlantis and forsaken its goodness, instead seeking to earn his fortune in pillage and war. And at that, he excelled. He'd conquered much of the lands when he turned his sights to his home, and his brother.

The mages warned the king for years that danger was on the horizon, but danger is always on the horizon, isn't it? The king was reluctant to take protective measures, and instead, let the dark storm build on the shores of

Atlantis, largely unknown to its people. Their magic was one founded in peace and fueled by love. It was their greatest gift, but also their biggest blind spot. For no matter how powerful the Atlantians grew, they simply couldn't imagine a force so destructive, so opposite. By the time the traders were warning of trouble on the shores, it was too late. The king's brother, Zyah, had massed his forces and prepared for attack.

The king called a legendary council, gathering advice from his closest advisors, even those in the King's Guard. He was afraid, yes, but he'd once been wise and knew how to gather opinions and look at all angles. All angles were equally grim. The King's Guard were not confident they could defeat Zyah, while being quite willing to fight and die for Atlantis. They were sure death would be the outcome, and it was not one the king could stomach.

So, he turned to the deep magic of the mages. Perhaps this doesn't make much sense in a land devoid of magic, but on Atlantis, their visions of the future held great weight. Sometimes those futures were able to be swayed, but sometimes they just had to be lived through. Through them, the king saw the pillage and destruction of his land. There was nothing left for his brother to rule over. Atlantis would be hazed to the ground. Sunk underwater. He sought another way, but even magic has its limits, and fate is not an easy opponent to fool.

Ah, but perhaps it was only Atlantis' time? Everything has its limit. Perhaps the city would have been razed and built again? We will never know. What we know happened was the king gathered those with the strongest magic and locked them indoors until they came up with a solution. Legend has it, those solutions were unpredictable and dangerous. Sinking the city was one, but there was never a way to guarantee the citizens safety under the water. Invisibility also had its problems. And so it was that the mages looked to the sky.

The magic was like nothing Atlantis had ever seen, for this was not magic built on love, but that built on fear. The king had plenty of fuel on his own, but for good measure he threatened his sorcerers. Locked them away. Even the King's Guard did not get out unscathed. Five good men lost their lives that day, and none would risk making the king unhappy in the many years after. Their fear allowed the city to take flight. And the king? Well, he was content to stay in the sky, never to confront his brother. Never to return to a world so devoid of love and magic.

"At least until…" At this point Hawk paused in his story. He realized there was still liquid in the glass he clutched. He swirled it around. A beam of light reached the glass and set off a rainbow on the table. He swallowed the drink down as Ember realized a tear had escaped the corner of her eye. She hastily wiped it away.

"The sorcerers told the king that Atlantis would one day return when there was one born who held great enough magic to heal what's been broken and bridge both worlds." Hawk looked at her pointedly. There were shadows on his young face, and whisps of his blond hair escaped the tie he'd used to hold them back. "While the people of Atlantis think he's been looking all these years, he hasn't, at least as far as we've heard." He walked back to the decanter and filled his glass again, giving Ember time to take in what he was saying. She watched his hands shake as he poured the glass. She watched his eyes glass over as if they were so used to holding back tears they could hardly produce. She watched him look at his reflection in the glass, sigh, and put it down again.

"How long has it been?" she asked quietly.

He closed his eyes. "Centuries," he answered. He forced a smile. "Though I, myself, have only been alive for a couple of those. You could ask your friend there about that." He tipped his head toward Shep and turned his back to them.

A soft knock interrupted them. Paine stuck her head in and gaged the seriousness of the conversation. "The crew is arguing about direction," she told Hawk, while eyeing Ember with questions written all over her face.

"The direction is up!" Hawk said dramatically, but he sighed, placed his cup back on the desk and made his way over. "I'll take care of it." He gave Shep a look on the way out, one that was readable. But the expression on Shep face was not, and to Ember, it had guilt written all over it.

"What did he mean?" she asked carefully. She'd always been careful around this man. Not because he was breakable. Not even because she was afraid of him, though there was an impenetrable shadow around his every move. No, it was because she couldn't read him, and she could read everyone.

Shep met her gaze this time, dark and apologetic. Was she imagining or were his walls down just a bit. The magic that surrounded him, his aura, deep and blood red. She blinked and it was gone. "I have done great and terrible things," he admitted, his voice dropping an octave, "in order to return Atlantis to the ground."

Ember was able to rise without dizziness. Indeed, the weakness that had passed had left her with more strength, more security that she could wield this magic. But Shep, what could he do? What could they do together? His brow furrowed as he watched her take in the words great and terrible things. She remembered him as he'd walked into her store. He'd become so much more than a category five.

"What things?" she asked, forcing herself to sound braver than she was.

He took her hand, his was much colder than the room. "What would you do to rescue one that you loved?"

She considered the depth in his gaze. "Anything," she admitted. He tugged her a little closer.

"I have done much more," he whispered in her ear, and in his words, she felt the language of the dragons, like the way she communicated with Draco. She saw pictures of lives. Her life. His life. Almost intersecting but not quite—on fields in battle, on farms, in cities. Once, even, killed in a cradle. She felt what he felt, not quite anger, but frustration each time. Helplessness. The sparks extinguished from her lives one by one until there was only one left. His. And he was holding a child. Bidding her farewell as he turned to leave. The city rising behind him as his heart broke for her.

"A baby?" she asked, her heart softening. He was still holding her hand, but his had warmed. She squeezed it. "That's who you want to find?"

But when he pulled back from her, it wasn't love or longing on his face. It was regret. Etched deep in the lines around his face. "What did you do?" she asked.

He touched her cheek gently as the ship buckled. "What I needed to do to find you," he responded. He rested his forehead on hers. "But you have become so much more than I anticipated. The danger of returning Atlantis is great, but perhaps…"

He didn't have a chance to finish before Hawk barreled into the room. "We have a problem," he said. He looked at the half-empty decanter and frowned.

She reluctantly let her hand drop from Shep's. She'd found a certain steadiness in it, if one laced with danger. "What's wrong?" she asked.

"It seems your magic only keeps us afloat when you are engaged and present," Hawk said. He took one last drink and downed it much easier than Ember had. She jumped when she looked out the portholes and saw water close.

"We're sinking," Shep noticed.

"It's all right." Hawk flopped dramatically into his chair and pretended to consult a map on the wall behind him, but they could be anywhere in the world right now. Where they needed to be was up. "We've outrun the hellhounds for the moment, and the ship will sail on water. Perhaps you should rest, seeing as you're our strongest magic and we may need you."

Ember had come a long way from restocking he store shelf to being the most important magic on a floating ship. Draco stuck his head in the door, but it would have been a tight squeeze to go through. She crossed the room and patted his head.

"I'm not your strongest magic." She turned with a smile. "For that, we have to work together."

Chapter 17

Sierra's dreams were filled with the kind of magic she'd never known in life. She was dreaming, she was sure of it. For where else did you wander a city floating in the sky, passing magicians and dragons and magic of the most fun and dangerous kinds? The fun kinds were practiced by day in growing flowers or food, or enchanting toys for the children, who either aged very slowly or not at all, at least as far as Sierra could see.

But the dangerous magic? Well, she tried to avoid those shops when the island was passing through the night sky. She'd always been able to feel things and read energy. Ember had the gift too, though she'd never known how strongly Sierra felt it. And in those shops, she felt something. Something unnatural that whispered seductively. That energy would see her, if she so chose, but she'd not like to be seen by such things. She kept her distance.

Instead, she passed the streets and backroads of the city every day, a ghost in plain sight. She was a prisoner of the king's, one who could not escape. He watched her from on high, for no one else could see her. Not the mages. Not the sorcerers. Not even the king's own wife or her guard, though Casius had been sent to find her. He would not find her above in the floating city, for she was invisible. And he would not find her on the land below, for her body was only a shell. The accident that had put her in the hospital was no accident. It was a spell, made to enchant and entrap her, and it had worked.

Or perhaps, it was one long, terrible, beautiful dream of which she could not wake? And how she longed to wake.

She remembered the taste of the beautiful fruits they sold in the markets. She could smell them, the strawberries and tangerines and melons, enchanted so they were just the right amount of ripe. Her mouth would water, if she could do such things, but her hand went right through the stall as she went to grab them. She could not taste, not a strawberry or a melon or the kiss of a lover, and she didn't know which she missed more. In so many years, she had not felt the touch of another nor heard their voice addressed to her. The king was the only one who could meet her eyes. He was locked away in his enchanted castle, and that was the only place she could not get to. He was hiding from her. He was afraid, though of what she did not know.

She passed through a cloud, then by a tavern that the King's Guard would play for coins when it was evening. Not that the word evening held much sway. People ate and slept and gambled as they wished, and the city passed through day and night as if the words meant nothing at all. The light in their eyes dimmed. Even their magic was waning. And still, they flew, Sierra every bit as much of a hostage, though she'd never known why. Perhaps this was heaven, or even hell? Perhaps she'd be trapped between forevermore? Not good enough for above, nor bad enough for below. She was just a girl, and a boring one at that. At least she had been when she'd been alive, truly alive. Sure, she'd liked to party in the woods on the island on weekends. Who didn't do that? And she could be kind of a bitch to her sister. She regretted that. But she liked to think she had a big heart and was kind. Did those things mean anything, she wondered, trying to kick a stone but only passing her foot right through.

She sat at the end of the tree line where she'd seen the queen oftentimes, in contemplation or meditation. Oh, how she wished she could reach out to Queen Aura. She sensed in her a kindred spirit. A heart that wanted justice. But no matter how Sierra screamed or yelled or clawed, her voice was swallowed by the void between them.

She was alone today. She was still connected to her body, but something felt off. She couldn't see it. She didn't even know where the island was, but they were close. Her body called for her, but she could not get to it. She'd tried jumping, more than once, only to bounce back to her own personal hell. She was tied to the fate of the island.

The grass shifted. Something drew near but Sierra didn't have to be afraid of even the tiniest of spiders. For in fact, they were the only thing she could pick up and she spent days trying to make something of that. It was what it was. She was in a prison. Her body, below, was telling her she was in danger, and she could do nothing about it.

She stared wistfully at the water and shoreline below, wishing desperately to fall.

Chapter 18

Days passed. Ember grew in her power but also in her frustration. What good was power with no direction? She and Draco kept the ship in the sky, there was that. They flew an endless loop to keep away from the hellhounds. At night, she could sometimes hear their brays.

"Who sent them, anyway?" Ember ducked to avoid a jab. She'd taken to training alternatively with Shepherd or Hawk or one of the crew. Today, they were sparring on the deck under a cloudless sky. Though she spent more and more time with Shep, he skirted any questions about his history on Atlantis or his long life span. Immortal? She couldn't answer that. None of the blows seemed to affect him, though admittedly she rarely got any in. Shep was much better than he let on, only occasionally letting the crew best him.

He rolled his sleeves up and watched Ember spar with Hawk from the shadows, occasionally giving tips to one or the other. His hair had grown longer, and he had the shadow of a beard. The biggest change was his occasional, even frequent, smile. Ember caught that smile and flushed. The ship was so attuned to her feelings it shuddered in response, though thankfully no one seemed to notice except Draco, who puffed smoke out as he made lazy circles around the ship.

She ducked at the last minute when Hawk parried with a wooden sword. "I told you." He answered. "We think it's King Zyah, but there's no way to tell. Someone has been after the ancestors of Atlantis since as far back as we remember."

She dodged right. She'd long since stopped feeling silly about sword fighting. What else could they do to pass the time? Her magic had grown exponentially, and so had Draco. The dragon was the size of a small horse and could barely land on the ship anymore. He let out a roar of true fire. She was glad they'd taught him to direct it away from the ship, though she'd learned how to control the flames with nothing more than a flick of her wrist.

Shep stepped out from under the eve of the deck and stood next to her, pointing out Hawk's weak spots. Shep was thorough and analytical. Controlled. Though she felt that control weaken when he put his hand over hers to show her how to clip Hawk on his left shoulder. She hardly felt the blow land.

"Two against one." Hawk rubbed his shoulder, more for theatrics. She'd barely tapped him. "I see how it is." His dark blond hair had escaped the tie, and he had a deep tan from the time out in the sun. His grin was warm and genuine, even though he'd technically lost. Ember caught Paine's gaze from the doorway and they both laughed. This could be her life. Keeping the ship afloat. Dodging danger. Saving whatever survivors they could manage to find on the ground. That had been the crew's life before they found her, and it had been a good life for them. With her magic they'd be safe, but safety came with a price, and a high one.

She'd accepted, before, that her life would be no more than that of an orphaned bookstore owner, and a failing one at that. That the only adventures she'd have were the ones she read about. Adventures that were impossible or improbable, or meant for other people. She wasn't the kind of person who would find love when she wasn't looking, not in a fairy forest or an enchanted castle, or even a bookstore. She wasn't the kind of person to visit a magical island, at least outside the pages of a book, much less save one.

But her heart hadn't accepted that fate, not really. And those nights she cried herself to sleep, her soul told her there was something else out there. *Someone* else. A part of her had held on to that hope through the long, lonely days at the bookstore. Years of them. And when she would see the man in the red cloak in her dreams or catch a whisp of a spire in the swirl of a cloud, she knew for a moment that she was destined for more.

And still, she was destined for more. Not just destined. Expected. If she stopped now, the price would be Atlantis itself. If not forever, at least for this lifetime until Zyah could hunt her down in the next and the next after that. The cycle would continue until she was strong enough to stop it.

She looked over to Shep, who gripped the rails and looked up as he always did. Searching the sky for whoever he'd lost. The price would be Shep's heart, and that was not one she was willing to pay.

Paine took up the wooden sword that Ember had tossed to the side. "I'll take you on, Captain," she said to Hawk, a twinkle in her eye. Ember moved out of the way.

Those two could go at it, and she didn't know who would win, only that someone might need a healing spell later. She left them to it, following Shep to the bow of the ship.

The crew's magic kept the decks pristine. Well, that and their constant cleaning. Hawk kept a tight ship, but not because of control. She knew what was in his heart. The work kept them busy. It gave them purpose. Even those silly shows put on by "entertainment." What else did they have, except endless searching or longing for home? She wouldn't be able to leave them to such a fate any more than Hawk. Only she could do a little more than put on a show. She could return Atlantis home.

Her boots squeaked on the white deck. Flying so far above the sea was oddly silent. There was no spray of the water. No waves. Even the wind was subdued, barely brushing her long bangs off her cheek. Her hair was growing in dark brown, in contrast to the jet black she'd dyed it before and already reached her shoulders. Those external changes were only a hint of the changes inside her. The strength. The confidence. The magic.

Sunlight played off the deep blue of the ocean, broken up by lines of whitecaps. In the distance, the peaks of the island rose, and then there were the clouds. They were light and high today, not capable of hiding a city. No, Atlantis was far away. She could barely feel its pull, only a soft whisper that said: *I'm here. Come for me.*

Shep had his back to her, his elbows on the rails with his shirtsleeves rolled up. She passed by the crew's bubbling hot tub, which was thankfully empty, and approached him with hesitation, startled to see his expression so downtrodden. If she wasn't mistaken, he'd been crying.

What did you say at such a moment? Ember hadn't the best social skills in the best of times, and these? Well, she'd hardly call them the best. Shep always referred to the choice to return Atlantis, but it had never been a choice for her. She knew it was fraught with danger but perhaps she had underestimated how much.

Shep caught her glance and didn't look away. He had something about him that was more than magic. Power, perhaps. Presence. He could wield the world with just a note, but he couldn't play the song his heart desired. "You'll die." His voice cracked on the last word. Still, he didn't look away.

"Everyone dies," she answered, her own voice steady enough not to betray the beat of her heart. The wind ruffled his hair. Even that little gesture made him more human than she'd ever seen him, but was he? He'd lived more lifetimes than any of the crew. He'd seen Atlantis in the flesh, and yet he was still young to her eyes. What had he seen? What had he done?

He exhaled, a storm brewing in his eyes. Was he considering telling her about the awful things in his past? Or perhaps, throwing her over the edge as a sacrifice.

She was wrong on both counts.

He crossed the space between them as if it were nothing, and perhaps it was. His boots didn't squeak. He moved with purpose and lifted a hand to her cheek. "I cannot sacrifice you," he said all in one breath, searching for her reaction. If he thought she was scared, he was wrong. If he thought she would back down, he was even more wrong. Instead, she covered his hand with hers.

"I don't accept that fate," she said, trying to force down the small smile that pulled at the corners of her lips.

"It is not yours to accept or deny, I'm afraid." Still, he didn't look away but frowned. "The prophecy…"

"… is bullshit," she finished. His eyes widened in both surprise and amusement.

"I've heard magic described as a lot of things." His hand slid down to her shoulder, and she let hers linger on his arm. His eyes twinkled. "But not bullshit."

"I don't believe in fate," she said, but she didn't have to believe in fate to be afraid of it. Her expression wavered just enough for him to understand. He gave her a sad smile and pulled her into a hug.

"Perhaps it's time for me to explain what the mages predicted," he said with sadness. She looked out over his shoulder at the endless ocean, as endless as their quest for Atlantis.

"I think…" She reluctantly pulled back. "It's time to explain a lot more than that."

Chapter 19

They'd taken to meeting in the captain's study, and at the moment Hawk was still parrying with Paine. Paper crinkled lightly as Shep ran his hand gently over the map on Hawk's desk before dipping his head to tell his story. Ember perched on the arm of one of the chairs.

He was known as Shepherd in this life and in many lives before this, but once upon a time, on an island filled with love and hope and magic, he'd been Casius, and his job had been to protect the king and queen.

There were no castes in Atlantis, no social tiers. Everyone was an equal from farmer to soldier to mother, even child. But within that there was magic. Each person born of Atlantis had some magic skill. They were chosen, the queen would say, but chosen by whom and for what they never knew. Only chosen to make a perfect society, and indeed it was for a long, long time.

Cas was born and raised by a family close to the palace. He was not the only protector in his family. He'd come from a long line of soldiers and healers. His own parents, in fact, though when they'd fallen in love, the king gave his father leave to raise his own family and his mother made their living as a mystic and a healer. No wonder Cas had been born so powerful. Fate, you may have said, though over the years Cas had doubts about such a thing as fate. At any rate, it had sorely tested him, and sometimes he wondered if he'd failed altogether.

Ember leaned forward as the candles flickered on the sconces on the wall, putting Shep's face in shadow. The ship softly swayed side to side like a cradle, but it didn't lull her to sleep. She was constantly on alert to keep them in the sky. Shep turned and sat on the desk with his head in his hands.

"You've hardly failed," she told him. She moved to perch next to him on the desk and touched his cheek gently. It was covered in a shadow of stubble.

He lifted his head and gave her a slow smile. "I've hardly succeeded," he responded. She let her hand fall so he could continue.

Shep's gifts were clear at a young age, though by then, the king's brother had been born without magic. Or at least so the palace said. The rumor was he'd been born with dark magic, and a prophesy was placed on his life. One of a heavy fate, destruction and chaos. Perhaps without such a weight, Zyah could have grown in love on Atlantis, with or without magic. But as it was, his own parents feared him. They believed the mystics over their own child, and so the prophesy became self-fulfilling.

"What was it?" Ember interrupted.

Shep smiled. "Mystic's prophesies are filled with riddles and half-truths, but there is often some truth to be found in them." He began to recite it in part:

Second son of a king.

Born under a blood moon, on a dark spring night.

He brings ill tidings. The fall of Atlantis.
The dark consumes him.
Blood in his heart. Blood on his hands.
He kills without remorse. Over and over.
He heralds the downfall of Atlantis.
Unless and until
Far in the future – hazy, at best
One returns with love to complete the circle.

The mystics all repeated it, over and over until the king's mother went mad from the choice. She bore it until she could no longer. The magic of Atlantis is one of love and hope, but there are places even love and hope cannot flourish, and the queen's heart was one. Perhaps it had been that way from the beginning. The king fought to raise the child, teach him the ways of Atlantis, but perhaps therein lie their mistake. The queen would have nothing to do with her second son, instead doting on the first, and Zyah was raised an outcast for his first ten years. This settled his destiny even more than any prophecy.

"And his brother?" Ember asked. She thought of the jealousy she had for her own sister, though she'd never felt like Sierra was chosen or she was less. She couldn't imagine.

"Corin was a just and loving child who tried to include his brother, but his mother did all she could to keep them apart. The seeds of Atlantis' destruction were planted by her. She spirited the child away in the night. His father thought she'd had him killed and spent his life searching. His mother locked herself up in the tower. Some say she died thereafter. Some say she is still there, keeping Zyah away from the city."

Ember rubbed her arms. "That's a terrible story."

"Indeed, it is," Shep agreed. "I was raised with Corin, but I never saw much of his brother. What I did see was sadness. It was a weight on Atlantis that has yet to be lifted. When Corin ascended the throne at a young age, assisted by the sorcerers and mages, it was I who was by his side.

Shep paused, his gaze far away. "He was wise, to begin. He took a beautiful bride, Aura, which is why he stayed as sane as he did for as long as he did. When rumors of Zyah began to pop up, he ignored them. But she did not. She was intuitive and knew in her heart there was a choice to be made. It was she who called the council that decided to raise the city. For prophecies may be untrustworthy and weak, but when all the magic of Atlantis agrees, that is something strong. Zyah would have burned the city to the ground. Perhaps rightfully so."

"And you?" Ember asked.

"And I," he said, "met a woman. I stayed by the King's side while our child was born, which was strictly speaking against the rules, but Corin would not let me go." He paused. "She was a mystic. I never knew the things she saw, only that they made her sad, and I, somehow could ease her burden. When she died in childbirth, it was as if she'd given up on this world and was ready for the next. I raised our daughter as the threat to Atlantis grew. When we were cursed to the skies, I knew the king would never return. The queen sought me for a mission, to find the one with enough love and magic to pull the city home. To bridge our return."

Ember leaned back. She couldn't tell him that it wasn't her, that she had as much love and magic as the average person, but then, she did have a dragon.

"I sought her, chasing magic at first. Following every lead until I could feel the energy of the one and I chased it, arriving too late in every lifetime. She had been slain by Zyah in mundane and gruesome ways I'd not concern you with. Lifetimes went by like this, with me just a step too late."

She narrowed her eyes as the candles flickered. "Lifetimes?" she asked softly for here she got to her real questions. Atlantians lived long lives, this she knew, but this long? He'd traded something for it. She held her breath.

A shadow crossed his features. It was clear this was not something he wanted to discuss. "Lifetimes," he confirmed. He met her eyes, within his was the sadness of a million near misses. Of a child he'd left behind. "I aged much slower than those on the surface, but age I did, and I began to fear I'd never complete my mission. I'm not proud to say I spent some years lost to sadness, fighting hopelessness and desperation. I did many things I'm not now proud of.

"It was during that time I was introduced to a way to boost my magic. To increase my lifespan… exponentially. I brushed it off. At that time, I was looking to die, not to live. But the more years that went by, the more I thought of that woman who offered me this curse and gift. I knew what it entailed, but I had already walked through the dark. This? This was one more step. One I would willingly take if it meant a chance to see her again."

He'd lost himself for a moment in the memory of those years. For a moment Ember saw the dark side of him come through and trembled. She took a deep breath, feeling the mist that was falling outside as they cruised through fog. No longer did the fire inside her keep her warm.

Instead, a chill had formed deep inside her bones. She suspected where he was going, but she'd always thought such folklore were tales from old horror novels. But if hellhounds and magic and flying ships were real, and Atlantis was floating in the sky, what else was possible? Monsters? Perhaps she was even sitting next to one, but she did not scoot away. She did not even let go of his hand, cold as it was. She knew his heart, even if she suspected that technically it wasn't beating. Not like a normal human heart.

He took back his hand and pulled the collar down on his shirt to reveal two deep scars. Puncture marks, if she had to guess, and old ones. They looked rough but healed, and the skin surrounding them papery white. She raised her hand to touch them, and he didn't pull back, but winced as if from emotional pain rather than physical. Her senses heighted at the touch. She felt his longing, years of it. She felt his loneliness. She felt the weight of the decision to keep her safe. He covered her hand with his.

He covered the scar but the memory of it remained between them. "It's not like the books of this age, or the movies. It's… hell." He closed his eyes. "It's not you the hellhounds seek, or at least not only you. They seek me. I have cheated them for so long, but I was so close this time."

Her palm was still on the collar of his shirt. She felt the eerie stillness underneath and wondered at all the silly superstitions she'd heard. He walked in the light, she'd seen him. She'd even seen him eat and drink, though admittedly not much. Her hand slid down his shirt until it was resting at his side. She lifted it and looked at the blue veins under her wrist, watched her pulse throb. Did he…?

He covered her hand and pushed it away, getting up. The air had cooled considerably. The day turned dark and damp. They were alone. She got up, rubbing a circle in her wrist with her thumb. "Do you… need blood?"

He gave her a sad smile. "No, Ember. I have my own ways, and they are not ones I would share right now."

There was only a space between them, and somehow it was crossed though by him or by her she wasn't sure. His gaze traveled over her. "I thought I needed your magic, Ember Weathers." He touched her cheek lightly. "But it turns out I need so much more than that."

She'd touched him plenty over the last few weeks. Lightly, on the arm when sparring. In jest. He'd helped her up and held her hand, maybe a little too long. She'd placed her head on his shoulder as they looked over the rails at night and dreamed of Atlantis. She always thought he had a lover back on Atlantis, but then sometimes she'd catch him looking at her and wish it were different. In an instant, it was, and when those walls broke down a flood of feeling came with them. She'd known he had secrets. She'd known they were as deep and dangerous as the look he was currently giving her, and still she wanted him.

She thought his lips would be cold, and his touch too, but it was nothing more than a boy reaching out to a girl and feeding a fire that had started when he'd blown into her store. This was more than the flames she could pull up with magic. This was something that started deep inside and traveled right up her spine to where his lips met hers. Soft. Inviting.

He ran his hand up her arm, and she shivered in response. The cool night faded into the background as he deepened his kiss, as if inside her was the very air he needed to breathe. Or blood, she corrected. He reached around with his other arm and pulled her in close. Far away, Draco roared in warning, but she was already lost. At least until shouts rose from the deck.

Draco roared louder, and closer. Shep balled his fist before he let her go. "There's more…" he said, but there was no time for more. Draco was circling the ship, blowing flame at the deck and shouts rose from above. The ship rocked. They scrambled out of the office and onto the front deck where the crew was watching Draco set his golden irises on a target. They had surrounded something on the deck. Blood pooled.

"Stop!" She waved her arms at Draco and the circle opened. Paine stepped back and met her gaze.

"It can't be…" Ember saw the writhing mess on the deck.

Paine didn't even turn her head. "We flew too low." She waved her sword as the hellhound got a look at Ember. "It's only one, but he's a fierce bastard."

Captain Hawk had taken slow steps toward it, parrying his own dagger. "What's he doing?" Ember asked, shouldering her way toward them despite the abject terror the hellhound brought up. It was only the size of a dog but struck terror in her heart with its jagged teeth and spiked nails and a swishing tail. It bore those fangs at Hawk, and if she wasn't wrong, enjoyed it.

"Look out!" Shep had pushed Ember aside, but he was too late for the barb of the tail to hit Hawk square in the chest. He was thrown back and fell. Paine cried out and ran to him, but Ember's attention was on the hellhound, who finally had Shepherd in its sights.

Chapter 20

Shepherd was calmer than she'd ever seen, as if he fought hellhounds every weekend in his spare time. It was the first time she'd seen one up close, and the beast was just as terrifying. Not in size, for it could be compared to a boar, but in the craze of its red, bloodthirsty eyes. It was in the size of its teeth, all fanged and long enough to rip her head off without a thought. Its tail was barbed, and it issued a low growl as it paced and took stock of Shep. More than that, the beast exuded a stink of wrong. Not just in odor, for it reeked of rotten eggs, but its body blurred and shook as if it had trouble containing itself to one point. Even the fur on its back looked barbed and sharp, and the drool down its chin sizzled on the floor. It let out an earsplitting bray.

Half the crew had gathered around Hawk, so Ember couldn't see his wounds, but she felt their devastation. The other half of the crew had bravely lined up around Shep with various useless weapons, but Shep himself kept his eyes trained on the beast. He stopped to pick up Hawk's sword and gave it a light toss from one hand to another.

"Not my choice for a weapon but it will do," he said.

Ember stepped up behind him. "Magic?" she asked.

He shook his head. "That will not fell this beast. No..." He paced, the beast matching his stride. Studying him. Its tail swished back and forth and almost caught one of the crew before he jumped back, slipping on the beast's drool and scooting himself back. Another of the crew parried the beast off, but it seemed content to play with them. With its fangs and speed, it could take them all out and quickly. Ember's heartbeat raced. She felt the very blood going through her veins. Magic struggled to come out, but what type of magic would stop this? Already it had broken through her wards.

"The only way to defeat a hellhound is to behead it. Keep the ship afloat so no more come on." He didn't turn his head as Draco issued a loud roar, but his flames didn't reach the deck. Ember had long since warded them, but her wardings hadn't kept the hellhound away.

She stepped back, avoiding the circle around Hawk but hearing Paine's shrill cries. "Draco!" she climbed on the rail. "We need height!" She hadn't noticed how perilously low they'd been flying and cursed herself. Flitting around while Hawk was defending the ship was inexcusable. Draco flew down next to the ship, and she climbed on his back. They'd practiced this, but barely. She'd only flown him for short times, but their magic was stronger together and they needed to pull the ship.

"Up!" she told him, and the dragon took off in a straight line. She weaved magic to pull the ship with them, and despite Shep's warning, worked on a hex to send to the hellhound. Perhaps it wouldn't work, but perhaps it would aid his combat. "Live through it," she pleaded to Shep through clenched teeth. The wind rushed past her face and rain pelted her as they flew through the low clouds, emerging into a blue, sunny sky.

"That's far enough," she coughed. She blinked the light away and concentrated all her energy on rising the ship to them, but it was slow and unwieldy with the weight of the hellhound dragging it back. Its weight was like an anchor through the sky, the hellhound pulling back as hard as she pulled, and even with Draco's energy mixed with hers, she could only pull the ship up so that the top of the white-sailed masts peaked through the clouds. They flapped in the wind, and one tore from the effort.

"Come on," she pled through gritted teeth. What had Shep said about magic? That it was fueled by love. She concentrated on protecting him, on the kiss they'd shared. The lifetimes he'd been trying to find her. His daughter. His touch, still burned into her skin.

The ship rose slowly, and she was bowled over both with gratitude and fear, for she felt their souls and their emotions. Not all the crew had made it. She couldn't feel Hawk and her heart went cold. But Shepherd was on the deck sparring with the hellhound. As it peaked through the clouds, Draco circled back to the deck where she jumped down quickly, slipping in the blood of the hellhound, who's body convulsed as the crew pushed it to the side then off the deck. It fell down and through the clouds. She found Shep, who was across the deck wavering on his feet, the head of the hellhound by his feet. It's mouth was still open and full of blood.

"What happened?" she asked, but the closest crewman only retched. He had a long gash down the side of his cheek. She only felt stony coldness from Shep.

"It was not only one," he spit blood, which mixed with the other on the deck. His shirt was cut and gashed, and his face swollen. At his feet lay the bodies of two other hellhounds.

"*Three*?" She pulled all the healing energy to her that she could, but how did you heal such a man? She barely understood magic as it was. She placed a palm on his collar where the deepest of his injuries looked, but the wound seemed to bite back, and she cried out. He wavered and she caught him under his arm.

"I'll heal, but it will take time," he breathed out. He barely moved his legs to help her get him in Hawk's office.

"Captain Hawk?" She looked back at the blood covered deck, half the crew was in various states of wounded. They needed her.

"The captain will need you more than I do," Shep answered. He barely made the office and stumbled onto Hawk's couch, his hand covering the gash on his shoulder. He closed his eyes. Was he breathing? She didn't know if he needed to, but his breath came in rasps. She knelt before him.

"Let me see." She carefully pried his hand off. The sight of blood had never bothered her but there was so much. His shirt was torn enough that she only had to gently remove it, and she held back her horror at so many wounds. The hellhound must have raked his skin. She gathered as much magic as she could, but it only slowed the wounds.

"You need..." She swallowed. Blood. He'd need blood, and lots of it.

He took her wrist in an iron grasp. "Bring me Hawk," he said, his voice fading.

"How will that help?" She shook her head, but she couldn't pull out of his grip. "He's..." She swallowed, but she couldn't finish the sentence. Was Captain Hawk dead? She could no longer feel him.

Shep struggled to prop himself up on his embows. "Ember, I need you to trust me. Bring me Hawkins, or his body. Quickly." He let go and gave her a little shove, falling back on the couch. He closed his eyes. He wouldn't have long, and she couldn't heal him. She scrambled back out, wiping blood on her pants. Her eyes were filled with tears. Outside Draco was frantic, circling the deck and breathing fire, but they were in the air, at least, and high. How had this happened?

She slipped through the gore on the deck to where the crew had assembled. Pushing her way through, she saw Paine cradling Hawk. Tears streamed down her face. Ember knelt and met her eyes.

"He's… gone," Paine told her, her voice cracking. Ember took her wrist as Shep had taken hers.

"I may be able to help," she said. Paine's eyes widened. Ember swallowed. It was too late to go back. "But you'll have to trust me."

Chapter 21

Paine moved quickly, bracing Hawk under one arm while Ember took his other side. The crew trusted her, but she had no idea what she was doing. What was Shep getting them into? What had Ember got them into? They were flying around just fine before she dropped into their lives. This was all her fault.

The crew had made a circle around the bodies of the hellhounds. The smell still turned her stomach, and the sight of their remains made her shiver. "The captain thinks the hellhounds had help getting on board," Paine grunted under Hawk's weight, but he hadn't moved. He hadn't even breathed.

"Why would anyone do that?" she asked. The rest of the crew had stepped in to tend to the wounded, but hellhounds wounds were deep and hard to heal. Best they could do was to bandage them up until Ember could draw enough magic to heal them, and Shep, too. If he made it. Her eyes misted over, and she blinked it away. Hawk's body was heavy and unwieldy. They made slow progress.

"I don't know," Paine answered as they reached the door. "But the captain is usually right."

Shep had managed to sit up, but the look on his face was one of pure pain. He opened his eyes as they came in. His skin had paled, and he'd lost more blood. It pooled on the couch and the floor. She almost dropped Hawk's body but managed to drag him to the sofa. His head hung off the edge. Blood matted his blond hair and his eyes, usually the palest of blue, were closed. She detected no heartbeat. No soul. It was enough to almost drive Ember to her knees. No magic would bring back the dead. Hadn't Shep said as much?

"Leave us." Shep placed a hand on Hawk's chest where it remained oddly still. The gash on Hawk's neck had stopped bleeding and his skin started to turn ashen.

Paine looked from Ember to Shep, avoiding Hawks body. "What's going on?" she asked. Tears had streaked her cheeks, but her pain did nothing to dull her suspicion. She pressed her lips together, but what could she possibly do? Hawk was already dead.

Ember took her hand. Paine's was so cold and flaked with blood. "It's okay. He's not the spy," she said. Shep's eyebrow picked up on that word, but she didn't elaborate. "He's right, it's best we're not here for this," she said, though she desperately wanted to be there. What type of magic was this at his disposal, and how would he wield it? While Paine looked at Ember, Ember caught a glint of a fang in Shepherd's mouth. "Let's go," she pulled Paine along. "The crew needs us."

Paine moved slow. She turned back to look at Hawk. Ember had known her friend was in love with the captain. She'd known it in a million little smiles and gestures. The way they looked at each other. The way they communicated without talking. Not to mention all the times they snuck off together. "Shep will do what he can," she told Paine gently, but still, her friends heart broke. Of course it did.

"What can he possibly do?" Paine asked, the hint of fear in her voice. Ember couldn't deny she was afraid too. She didn't know what Shep was capable of either, but if they didn't move fast both men would die.

"Hawk would want us to see to the crew," she avoided answering. That got Paine moving. She wiped the back of her hand on her forehead and managed a quick look back. She'd made it through the attack without being injured herself, but Hawk's blood covered her head to toe, a stark reminder that their captain was, technically speaking, dead. Ember closed the door behind them, praying Shep could do something to help, or at least that he wouldn't die too. She needed him more than she wanted to admit, and not just because of Atlantis.

Their crewmates ran back and forth on the deck, unsure what to do to help. The hellhounds had inflicted magical injuries which were not easily healed. Many were life threatening, and some had already claimed some of their friends. Paine swallowed when she saw Nat from the kitchen, lying still with his neck at an odd angle. Ember pulled her friend away and tried to think what Hawk would do. He'd give them purpose.

"Bindings," she said. "Bandages. Fresh water. Gather any crew who are able." The magic of healing would have to be done by her and Draco alone, the rest simply weren't powerful enough under these circumstances. Paine's face took on a green tint. Ember shook her shoulders. "Paine!" she called, wondering if this was the first time the ship had seen actual battle. It lurched back and forth as if it were riding high seas, but in fact they were as high in the clouds as they'd ever been. The sun shone strong on all the damage the crew and ship had taken, but it did nothing to warm them.

"Bandages, right." Paine shook her head. "Lucas! Jamie, come with me!" She gathered the closest crew who were milling around in various states of shock and injury. Lucas looked like he'd taken a blow to the head, but Jamie was only catatonic. Somehow, they'd managed to put a group of the worst off together. Two were passed out from extensive injuries. Blood loss, she though, looking from one to the other. Blood from… everywhere. The others were banged and bruised almost as bad. One moaned and lay on her side, Ember couldn't see her wound, and another rocked back and forth, his injuries in his mind.

She called to Draco, but it didn't take much. The dragon hovered by the side of the ship. She felt frustration ripple through her friend, and he flew close enough for her to climb on his back. His once soft feathers had turned coarse and sharp. She avoided them the best she could. "There's nothing you could have done," she said, assuaging his guilt, but she received back an image that was both confusing and infuriating. Draco had accused one of the crew of letting the hellhounds on, and it was unexpected, indeed.

"Are you sure?" she asked, looking back. Draco was sure, and angry. "Okay, let's heal them first, then we can deal with that." Though Shep usually assisted in her magic, she didn't dare reach out to him now. No, this would be up to her and Draco alone.

Traditionally she'd have to be with the crew to heal them, but in order to call forth such strong magic, she'd need peace and concentration, both of which she could only get away from the ship. Just binding their injuries wouldn't work. She'd need to pull the hellhounds poison from them, then rework on the wards. There were more than three hellhounds out there.

Draco flew as high as he dared. It was as close to the sun as she'd ever been, and she felt the trail of Atlantis here. If they could only go south for perhaps a day or two, would they see the great city? Or was it still cloaked to her eyes, lost in time and space, forever to wander? Somehow, she would pull the city home this way, but now, she only needed to take from it.

"Be still, my friend," she told Draco. The dragon flapped his great wings and flew a slow circle. She saw the ship far off, felt its pain and chaos, and tried to recenter herself around the lost city. It's magic. It's hope. It's love. Slowly, her heart opened, and tendrils of magic swept in, looping around her body. They were light and freeing. Open. She felt, again, like anything was possible. She felt love. She felt... Hawk?

"He's done it," she breathed. Draco dipped, unsure, but she had what she needed. "Return to the ship. Hurry." She leaned down flat on his neck as the dragon swept off. This was her favorite part of flying. She could have ridden Draco all night, but there wasn't such time. Clouds were forming on the horizon, and not just the ones in the sky. Something was waiting both for Atlantis and for them. Something explosive.

Chapter 22

Hawk didn't just blink his eyes open as he did every day, both blessing and cursing the fact his crew were still alive and in the air. Safe for another day. No, his eyelids flew open, and his sight was sharp. His other senses took another minute. Why was he in his office, the faint smell of copper and pine cleaners? He clenched his fist, wondering at the power thrumming though his arms. Was he dreaming?

"It's not a dream."

He startled at the sight of Shepherd behind his desk, the familiar decanter in his hand. Shep didn't seem to be drinking from it, only swirling around a thick, red liquid that both fascinated him and turned his stomach.

"How did you…" His voice was sharp for so early. He ran a hand over the stubble on his chin and felt nothing out of order. No lumps or bruises. He swallowed. The last thing he remembered was a battle.

"We have a connection now, for better or for worse." Shep's own voice sounded tired and far away. He was paler than Hawk remembered. Hawk sat up quickly, almost too quickly, but he wasn't dizzy. No, it was energy he felt, and it was so amazing he barely recognized the depth of Shep's words or the pain behind them.

He raised an eyebrow as Shep offered him the glass. "You can read my mind?"

"It's not brandy, I'm afraid…" Shep didn't have to read his mind. His expression would do. "… but it will help." Shep sat across from the couch as Hawk took the glass and sniffed the sharp smell.

"Are you crazy?" he said, but his stomach growled. He got up and bounced on his heels. "What happened? What is the status of the ship? My crew?"

"Sit down, Captain Hawkins," Shep answered sharply. "It is a long story and one that must be told properly. Your crew is safe for now." He sighed. "What remains of them, anyway."

Hawk forced himself to sit, but he couldn't force himself to drink. What evil had befallen his crew? Himself? His very body called out to drink at the same time as his mind was disgusted by it.

"You died," Shep stated, as matter of fact as if he were talking about the weather, which Hawk knew, without even looking was cloudless and dark. Cold. He felt it, but he couldn't say how. Someplace deep inside him stirred with a deep knowing, one that left him dizzy and breathless. If he weren't sitting, his legs would have given out under him.

"So, you, what? Performed CPR?" he asked, but the look on Shep's face said that no, he hadn't performed CPR or had assistance from any other modern medicine. No, what Shep had done was ancient and dark. He bore into Hawk with a deep gaze. The whites of Shep's eyes were tinged with red, and Hawk felt Shep's heartbeat, slow and maddeningly delicious. He felt regret pouring off his friend. Sadness. Whatever Shepherd had done to save Hawk's life had cost him greatly, if not physically then mentally. And if it had cost Shep, what would it cost Hawk?

"It seems I owe you a thank you," Hawk said quietly, looking at his reflection in the glass. The candlelight flickered behind him, and Hawk realized how dark it was, though his eyes had adjusted as if it were the middle of day.

"You are indebted to me and connected to me, but as for a thank you? No, I'd not accept that. It is more of a curse than a blessing, Captain, but this ship needs you. Atlantis needs you, and we are close. I'd not have you dying when we are on the brink of its homecoming."

The hunger was becoming obvious and overwhelming. Hawk's stomach made a noise that was between a plead and a grown. It demanded the glass. It demanded blood.

"What have you done?" he asked, bringing the glass to his lips, both savoring the smell and hating himself for it.

Instead of answering, Shep rose. The actual decanter still contained brandy. He considered it, then drank from the very container itself not bothering with such niceties as glasses.

"Gods." Hawk drank. At first, he choked on the taste and the thickness, but soon it slid down easier than the brandy that Shep so casually drank. It seemed to fill him from head to toe, and somehow, he was even more energized and powerful than he had been before. He filled himself quickly, then put the glass down, careful not to break it, and forced himself to sit still. Was he dead already? Was this hell?

Shep was equally still. The decanter empty, Shep returned behind the desk. A ridiculous map laid out over it. Hawk had been mapping their circles, but what did any of that matter now?

"It's a story that must be told from the beginning," he told Hawk slowly, judging his reactions. He wondered how other people reacted to such news. Did they rail? Scream? Beg for death? Or did they celebrate this new power? Revel in it. He could not pinpoint his own emotions, but he'd say they were somewhere in between. Closer to fear than glee. Much closer.

Chapter 23

Shep had left out so much of his story when he'd told it to Ember. She was brave, and she was strong, but was she ready for this? He watched Hawk dip his head in his hands and struggle with his emotions and his newfound strength. The smell of blood was in the air, but Shepherd was long since used to that. He twisted the decanter so it caught the light and beams shone on the map in front of him. The brandy had not even made a dent in his demeanor. If only it could.

No, he would not burden Ember with this. Not if he could help it. She had enough to deal with already – and vampires? He almost laughed out loud at the absurdity of it.

"The bond between us will never weaken, but you'll get used to it over time," Shep promised, but his words were empty. Hawk would get used to it, but if he were anything like Shep, a man who craved his freedom, he'd curse it every day.

"Who is it that so binds you?" Hawk lifted his head and spat. His eyes were tinged with red, and he was holding back tears. A red stain formed on his shirt where he'd clumsily spilled the blood.

Shep took a measured breath, for indeed, as Ember found out earlier that evening, even creatures of the night had to draw breath. And he'd come damned close to stopping that. Not as close as Hawk. His friend had been technically dead. Their blood had healed each other, if that's what you could call it.

"Her name was Mirabal, and she lived a long time ago," Shep said. How many years had it been since Atlantis had been cursed to the sky? So many that he'd lost count of even the generations that had passed, and all that remained of his home were whispered stories of a city in the sea.

"You feel her?" Hawk asked, his voice pleading, "like this?" He held a hand over his chest, where Shep knew he could feel both their heartbeats. It was chaos, now, but one day they would be synchronous. They'd beat in time. Though if it were Hawk's body that would acquiesce or Shepherd's, he did not know. Nor did it matter. There was no undoing it now.

Shep placed a hand over his own heart. Yes, he felt her. He'd done everything he could to sever their connection, but the link was still there. Old, but powerful. How many years had it been, now? How many centuries? How much death had come between them?

"Unlike you, I chose this," Shep offered with regret. He pulled a chair up opposite Hawk, observed the tremor in his friend's hand, the wild look in his eye. He would need to feed again, and soon. Baby vampires were needy. Shep would not have turned him if there were any other option.

"I did not know what I was choosing," he continued. "I…" He looked out the porthole window and remembered her. The curls in her dark hair. The azure blue of her eyes, a color he'd never seen before or after. She had an energy that was both calm and chaos. Shep had thought she was a witch when he'd sought her out.

"I cannot help you," she told him, but she reluctantly let him in. Her home was a cottage in the woods, tucked away by the river. He'd heard rumors of a sorceress, a healer – a witch that could stop time itself. He'd sought her for many years, finally reaching a village at the end of nowhere. Without even a name.

"Please." He fell to his knees. "I seek Atlantis."

She stirred her cauldron, unmoved. It smelled of lavender and spices. "You seek Atlantis. They seek Atlantis. Everyone seeks Atlantis." She threw something into the potion, and it popped and let off green smoke. She swirled it in the air with her finger and it seemed to follow her whim before disappearing. She pinned him with that deep blue gaze. "I cannot give you Atlantis," she said, "any more than I can give you the stars themselves. They are both out of our reach."

But there was kindness in her eyes, and she stooped to gaze deeply at Shepherd, as if she could see into his soul. She touched his cheek gently. "Ahh, but your intentions are so pure, child." He'd bristled. At that point he'd lived a hundred years or more but compared to her, he was only a babe. She took his elbow and helped him stand.

"It's a child you seek?" she asked. She turned, but not before he saw the flash of sadness in her eyes.

"Yes," he said simply. "My daughter."

She nodded. She began taking down jars which lined her shelves, but there was no order. She'd take one down and place it back. She was buying time. Finally, she turned and wiped her hands on her apron.

"I can offer you time." She looked down, her long lashes framing her eyes. Her beauty was timeless. "But it comes at a great cost," she added.

He would have agreed to anything, but how could he have known, then, the true cost? On his physical body, yes – he'd seen generations come and go. But on his soul? The things he would have to do to feed. He shivered when she took his face in her hands. Her palms were ice cold, despite the fact she'd just stirred the fire.

"The cost is your soul," she said, and she kissed him gently. Her lips were as cold as her hands, but Shep felt a fire in him, nonetheless.

"I will pay it." He covered her hands with his.

"That is a damned good story," Hawk interrupted. He stood on shaky legs. Blood matted his blond hair. "Romantic, even." He held the wall to steady himself. Shep looked on sadly. There was no steadiness in Hawk's future. Shep had gotten the blood from the dragon, but Hawk would require more and more. He shook his head.

"I promise you, there was nothing romantic about it. She bit me, then and there. I fell into a stupor. When I woke…" He looked out the window to his past. "I was in the middle of the woods, alone. I could never find the village again. I could never find her. Though what I would have done…" He turned to look at his friend: shaky, trembling, gray – but alive. "What I would have done I do not know."

"Blessed that you had a choice, mate," Hawk replied, but his tone was without cruelty. Without gratitude, indeed, but there was a resentful graciousness.

"Blessed or cursed," Shep replied.

Hawk tipped his head back and rested it on the wall, closing his eyes. "Now what?" he asked. The door flew open and behind it stood Ember and Paine. Ember strode in with her hands on her hips and fire in her eyes. She'd heard. He'd known she wasn't far. Paine pushed her way around Ember and right up to Shepherd's face.

"Now what, indeed?" Paine looked at Hawk with concern then turned on Shep. "What will happen to him?"

Shep tipped his head. "The same as happens to all of us. He'll age, though much slower."

"How much slower?" Her voice softened, and Shep detected a tremor. Ahh, that was the rub, wasn't it? Hawk would watch her grow old and die.

"Slow enough." He rounded the desk to sit behind it. Hawk had accumulated an impressive array of maps showing the places they'd sought Atlantis, but they were always too slow, or too late. Now, though? "Unless…" Shep added. Paine had gone to Hawk's side to help him sit. He dipped his head in his hands and spoke to her low. It was only Ember listening and despite the circumstances, she had a smile on her face.

"Unless we find Atlantis," she said. He nodded.

"And I think we can." He looked at Hawk's map again. "I have a plan."

Chapter 24

"There is some special magic above your island, that is true." Shep turned to the shelves behind the desk, running his trembling fingers over the spines of the books Ember's mother had sent Hawk, finally settling on a small, familiar volume.

"The history of the island?" Ember asked. She had, indeed, heard most of Shep's story, if not all. She felt marginally guilty for spying, but Paine was so worried about Hawk, and Ember? Ember was a mix of worry and curious. She wasn't sure that something such as a hellhound would be able to take down Shepherd, but the last she'd seen him, his skin had been pale gray. He'd taken on color now, and his countenance was animated. He had a plan indeed.

"In all the places I've sought, in all the lifetimes ..." He flipped through the book, but what he was looking for Ember didn't know. "There was no magic such as this, but something is missing. Here. What is this place?" He stopped at a page close to the end, an index of sorts of places close to the island but not quite on it.

Ember swallowed. "The cliffs?" she asked. She met his gaze and saw her own fear reflected back. It wasn't fear of hellhounds or vampires or even fate, but something much more real and human. "The shore of the mainland north of the island." She took the book from him, read over the small passage. "There's a rumor the two once were connected, though they don't say how. The stories…" She smiled. "The stories were that a great bridge was sunk, though no one really talks about it now. Since they built the hospital, the place is desolate. My sister is there." She flipped a couple more pages that talked about more populated places on the mainland. "Here."

The building was stark. Industrial. With it's stone façade, she'd always thought it looked older than it was, but the hospital was built only a couple years before Sierra ended up there. They'd reached out to her when they heard about the accident – island news travels fast. She'd once thought she was lucky that the place had been built for long term care such as Sierra's, but now the timing made her wonder, especially since her insurance didn't bat an eye at covering all of it. Or at least she'd never seen a bill.

"I try to go sometimes to visit," Ember said, "But…" What was the but? Her life was busy. She was the only one who ran the store. That wasn't her excuse. She bit her bottom lip. "But it's a sad place. Gray. Quiet. Outside time even. It gives me the creeps. And she doesn't know I'm there anyway."

Shepherd tipped his head as he considered her. "Doesn't she?" he asked, seeking answers in her eyes and not in the book. "I wonder?"

She didn't have a chance to ask what he meant. Hawk's knees gave out and he begun convulsing. He fell to the floor despite Paine trying to hold him up. "What's happening?" she cried. Hawk's eyes rolled back in his head, and he issued a low, guttural growl.

Shep rushed to his side. Hawk's mouth opened slightly enough for them to see sharp incisors. Paine fell back.

"He must feed again." Shep turned to look at Ember, a plead in his eyes. "You should go. So young like this… he is dangerous." Hawk continued thrashing and the expression on his face screwed up in both pain and frustration. Ember took Paine by the elbow.

"He's right," she told her friend. "There will be time for explanations. Right now, we should help the crew."

That got her friend moving, but only just. On the floor, Hawk writhed and growled. Tears formed in Paine's eyes as Shep held him close. "Come on," Ember moved her along, sparing one glance for them on the way out the door. When Shepherd met her gaze, his expression was filled with pain, and for a moment she felt the weight of all those lifetimes, though still… she didn't know if she was the one he sought. If he were to fail again, she wasn't sure he would make it.

The deck was still in chaos though the hellhounds were now gone. Ember put Paine to work on binding injuries, something she knew would hold her friend's attention. But as for her own? It was distracted. Focused on the accident that wounded her sister.

Magic takes love to heal, and that she had in abundance, but their injuries took longer than usual because she was lost in her memories of growing up with Sierra on the island. Sierra was two years younger than her. Blonde to her brunette. Outgoing to her introvert. Everyone knew the island would never hold her, but she never had a chance to find out.

Ember had always assumed they were on a college tour when they ran off the road, but why had she assumed that? Because the timing was right, though she hadn't heard from her folks that whole week, and when she had they'd been distracted. She'd spoken to Sierra and her usually bubbly sister had seemed sad. Ember had always thought it was because of her senior year. She'd had a boyfriend on the island she was sad to lose. She'd lost track of Brad in the last few years, and his folks had moved off the island. The memories were probably too much. She understood.

She wiped blood off her hands with a rag someone had given her. Draco pressed into her thoughts. She gladly shared their magic, but as for her thoughts? They were hers alone. Thoughts of she and Sierra playing dolls as kids, or pretending their back yard was a carnival fun house. Sierra jumping out to scare her, as if Ember couldn't see her blonde hair behind a tree. Good memories, mostly, but Sierra could be moody and broody. She kept secrets, but Ember had never had the heart to look for her journal. Perhaps it was in the house still, holding on to her secrets.

"Oy! A little further north if you don't mind!" Ember looked down and was embarrassed to see where her hands were much lower on Liam's abdomen than his gash, which had stopped bleeding but was oozing a green puss. Liam was an unlikely member of the entertainment team, gifted in song and piano. He'd be a movie star back home, she thought, with his mop of black hair and perfect smile.

"I'm sorry." She wiped her forehead with the back of her hand. Her hands shook. She was more than just distracted but spent. "Here." He winced as she placed her palm on his stomach. The wound sizzled as it stitched itself closed. Liam hummed something between clenched teeth. He was always humming something.

"What song?" she asked, mostly to keep herself focused.

He opened his eyes. They were the deepest blue. "It's from Les Mis," he said. She smiled. Of course it was. She was familiar. ""Bring him home". It's about someone who's worried about someone they love." She sat back on her knees and Liam struggled to sit up. "The captain?" he asked. There was little hope in his eyes, and she struggled to answer.

"He's alive," she said, but was he? What did you call the curse he fell under? Liam let out a breath and laid back. "You should rest," she told him. She looked around. They'd bound most of the crew. The rest had fallen back. It was evening now. They were high enough in the sky the hellhounds wouldn't find them. She called to Draco, who was close by.

She wound through the remaining crew and touched Paine gently on the shoulder. "I'm going to take Draco out," she told her friend. She needed air and clarity, and there was a place she thought she might need to go alone.

Paine's eyes were red from tears. She covered Ember's hand. "Will Hawk be alright?" she asked.

Ember frowned. They were all asking her questions she couldn't answer. "He will be," she said, gently removing Paine's hand.

She turned her back and headed to the bow of the ship where Draco took up most of the deck. He swished his tail nervously and Ember had to dodge it. She buried her head in his coat, avoiding the sharp parts of his scales and instead burying her hands in the fur underneath.

"You know where we need to go, don't you?" she asked her dragon. He dipped his head. He'd always known. She climbed on his back. "Take me there," she said, and the dragon pushed off with his back legs and flew off into the night.

Chapter 25

She'd been afraid the first time she sat on Draco's back. He was small then, and she thought she would break him, but magic works in strange ways. Draco could hold a lot more than her weight, not that she'd tested it. The beast felt solid, and on his back she was as safe as she'd ever been on land. She ran her fingertips absently over his scales and felt the energy between them. Draco flew higher through the clouds in the direction of the mainland. The clouds shifted and parted as they flew through, and soon she couldn't see the ocean below them at all, only the stars above. How often she'd wished on them. To get her family back. For fortune. A change of direction. The dreams of a little girl. She was grown up now and found her dreams were much more complicated. She hoped she would see her sister again, but if Sierra did wake, things would get much more dangerous. What her heart wished for now was something not even magic could provide, at least not the kind she could wield.

Draco flew the long way around, wind whipping Ember's hair around her shoulders. She'd taken to wearing it long and held back with a band. It had been short for so long, she was surprised to find it had such a curl, as if even her hair was waiting to grow up. She tucked it out of her face.

"What do you think, Draco? Is it Sierra that Shepherd seeks?" She tamped down a flame of jealousy. She and Shepherd had grown close, that was true, but she had no ownership over him, and she didn't delude herself. His heart only wanted to return home to his daughter. She was a means to that end in this lifetime. Or perhaps, her sister was.

Draco huffed noncommittally. He understood, but the dragon had no more answers than she did. If she could find understanding in the night sky she'd fly forever, but the answers she sought were decidedly on the ground in a place she was loathe to go even on the best of terms.

Draco flew up the mainland, far enough from the coast he wouldn't be seen but for the most abject of skywatchers, and even then, he had a special magic that encouraged them to look away or if they did see – register only a shooting star or a comet. Perhaps a child would point, somewhere. Perhaps a lover would make a wish. If only she could grant it.

Sierra. In Ember's memory, she was perfect in the way only a sister can be. Perhaps some of that was jealousy. Of the way people had just taken to her. Of her beaming smile and golden hair. Of the way she never seemed to get bored or mad or irritated, but knew how to cheer Ember up when she was in one of her dark moods. She'd always try to get Ember to tag along with one of her summer friends, even after she met Brad. They invited Ember to ice cream or an outdoor movie or the beach… until they didn't. The last year Ember was on the island they'd grown apart, and then Ember moved away to college. She wasn't proud of the way she'd all but dumped her sister. She noticed each time they spoke, Sierra's voice getting more and more distant. More and more sad. And then, she was gone.

Ember shook her head. The peninsula was in view. She pulled back on Draco and he flew farther away. She wasn't ready to approach it, not yet, but she had to get a look. The institute was set on its own down a long drive that snaked through woods. Heavily wooded on each side, with no beach access or towns for miles. The Maine coast could be that way, but even boaters or explorers tended to stay away. Magic, Ember realized. Now that she could feel it, the magic was as clear as day, but wrong. It was not protected by magic that was borne of love, but a kind Ember had never felt. Restless. Painful. She turned, but she spied the stark building as it overlooked the sea. Lights shone in the upstairs windows. Was Sierra in one of them? Had she been waiting for Ember to wake her up?

She reached out but felt only walls. Behind one of them, her sister waited for her. But not yet. She reluctantly turned the dragon back to the ship. She'd need more than a hammer to breach this wall. She'd need an army, and she thought maybe she knew where to find one.

Though she tried to keep her mind off Shepherd, thoughts of him filled her head like the wind that whipped past her face. Of his kisses, but also of the brushes of his hand, of the way he watched her when he didn't think she was looking. She couldn't read him, or at least she didn't trust herself to read him. What she felt was hope. Was there love under there too? She didn't trust herself enough to know.

He'd been known as Casius once, though he'd told them scant stories of Atlantis, preferring, instead, to hear of their own heartbreaks and troubles and hopes and dreams. Ember had done more than her share of talking. It was time for him to tell her all he knew.

Too much time had passed. Ember had known this. Though she'd peppered him with questions about Atlantis, he'd rarely opened up. If they were going to return Atlantis to the ground, she had to know much more than what the city was made of. She had to know his heart, whoever he was.

The magic of Hawk's ship lit up the night sky in a way she could only see now that she was attuned to magic. It was the same way she knew Atlantis was north, somewhere, and if they flew, she could find it. But what she'd do when she got there, she didn't know. The ship cut an impressive form. Looking for all the world (at least those who could see magic) as an old, wooden battleship, with sails unfurled and lights on the deck and in the windows. But inside was so much more than that.

She worried about Hawk, indeed, but it wasn't Hawk on her mind when Draco circled the deck. They'd cleared off a space for him to land, and Ember wondered what would happen when the dragon got bigger. Perhaps they'd have no need of the flying ship by then. Perhaps Atlantis would be home.

"Thank you, my friend," Ember told Draco, who bowed and batted his great golden eyes. She rested her head on his. The rest of the journey would not be an easy one. Indeed, the rest of the evening would not be an easy one, but they'd come so far already.

The deck had been emptied and cleaned. No sign of the blood or the hellhounds or the injuries. Or anyone at all, really. Curious. She felt them and walked the deck to seek them. She crossed the main deck, past the steps that led to Hawk's office, which was empty. She climbed further down one deck where laughter was echoing out of the auditorium. She walked past the hall where Shep was leaning on the wall, Paine beside him.

Shep had a faint smile on his lips. On stage, Hawk was putting on a play with some of the crew. "Shakespeare?" she asked, recognizing *A Midsummer Night's Dream*. Hawk was Puck. Of course he was.

Paine shook her head. "He's doing what he always does," she said. "Taking care of the crew. They needed to see he was okay."

"Is he?" Ember asked.

"That is complicated," Shep answered. "But for now, yes." He pushed back from the wall and wavered on his feet.

"Speaking of that, I need to speak to you," Ember said, pulling her attention away from the stage. They had a good production, she had to give them that.

Paine looked from one to the other. "Will the captain be okay?" she asked. "With the... you know... blood thing?"

Shep offered a sad smile. "He is in control for the evening. I can feel him, but as for these questions..." He met Ember's gaze. "I suppose you're right. It's time."

Paine gave a nervous look. "Where should I find you if I need you?" she asked. The audience laughed.

"You won't need to," Shep answered. "I'll find you."

Chapter 26

Shepherd turned them past Hawk's office and toward the deck where all the carnage had been only a few hours before. She was loathe to go, but he said he needed air. What else did he need, she wondered?

The white floors had been scrubbed as best they could, but there were still puddles here and there. They'd taken the wounded to the decks below, and the dead? Well, she didn't know what they'd done with them, but she felt the absence of their energy on the ship. It faltered, and she struggled to keep it afloat.

They reached the rail. The ship pushed silently through low clouds, splitting them. Ember stifled a yawn, for her human body still needed sleep and, at the moment, it was sorely lacking. Somewhere Draco hunted. Dawn hadn't yet broken the horizon and there was still a chill in the air. Shep's breath frosted.

"What would you know of me?" he asked. She sensed more in his words than just the way his lips formed them. There was fear, perhaps that she wouldn't accept him. There was hope that he could finally tell his story—and behind all that there was—purpose of bring his city home, completing his journey. And there was love, she was sure of it.

She watched the stars, the way the clouds lazily moved around the ship. Her magic kept them afloat, and it tired her.

She knew of the history of Atlantis. She knew of the king and his queen. His brother Zyah. The curse that lifted them to the sky. The king's reluctance to return and Zyah's blood lust. But those were all facts. What she didn't know was the heart of the city she was tasked to return. The heart of the man tasked to find her.

"What was it like?" She turned and leaned on the rail. "Every day? What was your life like? What did you do? What did you feel?"

At this, a smile crept on to his face. "Before I met you, it had been a long time since I'd felt anything, but you have brought back the memory of that place. It's magic. It's love."

He looked off toward the direction of Atlantis. He could feel it too. Of course he could.

"I can only tell you my own story," he answered. "But it is not facts you're looking for, I think?" He grinned. "If only I could put the magic of Atlantis into words. The life people live there. The magic. The love. You have to feel it, Ember, and I think you do. Here." He tapped a spot in the middle of her chest that lit up with his touch. She took his hand in hers. There was more than magic at work.

"Even without magic, it is the best of this world," he said. "It's the kindest of gestures, done anonymously. A coin given to a stranger. A smile that lights up a room. Kindness. Equality. Love. Creativity. Service." He pulled her into his arms. She wondered if he was realizing he'd done so, but indeed, he did. He held her tight so that her ear was against his chest, where his heart would have beat.

"I know not if I can return, in the condition I am in," he admitted. His hold on her didn't falter. "But yet I want to right the world just the same. Even if it cannot be for me, even if I am among the damned that can't walk the streets, I'd have the world put back into place. For my daughter, and all the others."

Ember had enough slack to pull back and look up at his face, screwed up in pain. What a burden he must have carried all these years. "What about those other lives? The girl you sought to return Atlantis?" she asked, for she'd been curious.

He opened his eyes, a ring of red had formed around them. "It was you, Ember. Always. I've felt your energy since I fell from the sky, and I sought it, always arriving too late. Perhaps I needed to be this man in this lifetime, and you this woman? Perhaps there is magic in our timing?" At this he smiled, but his smile was tinged with danger. With adventure. With love, even. It was more than Atlantis that pulled them together.

She wasn't sure where the words came from, but the threat of his damnation had hit her hard. His sacrifices, made for everyone else. "If you cannot enter the gates of Atlantis, I will wander this world with you," she promised. She reached up to touch his cheek. "There are some places, I think where we could be happy. There are some places we could get in some trouble." There was a twinkle in her eye. An invitation.

"Falling in love with you was unexpected." He cupped her hand on his cheek, kissed her palm gently. "And it makes me fear for you."

"I am not afraid," she said, and for once, she meant it. She wasn't the same girl that he'd met in the bookstore. She'd trained a dragon and fought a hellhound and gone back far enough in her own memories to question her own existence. But could she love?

Yes, she thought. Perhaps their timing was indeed perfect. And so were their kisses. She knew when he pulled her in, his hand on the back of her neck gently guiding her. His lips, soft and gentle at first. He watched as her eyes fell closed and she saw more than desire reflected in them. A fire to match hers. Magic, yes, but what was love if not magic? Magic of the kind that would rival Atlantis. She wrapped her arms around the back of his neck and clung to him as he deepened their kiss. The wind picked up and the ship sighed. She would stay afloat for a few hours. Draco would see to it. Ember reluctantly pulled away and took his hand. There was a question in his eyes but no regret in hers. He let her take the lead. She tugged. He followed.

They heard the echoes of laughter as they snaked down below decks, sneaking past the rest of the crew who all struggled with their own emotions of joy and sadness and fear and love. That was life, wasn't it? She opened her door with her palm and the magic of it yielded to him, as if the very room were in league with them.

The room took on a different feel with him there. Something had shifted in the very air. The ship flew strong and steady. Somewhere, Draco roared. The threats had been mitigated, and she'd never felt so safe.

He sat on the edge of her bed and watched as her insecurities bubbled up. "If it is my sister and not me who is destined to return Atlantis…" She threaded her fingers through his. He may not have a heartbeat but hers was racing. "Would you love me just the same?"

"Ember…" He tugged her so their bodies were flush, and she could feel his desire. "I know not if I sought you for Atlantis, or for my own heart. The city we shall return, one way or the other. It's our destiny, but you are my love. You are the woman I've been chasing through time."

The feel of melting into him was everything he'd described Atlantis as, and more. It was the feeling of love. It was desire. It was coming home. She had no shame or hesitation, not like the other clumsy attempts with boys on the island, but when she gave him permission, he took the lead. He pulled her up, rolled her over and lay on top as if he were claiming her for his own with every stroke of his hand, every kiss, every glance.

The ship held its breath as they came together, or at least she thought so because she'd forgotten where and who she was, and it was only thanks to the gods, and magic, that they stayed in the sky at all. But the dance they did was a kind of magic on its own, capable of more than holding a ship up, but binding two hearts together, and she yielded for him, and him for her, time and time again.

Chapter 27

The crew gathered the next morning to mourn the dead. Captain Hawkins led them in prayer, looking just a little peakish, but otherwise the leader they expected him to be. Ember studied him from the back of the crowd. He didn't waver on his feet, his voice didn't even crack when he talked about the two crew who didn't make it. Paine had told Ember their bodies would be burned. They had no families to mourn them. Orphans, all.

Shep led them back to Hawk's office, and Ember couldn't help remembering the first time she'd been there. In such a short time, she'd leaned and gotten more muscle. Her hair had grown, and she had become stronger. Strong enough, though? She wasn't sure.

The weather had turned colder, and though Hawk was able to regulate the temperature enough on the deck, often they flew through snow. It would complicate getting her sister. She ran her fingers over the map of the island.

There had indeed once been a bridge to the peninsula, but it was long sunk.

"Tell me again why Sierra is important?" Ember asked. It wasn't that she didn't want to use magic to wake her sister up, quite the opposite actually. She didn't want to put her sister in danger, and coming at her with a flying ship chased by hellhounds surely qualified as such.

Hawk shook his head. He was wearing his hair loose and it fell around his shoulders. His hands trembled slightly, and his lips were as red as she'd ever seen him. Paine watched him with sorrow in her eyes.

"I don't know, exactly." He looked up and met Shep's gaze. Something passed between them. Something regretful and sad, but also knowing. Paine picked up on it first.

"Care to clue us in?" She flopped down in one of the chairs.

"I'm sorry, love," Hawk touched her shoulder. "This feeling is new…"

Shep cut him off. "He was trying to say there is strange magic surrounding your sister. This place she's at is not even a hospital. It's a privately owned company, and its records are sealed tightly."

Hawk smiled. "All we can find is it's owned by a company called Skycity. Clever."

Ember shook her head. "Why would they be keeping my sister hostage?" she asked. It was well into evening, and she picked at a food spread without much interest. "Why not just kill her?"

"I have a theory," Shep offered, but he said no more, instead waiting for Ember to encourage him.

"This ought to be good," she said. She lifted herself up on Hawk's desk, so her legs dangled. "What is it?"

Shep pressed his lips closed. He waited long enough for Ember to wonder if she should be scared. "I think they tried. I think that's what the accident was about, but her magic is strong. I don't think they can kill her, but they can curse her." He pinned her with a stare. "Perhaps they even needed to curse her. To siphon her magic."

"Why?" Ember asked. "Why her and not me?"

It was Hawk who answered. "Shepherd thinks they might not have known about you. Your mother was protective. Secretive. They rarely went off island, but perhaps they were spotted."

Ember blanched. "You think their accident had to do with Zyah?" she asked. She'd batted the idea around, in fact she was almost positive that was what happened, but some things didn't make sense. "Why didn't he come for me?"

Shepherd narrowed his eyes. He touched her cheek lightly. "There is something about you that's protected," he said. He smiled. "Old magic. It's what called your dragon."

Hawk interrupted. "There's something about the island that's protected, not your girl." Ember blushed. It was the first time she'd thought to be called his, and while it felt right, she searched his face for hesitation and found none.

"I felt it," Paine paced, "when we picked you up, but I don't know how to explain it. I've never felt magic like that."

Ember had grown up around magic like that, but to her it was just second nature. It was the reason everything off island felt so wrong. Cold. The ship's magic came close, but nothing was quite like the air on the island. It hummed with magic. Filled her veins.

"Who was protecting it?" She picked a piece of lint on her sleeve. "And why?" She stopped herself before she could say some biting words about that protection. She'd grown up lonely and isolated and ended up orphaned. Some protection.

It was Hawk who answered. He flipped through the book on the history of the island. The statue on the common cut an imposing figure on the cover. "Perhaps your grandmother knew it. Felt it?" He tossed the book aside. "Or perhaps we'll never know. I just know your sister is important to this. We must break that spell."

Paine was the only one who truly understood. Ember felt it in the sad look they exchanged. While Shep and Hawk made plans to get close to the island, Ember got up to sit next to her friend and put her head on Paine's shoulder.

"She's been asleep for years," Ember said softly. "She doesn't even know about my parents, and this?" She gestured around. "It will be a lot to explain."

"It will," Paine agreed, putting an arm around her friend. She smelled like the sea and the wind and magic and freedom. "But you won't be alone."

Ember was comforted, but only slightly. The road ahead of them was likely to be harder than the one behind, like the way a mountain peaks as you get close to the top. And were they even close to the top? What would happen when she finally saw Atlantis? Returned it? Were they ready to change the world forever?

She had to be, because her sister's life depended on it, and so did so many more.

Chapter 28

They were going to have to split up. Ember had known it early on, much earlier than she wanted to admit, that she would have to do this part alone. Perhaps she'd read too many books about the hero's journey. Perhaps she'd just known in her heart that some roads you must walk alone. Perhaps, though, it came down to simply wanting to see her sister. At any rate, she wasn't surprised to find the ship couldn't sail anywhere near the facility. Some foul magic pushed it back.

"We'll walk," Shepherd argued. She eyed him with a smile. He'd acclimated to this world, but only just. There was still something off about him, like she'd noticed the first day. As if he didn't belong here, or anywhere. He was from the stars, but instead of returning to them he'd pull the stars back to them.

"*You'll* walk," Ember corrected. She'd already told them how it was going to go down. She was just waiting for them to catch up. "I have a dragon."

She was dressed, already, as if she were leaving that very moment. She'd said her goodbyes to her friends. To

Shep even. He'd been staying with her and how comfortable it would be to slide into this life. Stay on this ship. Rescue survivors.

But it was not her fate, and it never had been.

They stood on the front deck and watched the outline of the island spread itself out before them in the morning sun. She felt it. The goodness of this place. Atlantis would be home here, next to her. Shep pulled her aside.

"Your dragon can carry us both," he argued. Draco had taken to flying off by himself for long times. His form cut an outline over the ocean, making slow circles. He was waiting for Ember to give the word.

"He could," she agreed, "but he will not." Who had she become, that she was embarking on such danger alone? Months before, she had barely wanted to run the bookstore, her life an endless loop of monotony. If only she could go back and tell herself that everything would change. What would she have said? She smiled at the memory, and the words came to her exact. *Magic and adventure are inside you, and your fate will come to you soon.* The words were vaguely familiar and comforting at the same time.

"Ember…" Shep looked in her eyes prepared to argue, but instead she projected a quiet strength she wasn't sure where it came from. It was more than fate or destiny, silly things if you asked her. It was more than prophecy. Whether or not they said she was chosen, she was choosing herself. She was choosing to walk this hard road. She was choosing to save her sister, to bring home Atlantis.

She was choosing to love him and to let him go. For now.

He exhaled, feeling all of that in her energy. In the very way she squared her shoulders. He grabbed the rail and looked out over the ocean. Far off, a dolphin surfaced and dove again. "I wish sometimes it were different. That I did not choose this curse. Died as the rest, in my time."

She let him continue. He covered her hand with his on the rail. "But then I would not have lived to see such times. I would not have met you. Not in this lifetime, at least." He raised her hand and kissed it gently. "And that is worth every terrible decision I've made. It was worth every curse. Every scourge. Every pain… I love you."

They had danced around those words. What was love, anyway, but magic? And he'd showed her magic of the most beautiful and amazing kinds, but love?

She squeezed his hand. "I love you, and I will see you on the other side of this."

"Perhaps sooner than that." he smirked. "We walk fast."

They weren't sure how close the ship could get to drop them off, but they had a hike of many miles. Ember hoped to be in and out by the time they reached the facility. She wondered, briefly, if it was her in those past lifetimes Shep remembered. If she'd been born and died over and over again just for this moment. For this love. And she thought, maybe, it was true.

Draco was perched calmly on the deck. None of the crew was on deck, save Shep, Hawk, and Paine. Paine had argued strongly against this, and her face reflected such, though she chose to keep her mouth closed at this moment. But Hawk? Hawk knew sacrifice. Though he'd perked up since he'd been turned, there was a sadness that had settled in his bones. He hugged her tightly.

"I always knew," he whispered. His voice was such that it carried only to her. Some magic, maybe, or just

Hawk being Hawk. For he was still his youthful, caring self, with a strong sense of responsibility to boot. He pulled back and she noticed the red tinge to his eyes, though on the whole he seemed healthier than he'd ever been.

"You knew I was reckless?" She batted his shoulder as he let go.

He shook his head with a smile. The morning sun reflected on the gold in his hair. "I don't hold sway with prophecies, really. I mind my crew. Keep them alive. Rescue survivors." Paine watched from the rail while Shep readied Draco. Neither could hear. "But I knew the moment I felt your energy there was something different about you. Something lifechanging."

"That's a big responsibility," Ember pointed out.

"Precisely why I never told you until I thought you were ready," he answered. Across the deck, Draco fluffed his feathers and let Shep stroke his fur.

"And now?" she asked, distracted. She turned her gaze back to Hawk. "Now you think I'm ready?"

He nodded his head. "I cannot place the moment you realized your power, but there's no doubt you have."

"It's my sister they want." She looked out over the horizon, where somewhere Sierra was waiting for her.

"Perhaps. Perhaps not." He put a hand on her shoulder. "Perhaps it is your combined power. Or perhaps there's no such thing as prophecies or energy and we're all just bumbling along."

She laughed out loud, a most welcome feeling. "That is a great pep talk," she told him.

He hugged her quickly. "Safe journey," he told her. "We will be there as soon as we can."

She felt a flush of love for her friends. "I know," she told him, and turned before her laughter could turn to tears. Shep helped her up on Draco's back, sparing a moment to kiss her.

"Are you sure?" he asked. She was as sure as she'd ever been, and still so afraid. She nodded, not trusting her voice. He patted the dragon once and stepped back. "Then the hopes of Atlantis travel with you. I believe in you, Ember. You've got this."

It was a decidedly modern thing to say, and finally her eyes teared up. "Up, Draco," she said. The dragon patted the deck and rose into the morning sky.

Chapter 29

Ember flew Draco across the morning sky. She hadn't told the others exactly what her plan was, but the path she'd chosen would take some time. It had come to her when she read the history of the island. The bridge from the island to the facility. She saw it in her mind, and she knew it would take her there. How wasn't important. Sometimes you just have to believe.

The wind was chilly, but Draco's body warmed her. They flew just under the clouds, the world just a tiny anthill below. Life on the island probably went on, slow and lazy in the winter. Maybe someone had wondered why the shop was closed. Maybe not. Her old life had been so easy to walk away from, as if the new one had been just waiting behind a curtain, one that was impossible to go back through.

Draco projected images as they crossed the sky. She knew them now as Atlantis, though where the dragon had gotten them from, she didn't know. Muscle memory or history? Atlantis was a land full of magic and dragons. And while Shepherd and Hawk and all the books she'd read said that it was a land fueled by love, nothing is a hundred percent. There were seeds of unease. Unhappiness. Sorrow. Grief. It was a land filled not with love, but with *life* in all its depth and feeling and emotion. Perhaps that was their mistake after all, to discount what was uncomfortable, and focus only on love. Love can be found in sorrow, in grief, too. It can even be found in anger, but it must be grasped tightly. All must be acknowledged.

She knew this from counseling after her folks had died, yes, but she knew it in a place deep in her heart. She'd celebrated their lives. She'd mourned them. She couldn't be sure that she let them go, did you ever let anyone go? But she saw them when she looked at her mother's paintings, or when she saw a dragonfly outside the bookstore window. She saw them in the new bestseller her dad would have read in a day. She saw them in this adventure, one her mother was trying to protect her from and prepare her for both at the same time. Love and grief. Sadness and hope.

They were too high for birds to fly but they passed a flock of seagulls below that cawed mourningly. She patted Draco. She was afraid she would have to leave him and travel the bridge alone, in fact she was almost sure of it, but Draco wouldn't hear it, only roaring if she got close to the subject. They'd see him. If only they could just break in, but magic was the only way, and true magic. Atlantian magic. Draco could hold his own. He'd wait.

The dragon swept low as they got close to the island, just as they practiced. She felt a wave of love for the beast. Shep had been right, it was a connection like no other. Draco would die to protect her, and she him. How must it have felt to have his dragon slain? She couldn't imagine.

They'd chosen low tide on purpose. Draco landed gracefully on a pebbly beach down one of the cliffs, one she once would have walked to look for sea glass and to ask the spirit of the ocean to bring her purpose and love. Well, spirit had done all that. Now what was she to do with it?

"Maybe I asked for too much?" She patted Draco's nose as he dipped his large head. She remembered when he was once no bigger than a cat, and she was the only one who could see him. Had she dreamed all this up? If so, she'd choose to continue dreaming.

"Maybe I asked for too little?" She smiled as Draco projected the vision of Atlantis returning. She'd never dreamed that she'd save a whole magical city; she'd never thought to ask for it. But maybe it was time to embrace those big dreams? She'd take this destiny if it was thus given to her. But first she had work to do.

"I'll be back shortly," she told Draco. He remembered Sierra. He'd projected visions when she talked about her sister. Visions of them playing as girls, at least until Sierra got older and popular and got her own friends. And still, Ember had been happy for her. She did have a dragon, after all. She'd take that over friendship drama anytime, at least until she'd stepped on the ship. Paine and Hawk, and even Shep, they were friends like she'd never had before. She'd heard them described as ride or die, and never understood that until this moment. They wouldn't let her fail. They wouldn't let her fall.

And love? Was her heart ready to go there? Love was for other people. People with money, status. The tourists that frequented the island in the summer with their fancy cars and their yachts. The ones who could hire people to do the dirty work, so they had time—actual time—to spend with each other.

Ember's life was complicated. Before this adventure, she'd messed around on dating apps. Even hookups. But how could she drag anyone into this messy life of being an orphan, of running a failing bookstore on a quiet island? What did she have to offer besides a financial hole, and a crumbling life? A heart that was in pieces.

It wasn't until she fell into this adventure that she realized how much she embraced that mess. On the ground or in the sky. She would never be the kind of girl to keep a perfect house. She'd never be the kind of girl to hire someone to take care of the messy parts of her life, like the summer tourists, because messy was her heart. And she loved it, and anyone who loved her would have to love that about her.

The scary thing was, he did.

The remains of the bridge glittered out of the ocean in a way she knew she was the only one to see. Far off, the ferry blew its horn. Life went on. The bridge beckoned. Once, she might have been afraid of crossing an invisible bridge over the water, but she'd long gone past that. Fear was just excitement framed a different way, but in truth, she was both.

"I'll be back, I promise." She patted Draco's nose, but her heart was already on the bridge. It pumped wildly. What would it feel like? Slippery? Terrifying? She turned from her friend, his eyes wide with sorrow and he roared the other way. "Don't set the island on fire," she told him. She dipped her own head and projected love before turning and taking the next steps in her journey.

The first few steps were in the water and the waves lapped her calves before she took a step that was a little different than the sandy shore. Slippery? Yes, maybe a little. Terrifying? Definitely. But only in that way that your heart leads the way, and your head hasn't quite caught up. The bridge felt cobbled beneath her feat, and when it rose up just over the ocean, she could see the twinkle of magic and the ocean below.

"Don't look down," she told herself. She'd always been afraid of silly things in the water like sharks and jellyfish. She'd let those fears stop her from going any more than waist deep, even with her mother by her side. But now? Sierra needed her, and not just her sister. A whole city.

She placed her feet carefully, one in front of the other. The bridge wasn't exactly see-through, there were twinkles of magic she was sure would hold her up before her feet hit them, but who's to say that magic wasn't fleeting? That someone would catch on and strike the bridge, send her plummeting into the waters below. Cold waters. Shark infested? She'd not care to find out.

She guessed it was a couple miles and wished Draco could have gone with her, or Shep, or any of the others. It felt like it should be a special walk, it was a magical journey after all, but it turned out magical journeys are just one foot after the other, and after some time the novelty wore off and she was just walking. She felt for Draco, who was restless and anxious, and tried to project calm, but the beast wouldn't calm until she was back. She dared not look back. It was enough to look forward, the far away shore slowly growing nearer and nearer.

The waves beneath her were thankfully calm, though they'd taken on a deeper blue hue of the ocean.

Seaweed floated by, and here and there a bird dove down to catch a fish. There were no boats nearby, though she suspected she was protected by magic. Whether that would hold when she reached the shore would remain to be seen. She sure hoped so.

The facility itself was set upon a cliff face. She'd never approached it from this way, and it set an imposing silhouette across the morning sky, seeming as if it could reach the very clouds itself, and perhaps it could. Who knew what magic hid inside. The building was industrial, with long gray wings and architecture at odd angles jutting up. She continued walking as the sea breeze blew her hair. She tasted salt on her lips and wondered how she'd climb the cliff.

She was surprised to find she connected with Shep almost in the same way she connected with Draco. She felt his nerves. His fear. Even his love. She could see Atlantis through his eyes. She could see his daughter. She wondered if he could see Sierra, and if so, what he saw. She used it as motivation and soon she was stepping off the bridge into the water, which was murky and filled with seaweed. The bridge had deposited her at the bottom of a little cove. Her only option was to climb, and she let off a string of expletives and rolled up her sleeves. She was going to get dirty.

Chapter 30

Climbing had never been Ember's strong suit, and magic hadn't helped that. There was probably a spell or some energy that would make her feet lighter, her arms stronger, but she preferred to hold that energy until she really needed it. The cliff was tall but pocked with places for her hands and feet. It was like the bridge. One step after another. One grasp. Though it was chilly, she didn't feel ice, which she was thankful for. She only slipped once. That's all it took to be super careful. Perhaps her energy would keep her from plummeting to the ground. Perhaps it wouldn't.

Somewhere Draco was stewing and Shep was nearing with the others. All were nervous and she tried to project calm.

"Ninety percent of winning is your attitude," she quoted her dad. Her breath fogged on the climb. She'd made fun of him for his advice and his dad jokes, but she sorely missed him. Not just his quiet leadership at the store, but the way he'd ground all of them. Kept them steady. She secretly wondered if she never seriously dated because no one could live up to his image.

"I could use that guidance now," she said, nearing the top. She'd seen the back of the institute from Sierra's window. A grass area to the left with a stark parking lot to the right. They'd had a covering of snow. She'd be able to hide her presence, but she couldn't hide her tracks. She'd have to be fast.

She peered over the top. She'd never seen the institute from this angle, all odd angles jutting out. Institutional. Cold. The upper floors were what she assumed were rooms, dozens of them if she had to count. Not that she'd seen any other patients. The bottom level was an employee entrance and two cargo bay doors, which were open with a nondescript white truck unloading. She scrambled up, not unaware it could be a trap. She had to get in somehow and she wasn't climbing to a third-floor window. Her eyes flitted to what she thought was Sierra's room. The lights were on. Probably classical music was playing in the background. Nothing had changed in years, but it was about to.

The cliff had a row of hedges that she fought through and then emerged from. She kept to their shadow, eyeing the cameras all over the building but not seeing security, at least not here. The building had two wings that jutted out to prevent her from seeing the front, but she could imagine the long drive with pine trees on both sides. The immaculate landscaping.

The truck was empty. Whatever had been delivered had already been unloaded, and the engine hummed lightly waiting to go. She took her chance and slipped in next to it, but when she realized it was a uniform delivery, she climbed in the back and grabbed a package off the top shelf, jumping down just in time to hide behind a rack containing boxes as the driver came out whistling. He was wearing the same uniform in her hands, white on white, an interesting choice for a hospital. She looked around for cameras, and seeing none, changed right there and stuffed her clothes in a box, only pausing briefly to see beakers with a hazard sign on them.

"It's too late now," she whispered. The truck hadn't left yet, and the doors were still open. She took a breath and walked behind it and opened the door to the institute.

The bottom floor was nothing like the patient wing. It looked more like a hospital, with the white hallways and the smell of antiseptic. Somewhere off to her right, machines beeped. To her left, the sound of kitchens and the smell of bland hospital food. The hallway straight seemed to lead to offices, their doors paneled and covered in numbers with doctors names. The quickest way upstairs could be any of those.

She startled when she realized the magic here cut her off entirely from the outside world. She couldn't feel Draco. She couldn't feel Shep. It was funny how quickly they'd become a part of her, and it felt like something was missing. If this was what it was like to lose your dragon, she didn't want to find out. Her heart had a dull ache, like it was reaching out and fading away.

Straight was the least populated direction so she headed past the offices, some with glassed off doors that looked like they led to labs. She wouldn't have made anything of them, science was never her strong suit, but she thought she heard a sad wail behind one of the doors and repressed a shiver. Labs always had that effect on her. She'd been an English major in school.

She was halfway down the corridor when she heard voices behind her, and they didn't sound like kitchen crew.

She had the choice to book it to the other side or try to duck in a room. A woman's voice raised in argument.

"We cannot afford to lose our greatest asset…" Ember thought she vaguely recognized the voice, but she didn't want to run into them because the man's voice raised even higher, and his was filled with vitriol.

"I will take out the asset rather than see it in the wrong hands!" She looked to the left, windows with labs, and to the right, a plain wooden door that read, "Dr. Darcy." Thinking of Jane Eyre, she said a silent prayer and tried the door. It opened to a dark room smelling of antiseptic and she ducked in just in time.

They were still quarreling about the asset as they passed. She got a look at a tall woman with a gray bun, and a man in a dark suit. They were protecting some asset. Deploying all means necessary. Even fatal. Ember tried to swallow but her mouth was dry. She suppressed a cough.

She turned the lights turned on, revealing a large brown desk surrounded by bookshelves containing odd curiosities. An eye floating in a jar. A petrified hand. A tusk. It was the desk that drew her in though. Beside a fountain pen lay a plain notebook with the words "Known Survivors," on the cover. She flipped through. There was a description of Hawk, (who was called Michael Hawkins), Paine, and several other members of the crew. She flipped to the end where various ways to chase them down had been tried.

"This is where the hellhounds came from?" Ember asked, a bit too loud. If there were cameras in the office, they'd see her for sure, but there was deeper magic than cameras here and she was careful to keep her energy masked. She ripped off one of the pages and put it in her pocket, eyeing the strange jars with distaste.

She pulled the first paper out of the folder with the company logo and creepy mission statement, along with a graphic she couldn't place. It was opposite the Atlantis flag in every way, all sharp angles and corners. Placing it in her pocket, she turned to the side door. There was a keypad. Instead of placing her finger on it, which was sure to set off alarms, she concentrated down to the very magic inside and set off a little storm of electronics. It beeped in quick sequence then fizzled and the door popped open. Maybe it would also get her caught, but she'd get a head start.

"Thanks for the lessons, Shep," she said, missing him even more. The door opened to a long conference room, mahogany paneled with deep red curtains on the windows, but it wasn't the windows that called her attention. On the center of a long table was a model of an island. She held her breath as she approached it. She'd seen this place before. In dreams, perhaps in memories. There were tiny models of people in the small outer homes, and stalls in the shops sold tiny jewels and fruits and fabrics. A magician was in the town square in the middle of a spell to call up a dragon, and on the edge stood a castle with tall white spires that took up the whole top side, with its terraced gardens and stables along the back. In an upstairs window, a golden-haired woman looked sad. Of the king, there was no sighting.

"Atlantis," she breathed, and for a moment the city took to life. Laughter carried into the room along with clapping for the magician's trick, even the soft cries of the queen. Quickly the sound died off, but a bit of its magic remained in the air. The room was charged with it. Around the model were maps and calculations. They'd been trying so hard to find the city, and then what?

The magic must have damped the sounds outside, or perhaps her guard was a little down at the sight of the enchanted city. She reached out to touch the flag at the top which waved although there was no wind, when the door behind her opened and a familiar woman stepped in. This time her gray hair was tied in a bun, but she wore a sharp suit and looked more 21st century CFO than hippie, but there was no doubt it was Maryse, the woman she'd seen at her mother's house who'd tried to poison her. Behind her stood a much younger man holding a folder.

"You?" Ember asked, not sure how they connected.

"You thought you could sneak in, did you?" Her voice had the same melodious quality, but instead of charm it exuded strength and power. Ember was trapped for sure. Even her magic was chaotic now.

"What have you done to my sister?" Ember's voice cracked, for, despite everything, Sierra was the most important thing. What had this woman done to her parents was the next question.

"She's safe," Maryse ran a hand down the edge of the table. The city shuddered. "For now," she added. "Whether she stays that way is up to you."

Chapter 31

Ember didn't need to be told twice. Maryse wielded enormous power at this place. It was rooted in the other kind of magic, the kind not found on Atlantis but here, on the ground. Ember wouldn't classify it as rooted in hate, no, that was too simple. Fear, perhaps. Selfishness. Anger. She felt the energy of the world and all its wars and strife and conflict. Maryse could have propelled her feet forward if she so wished, and Ember would be helpless to stop it. How had she not felt it before? How could she have left her sister here?

Maryse waved a hand and a door on the far side of the room opened to a long lab. On the rectangular, black tables were instruments of the kind they didn't use in liberal arts school, but she doubted they used at regular colleges anyway. Some equipment had wires and beakers and bubbling liquids of all colors. Some were scopes with different dials. Some had writing she couldn't recognize.

"We're close to isolating the secret of magic," Maryse said offhand, waving her arm. Ember got a peek at the bracelets she wore under her blazer and wondered which was the real Maryse. The woman they'd met in the attic or this steely businessperson. The other man walked behind her, his shoes clicked on the floor, but otherwise he made no comment.

"Why would you want to do that?" Ember asked, watching a pink beaker foam and bubble as she passed. It felt sad.

Maryse reached the far side of the room and paused at another door. "For control, of course. If I can compel Atlantis to return, then I can control all its power."

Ember couldn't help the roll of her eyes. It wasn't just tyrants who did this. She'd seen it in the tourists on the island. Heck, even the students she went to school with had a pecking order. Was it human nature, she wondered, to crave control? And if so, why had that particular trait missed her? All she wanted was to live and let live. There's no reasoning with such instinct. Her whole life she'd sidestepped it, but if there was one thing she'd learned from liberal arts school it was that sometimes things needed to be faced head on. In the books she read, she'd know she'd prevail. It was all part of her heroes' journey. But here, in this mad scientist lab surrounded by the foulest of possible magic with a woman out of control, and a man who, she looked behind her, might or might not be hiding the worst possible magic (his aura was shrouded). Here, well, it didn't look good for her. She might die. She might end up like Sierra. She'd known it since Shep had walked into her store. Maybe since she'd begun to see Draco. And she wouldn't change it. There was a chance now to put things right. A spark. She had to blow on it.

"That is a completely normal thing to say." She tried to keep sarcasm out of her voice. Maryse might be bringing her to a dungeon for all she knew, and best not to poke the beast. But some things you can't help. Beasts are made for poking.

Maryse entered a complicated code, and the door opened to an elevator. "You still don't understand what's at stake, but you will." She gestured inside. The elevator was roomy and made of mirrors so she could see them at all angles. She straightened her shirt and tucked a piece of hair behind her ear. She sucked a breath in when she caught a glance at the man's aura, blood red.

"He's a vampire," she breathed. He turned and smiled revealing a fang. He winked.

"One of the first things we reverse engineered," Maryse said. The elevator began to descend. "Easy, really. It's controlling them that's more difficult, but with the correct motivation…" She shrugged. Ember swallowed. She hoped she wasn't about to be that motivation.

They settled farther down than she was comfortable with. Along with a fear of heights she also didn't like confined spaces, and this surely counted as one. The elevator seemed to descend as far down as Atlantis was up, a paradox that did not escape her. With every foot, she felt the weight of the ground pressing down over her. She'd never realized how much she loved air. She eyed the vamp in the mirror. Clean cut and young. Pale, but you wouldn't make any assumptions unless you saw the fangs. He caught her shiver and gave her a troublemaking smile, thankfully not revealing his teeth. Unlike Shep, he was someone who had chosen this without regret. What must it be like, she wondered, to embrace evil?

The elevator glided to a stop. Of course it did. This wasn't the place to jostle them. The doors slid open, and her stomach fell. It wasn't the four seasons, of course it wasn't, but a stark, gray, dark hallway that was decidedly underground. Far underground. Though they'd built in recessed lights, the illumination was low. Vamp seemed to pick up. He stretched his neck to both sides and gave her a little shove on her lower back.

"Atlantis went up," Maryse explained, stepping out. "We went down." Though she'd transformed to a professional, she was still wearing sandals.

Ember cleared her throat. She was miles away from her goal of freeing her sister. "Why?" she asked. Her voice cracked, betraying her fear.

Maryse led them down a hall lined with closed, numbered doors until she got to the end. "That is a long story." She scanned her eye next to the door, then looked back and sized Ember up. "Though I suppose you've earned it. We need you," she admitted. "And I think you'll come to realize our goals are aligned."

I doubt it, Ember thought. Again, the vamp pushed her when the door opened, and she gave him a dirty look to which he only smirked. *Dick.*

The room opened wider than Ember imagined was possible. Were they under the ocean, she wondered? Or had they tunneled under the mainland? Were they under some innocent person's backyard with their weird mad scientist setup? The room was wide and circular with workstations around the perimeter and on stairways crisscrossing, something she could only describe as a hole. A dark, black blob. The opposite of Atlantis, it exuded fear, but Maryse and Vamp seemed to thrive on it.

"We both want to bring Atlantis home," Maryse said. "This is how we call her."

Ember took a step back. She was smart enough to know she wasn't going to run out of there, but also smart enough to keep her distance. "This is how you make people think you're crazy." The words escaped her mouth before she could stop them, but Maryse only laughed.

"Perhaps I should have explained first." The static in the room had made Maryse's hair fall from the bun it was in. Strands floated around her face. Ember smoothed her own hair down. Vamp had enough product he didn't have that problem. Maryse began to walk to the right, though Ember noticed she also kept her distance. Near the blob, workers took measurements with electronics Ember had never seen.

There were more people in here than Ember thought. Dozens, maybe. The ones closest wore hazmat suits. Maryse came to a door and opened it, leading them up two flights of stairs to a conference room that looked over the anomaly. Ember noticed it moved, as if it were writhing, pleading that it didn't belong here. She could almost hear it but decided not to listen. It was the kind of thing that could pull someone in. She almost understood then, the pull of evil. Vamp took up position by the door. There would be no getting out. She'd have to hear Maryse through.

She pulled out one of the cushioned chairs. There was food on the table and though her stomach growled, she didn't take any. Maryse sat opposite her. "Leave us, Hugh."

Ember raised an eyebrow. Hugh? Vamp fit him better. He nodded and gave Ember a pointed look she couldn't read. She was getting tired of not being able to read people, and for a moment missed her old life and all the tourists with their see-through motives. Vamp closed the door behind them. The hum and hiss of the anomaly faded, though she watched it struggle.

Maryse watched it for a moment too. "Beautiful, yes, but sad, don't you think? A means to an end. We thought your sister would help us to that end, but she refuses to wake. We need you, Ember. It is time to return the city, and we need your magic to do it."

Chapter 32

Ember wanted the city returned, but this didn't feel like the way. Something was wrong about the facility and their tactics, this anomaly didn't help their cause, and oh, there was the little fact about murdering her parents and all the survivors. She bit her bottom lip. Sass wouldn't get her out of this.

Glass overlooked the rift, which writhed as if it were in pain. It let out an almost imperceptible high pitch that set her teeth on edge. How had she not heard it before? Ember hesitantly pulled out a chair while Vamp took up a position outside the door, giving Ember a little wink before closing them in. She rolled her eyes.

"What's my sister got to do with this?" Ember asked, trying to avoid the rift outside the windows to her right. In front of her, and behind Maryse was a bank of screens which were all blank. There was another door to the left which led further into the facility.

Maryse folded her hands on the table. Her fingers were filled with the same rings Ember had seen on her before, though her blazer hid the bracelets.

"Though Atlantis magic is strong, I hold no stock in prophecies. I never have. Some can see the future, yes, but it is always muddied and changeable. The gift is a warning, and not a fatal one. The king was a fool to put so much faith in his seers. He scared them so badly they tell him to remain in the sky only out of fear."

"Fear." Ember let out a laugh. "As if that's not exactly what you're doing here." One of the workers got too close to the anomaly and shouted. Electricity sizzled and she heard a noise like the bray of a hellhound before another worker pulled the first out, his arm burned and singed. None of it seemed to phase Maryse. She considered.

"You only have one side of the story, child," Maryse said, her voice betraying her years. She pinned Ember with a steely blue gaze. "The king's brother wasn't always the monster they said. Atlantis made him that way. His family made him that way, and his brother most of all. The king…" She let out a tut. "He wears the crown because he is older, but not because he is wiser. Nor is he more empathetic. Or kind. He was simply, born one year before."

Ember narrowed her eyes and tuned out the screeching. "You sound as if you knew him," she said. It was not impossible. Look what things Shep had done to stay alive, but Maryse didn't give off the aura of a vamp. Instead, the magic that clung to her was a deep, unreadable purple.

"Intimately." She smiled. "I met him when he was not much more than a boy. He'd escaped the castle prison he was put in. Not a difficult feat as he was smarter than his own guards, and his parents only cared that he stay unseen. But I saw him."

Maryse's magic was powerful, and she saw the scene unfold just as Maryse said. She was tending horses on a hill, and he appeared, watching her. Ember had only seen him as a villain in her mother's paintings, but here, here he was just a pained boy with a mop of dark hair flopping into his face and his shoulders hunched. She felt magic when they saw each other. Curiosity, yes, but something deeper. Like the feeling they'd known each other before or were destined to meet. Maryse smiled.

"He asked if he could help me. I was no fool. I knew who he was, but I was intrigued. My family were simple farmers, but our gifts were well hidden. I could see the future, manipulate energy, make things happen." At this she lost her smile. "But for all that, it went terribly wrong."

Ember gasped. "You were married!"

Maryse nodded. A tear formed in the corner of her eye. "Indeed, we were. That, more than anything was the reason we were banished. Perhaps the queen could have lived with a wife of a royal family. Perhaps my family would have forgiven me, but we will never know. We set out to build our lives outside Atlantis, but we were cast aside. Judged. Blacklisted everywhere we went. It caused a blackness in Zyah's heart he could not overcome. He became who they thought he was, but still... still, I saw him as that boy with the shy smile."

Her smile faded. "But there was a sickness in Atlantis. You do not see it because of the legend..." She looked away to the monstrosity they'd pulled up. "The legend talks of light and love and hope, but nothing is all goodness. It was a show, all of it. Zyah sought to expose it. His tactics were perhaps harsh, but Atlantis, too, was harsh to him. I would hold them accountable for all they've done."

"By killing the survivors?"

Maryse sighed. "Zyah thought it was his duty to stamp out magic. Not because he had none. No, he had a stronger magic than I've ever seen. But because he'd seen what it does to people in power. It destroys them."

Ember shook her head. She thought of all the people that had died for this madness. Her own family. "It sounds like magic corrupted him," she spat.

Maryse frowned. "I don't expect you to understand, but Atlantis must be held accountable. I promised him I'd see to it."

"Where is Zyah?" she asked. "I'd like to have a word with him."

Maryse's blue eyes misted over. "He's gone," she said simply. "I carry on his work. Imperfectly. But I carry it on."

Ember struggled between empathy and horror. Should she be sad this awful man was gone? She chose to stay silent. "I will not help you return Atlantis out of spite," she said, looking out the corner of her eye at the anomaly. "This is not the way. What even is that?"

Maryse smiled. "I think you will find our goals align, or at least I will make them align. Come. I'll show you." She pushed away from the desk and shouldered out of her blazer under which she was wearing a loose white blouse. She handed Ember safety goggles. "Here. It's the least of which will protect you."

"Protect me from what?" Ember stood.

"It's a density of magic," Maryse answered. "And it's meant to call Atlantis home."

Chapter 33

Density of magic was not what Ember would have guessed. It was something more grotesque. Like chaos incarnate. The magic of Atlantis was a beautiful, loving thing, at least what she'd witnessed of it. She'd never experienced this, and a drop of doubt blossomed in her heart. *Could Maryse be correct? Was Atlantis, if not flawed, human in nature? Both good and evil at the same time? Hope and chaos. Joy and sadness.* The thought hit her harder than she wanted to admit. She followed Maryse out the office and down the first set of stairs, still wondering.

Whatever the projection of Atlantis magic, this void was the opposite. The workers took measurements and occasionally seemed to restrict the object's growth with some kind of long taser, keeping their distance as much as they could. Ember stepped over a bloodstain where the man who'd lost his arm had been standing. Her stomach lurched. The very air seemed wrong. If this thing had an aura, it would be of nothingness. Desperation.

Maryse walked with reverence, keeping them close to the wall. She stopped to consult one of the workers while Ember stepped closer to the entity. It seemed to draw her in, bubbling and writhing as if it were trying to breathe and it was sick. She closed her eyes and felt a million bees flying in her head.

"How did you do this?" she asked, feeling her energy drain.

"That is where your sister comes in," Maryse had to raise her voice to answer. The bees weren't just in Ember's head. Everywhere buzzed with so much energy it set Ember's teeth on edge. The very room hummed. "And you," she added. She twisted an obsidian bracelet on her wrist. Ember wondered if it protected her against the energy. "It's where the hellhounds have come from. An unfortunate side effect, but one we've used to our advantage."

That was the noise and the energy that Ember couldn't place. That of the hellhounds. Even the smell vaguely reminded her of the beasts. The shouts and background noise grew distant as the humming climbed into her bones.

"Your sister's magic is strong," Maryse said. Her voice seemed to come from far away. "We'd hoped to use her as a tether, to call Atlantis. Bring the city down to face its crimes, but instead…" She gestured to the anomaly and shrugged. She took a step closer, taking off the safety goggles. "It's a thing of beauty," she said. "But we're still figuring out what it can do."

Ember took off her goggles. The anomaly was more than just black, but every color mashed into one. It reached to her, the way magic did, but its thoughts were pain and chaos. She'd not want to step into those, at least she didn't think so. Somewhere inside her the anomaly promised quiet. An end to all her problems. Solace, even. She shivered.

"Let her go then," Ember said, struggling to turn back. She hadn't realized she'd taken several steps closer. She could almost reach out and touch it, and wondered, briefly, what was on the other side. Atlantis? No, but something more powerful. More primal. Did the others hear it? Did it call to them?

"What would you be willing to do for that?" She thought it was Maryse who asked, but the words could have come from the anomaly. It throbbed and writhed, inviting her closer. In the back of her head, she remembered what happened to the worker, but that wouldn't happen to her. They understood each other, this thing and she. Outcasts, both. Out of place.

"Anything," she whispered, and wondered briefly if Maryse knew the effect this would have on her and brought her here on purpose.

"Good," the woman said. She turned to consult with one of the workers in front of her and Ember faced the anomaly head on. From this angle, she saw pictures in it. Pictures of her own life, but some from lives she'd lived before this one. Shep had been right. These people had been chasing her over and over and over. She witnessed Zyah, not as a boy, but as a man fully grown and seeking vengeance. Seeking to wipe out magic from the very world. He plunged a knife into her. He poisoned her. Drown her. She felt each death anew though she was scarcely older than a baby in some. Was he evil or was he protecting a world where people shouldn't have this much power? The anomaly seemed to agree, and it almost had her won over before she shook her head and stepped back. It cracked with frustration.

"Evil is evil," she said, looking back at Maryse. Revenge wouldn't bring back her husband or what he lost. And perhaps Atlantis wasn't perfect. Perhaps magic—in the wrong hands—was truly scary, but to kill to take it out of the hands of innocents? That was blood she wouldn't spill. She'd have to play along to get to her sister. The anomaly seemed to release its hold and exhale. A test, she wondered? Of what, and from who? She didn't even think Maryse knew, but the woman didn't know what she was working with, that was for sure.

"Follow me, I'll take you to her." Maryse turned. Ember watched the magic trail around her. It was complicated. Maryse thought she was doing the right thing, and Ember agreed Atlantis should be returned. Should they be working together, or were Maryse's motives enough to muddy her magic? She looked back at the anomaly that seemed to pulse with wrongness. She shivered.

They couldn't leave the workspace soon enough. Ember wondered what else this group had done and for how many years. How many survivors they'd killed in the name of protection. How many of her own lifetimes they'd extinguished. Had Sierra suffered the same fates, or did destiny just throw them together in this life?

"Your sister has been kept comfortable," Maryse said, as if that excused everything. She stopped by an elevator and scanned her hand. On the other side of the hall was a series of paintings that mimicked the outdoors in a funhouse kind of way. Still lives of farms. Far away castles. Had her friends made it yet, she wondered, and what would they find?

"That's great," Ember bit back what she really wanted to say: "That's great you crazy maniac," though she thought it came out in her tone. Her father had forever told her that her voice and face were expressive. She couldn't hide anything to save her life. She missed him, and his advice. *What would he tell her now*, she wondered? To save her sister, if she could, and he'd remind her how many lives rode on her decision. Entire cities. Worlds.

"You may not believe it Ember, but we have great empathy for Atlantians. You did not ask to be born with such a curse." The elevator doors slid open to a fancy mirror lined box. They stepped in.

"Some of us don't see it as a curse," she replied. There were no buttons. Maryse seemed to run the machine with magic. Of course she did.

"No, I suppose it would seem exciting to you, all that power." Maryse considered her as the elevator climbed.

Ember shook her head. "It's not power in the way you think," she replied. Despite everything, she wanted this woman to see what she had done. It could be their only chance, and it was a slim one. "It's the power to help, not hurt. To make the world better. To love."

Maryse smiled. "I used to think that," she said. "Then I grew up. Power corrupts, Ember, and don't you think it doesn't. It corrupts even the most gentle of hearts. Yours too, if you had time. That man you were traveling with. Ask him."

Ember frowned. "Shep owns his mistakes," she said.

"He benefits from them too," Maryse added. "It's impossible to separate power from corruption. You'd see, if given enough time. Since we don't have that, you'll just have to trust me."

Ember watched the back of Maryse's head as the elevator came to a stop and the doors slid open. Her aura was muddy, making Ember think there was still a chance. "It doesn't have to corrupt," she argued, but Maryse didn't even bother with a response.

They'd come out on the main floor, Ember could see by the bank of windows behind them, showing the same ocean she'd just walked over. It was angrier now, and the sun had dipped low. No sign of the bridge, but of course there wasn't. How long did invisible bridges last, anyway?

Ember recognized the pattern of the rug and the dusty blue painting of the wall. Here the art was of fruit and flowers, meant to project images of tranquility. They passed offices and a nurse's station where a woman worked at a desk. Maryse led them down a familiar hall that led to her sister's room.

"Are there even any other patients here or did you just build this for my sister?" she asked, as they waited for another lift.

At this, Maryse laughed but it was an empty sound. "You think Sierra is our first? Oh, poor dear. We've been doing these experiments long before you were born. While Zyah was still around. It was his idea to harness the power of those with the most magic. We thought Sierra would be our crown jewel, but you..." She reached out to touch Ember on the chin, but Ember stepped back. "You were hidden from us. Smart of your mother. But here we are now."

The elevator dinged and Ember's stomach dropped. She knew the way to her sister's room; she just didn't know what she would find when she got there.

Chapter 34

Ember had never noticed the guards around the facility, but then, she hadn't been looking. Every time she'd come to visit her sister, it had been a quick in and out. She'd stay and talk to Sierra or read to her, but how much reading could you do to an empty room? Sierra slept like Sleeping Beauty. Ember wondered if anything went on in her head. There was hope, the doctors said, or at least she'd thought they were doctors, but not much hope. Enough to keep her alive, but it was all a lie.

"What have you done to her?" Ember asked, her face flush with anger. They passed the nurse's station where Ember used to have to check in. She noted all the room numbers. There were hundreds. Sierra was at the end of a long hall. Her room had two banks of windows that overlooked the ocean and the woods to the north. They were on the third floor, there would be no escaping even if Ember didn't suspect the windows were sealed.

"She's in a stasis," Maryse responded. "It allows us to feed off her magic. Incidentally…" She reached Sierra's room and looked back, "your mother was given that option, also. She chose to fight." The lock popped open and Maryse pushed open the door.

"And my father?" Ember gritted her teeth, but Maryse only shrugged.

"An unfortunate casualty. He fought as well. Hard, for someone with no magic." She turned before she could see the flash of rage on Ember's face. Had her father known all along then? How different it would it be if she could talk to him. She needed him now, like she did so often when buying new stock or balancing books or finding money to pay bills. She missed her mother desperately, but she needed her dad.

She thought she saw a flash of purple swoop by outside the window before it cleared to a cloudy late afternoon. The air was heavy with anticipation, though if that was weather or something else, she didn't know.

"Good morning, Sierra dear," Maryse said. "You have a guest."

Ember hadn't lost the anger, in fact seeing her sister in such a condition just amped it up, but she held it back for the time being. Nothing would be gained by losing her shit, she'd done that enough times to know. But biding her time, yes, that would have been her dad's advice. A part of him was with her still, after all. Just as Draco was. The dragon pressed on the back of her mind, but she couldn't let him in. Not yet.

"Wake her." Ember summoned her power but found it fizzled here in this place. The lights flickered.

Maryse raised her eyebrows. "Impressive, but of course we have wards against that. I think you'll find your dragon can't come close, either. Although he is a most impressive beast. I have not seen one in years. Should he come close by, well..." She looked out the bank of windows. Ember tried to reach out to Draco to stay away but all she felt in her mind was static. "He will be most welcomed." Her smile sent chills up Ember's spine.

"Wake her," Ember said again, but without the energy it had before. Now, it just sounded like a girl begging for a second chance. It sounded, as she knew it would, like she was begging. Sierra, who once chased her around the house. Who drove her to school. Who played tag and dolls and hide and seek. Who, despite their differences, loved her in a deep, binding way. Perhaps she was the only one who had. Perhaps sisters were the only ones who understood that bond. "Please," she added.

Maryse pulled up a chair, but Ember spent no time watching her. She watched Sierra's chest rise and fall as she slept. She had been well kept. Her hair was short and trimmed, and it's golden hue still shined. Though her skin was pale, she had pink in her cheeks, and if Ember wasn't mistaken her eyes fluttered behind the lids. Behind which, they were a light blue, her mom's color. She rested in a pink blouse under a white sheet, with a blanket folded up at the edge.

"She will wake, if I request it," Maryse said, "but there are things we must agree to first." Ember felt her stare from behind. It felt like nails. What was she willing to risk? What was she willing to sacrifice?

Everything.

"We need you, Ember, to bring them back. For payment. For justice. To bring the world right. However you want to put it."

Ember rounded on her. "I will not consent to live like this," she said, but would she if it meant Sierra would wake? She wasn't sure if she had the courage to take Sierra's place.

Maryse shook her head. "Nothing so dramatic. Sierra and the others are asleep because they would not help us. This was the only way to access their magic. To call the city home. They have called, but Atlantis stubbornly refuses to listen. With your help, and your dragon, we will make them listen. We will pull them out of the sky, Ember." She sat at the edge of her seat. Her eyes blazed.

Ember swallowed. "The others here must be woken too," she said.

Maryse nodded. "When Atlantis is down, I will release them. You have my word."

There was a short rap on the door, and a gust of cold air. Ember felt Hugh before she saw him. He had that same smirk as he looked her up and down, pausing by Maryse to whisper something to her while keeping his deep, amber eyes focused on Ember. Ember turned her attention to Sierra. She sat on the edge of her sister's bed and took her hand, which was so warm.

"I'm sorry it took so long." She squeezed Sierra's hand. The same hand she used to drag down and into the woods, or around the bookstore. Sierra's nails were neat and trimmed. Her body was taken care of, at least. Her mind, well, where was she anyway? Her eyelids again fluttered. Was she having sweet dreams?

Maryse cleared her throat. "Your friends seemed to think they could sneak in," she said. Ember raised her eyes to the woman, her anger rising again. "If you help us, we'll let them go."

Hugh seemed to have lost the smarmy confidence that was last on his expression. If she could guess, he was worried. His dark eyes looked from the floor to her, seeming to ask her something. But this vamp's problems were the last thing on her mind.

Shep. Paine. Hawk. If she didn't cooperate, they'd all be in this stasis like Sierra. "How?" she asked simply. Maryse was right about one thing. They had the same goal. The fight would be won once Atlantis was on the ground. Not that she trusted Maryse, quite the contrary. But Ember thought the magic of Atlantis would be enough to overcome her. She hoped anyway, and sometimes hope is the only thing you have to go on. Another of her dad's sayings. She thanked him silently.

Maryse stood. Was it Ember's imagination or did the woman wince a little upon standing. She must be a million years old already, Ember thought. What had she traded for immortality, besides her own soul. She glanced at Hugh, still silently pleading. Maryse didn't give out the same aura. Whatever she'd traded had been deeper and darker than drinking blood.

She spared a glance at Sierra while Maryse led the way out. "What is your problem?" she hissed at Hugh as they were leaving. His arm shot out and he clutched her upper arm tightly before they could reach the door.

"Don't," he said in the smallest possible voice. He didn't need to repeat it. His eyes said it all. Maryse was halfway down the hall. Ember yanked her arm out of his grip.

"What's it to you?" she asked.

His eyes flitted to Maryse. "They're more powerful than you know," he said. "They'll destroy the city."

"Destroy it?" She narrowed her eyes. Maryse paused at the end of the hall, and they had to pretend to walk. "How?" she whispered.

"In the most violent, destructive, public way," he answered. "And she'll take us all with her." His voice shook, and if possible, his face had gone even more pale. She would have given anything for her father's advice, for her friends by her side. But it was only her. They reached Maryse who was opening a door to a staircase and began climbing.

"My office," she called down, "is on the top floor. We'll need to see the sky for this."

I'll just bet we will, Ember thought. She hadn't decided how to proceed, and hoped, somehow, that sky would provide some kind of divine intervention.

Chapter 35

In the books Ember read, divine intervention was a bad plot strategy, and nor did it often work. She could wish for Superman to fly down from the sky and suddenly save Atlantis but firstly, he wouldn't. And secondly, then what? Getting Atlantis back was only half the battle. The woman she was currently following was the second, and maybe bigger, problem.

Hugh walked behind her, his steps measured. He'd warned her that Maryse planned to use Atlantis to take over the world, and if there was a bigger evil fantasy she didn't know what it was. Hugh had an angle too. When they passed the glass windows that overlooked the ocean, she looked at his reflection. It wasn't there. Of course it wasn't.

What passed for Maryse's office was at the top of a winding staircase, not accessible by elevator. She didn't trust the technology. It was in one of the turrets Ember always spied when she pulled up. Majestic. Mysterious.

The room itself was curved, with bookshelves built in between wide windows. They were filled with books of various odd titles, mostly on fantastical lore or Atlantis, but here and there she'd spot a classic. There was a small sitting area covered with papers that Hugh cleared, and Maryse's desk was barely visible under the clutter.

"I've been at this a long time," Maryse admitted, moving a shawl to sit behind her desk. She took the bun out of her hair, and it flowed down. Behind her, the sun was setting over the water. Soon it would all be dark. She dared not reach out to Draco, but he was near.

On the top of the mess, the history of Devil's Island book sat, but not the one she'd seen. This one was hardcover and seemed to be handwritten. Maryse lifted it and opened the book to reveal beautiful, delicate illustrations.

"Your island was the key," she said, her voice wistful. "I could never find it though. Protected by old magic." She opened to a page showing the raising of Atlantis. Ember recognized the bridge she'd walked over that led to her island. Despite herself, she leaned in.

"Atlantis was on Devil's Island?" she asked, but no. She put it together as Maryse explained.

"It was here," Maryse said. "Right where we're standing. It's why no one has been able to build here, until us, at least. We knew the proper counter spells. We were able to harness the magic, but still, the land yearns for its soul. Do you feel it?"

Ember could. She thought the pull she'd felt, the sadness and emptiness, was from the souls trapped between life and death within the walls, but the feeling went deeper. A chill settled in her bones. "What will happen to the people here?" she asked.

"They will be absorbed into Atlantis," Maryse responded. "This facility exists outside space and time. It is part of Atlantis, and yet, it isn't. The anomaly we created keeps us anchored to the city, but not enough to call it home. Not until you."

Ember sighed. She was getting tired of this "chosen one" bullshit. She was just a girl. A girl who had been bullied. Orphaned. A girl who was lonely, and bored and had a creative imagination and only wanted someone to love her, and a life's purpose. Was that too much to ask?

But yet… her magic had kept Hawk's ship in the air. It had kept all his crew, most of them, anyway, away from the hellhounds Maryse had sent to pursue them. She thought of the carnage when they'd been caught. The crew they'd lost, and she lost all sympathy for the woman sitting in front of her. Maryse had had a long life. A sad one, maybe. But a lot of people do. It could have been so different.

Maryse spun in her chair and looked back. "We will remove the wards. Call your dragon. Use his energy to call the city."

Ember fidgeted. "If I knew how to do that, I'd have done it long ago," she said. In the corner, Hugh coughed.

"No, you wouldn't," Maryse said, "because you didn't know why. Revenge isn't your motivation, it's mine. Perhaps the idea of setting things right appeals to you, perhaps it doesn't. I've studied you, Ember Weathers. Your motivations are as true as I've seen. I could offer you riches. I could offer you control. You could rebuild the entire world with me. None of that would appeal to you."

She turned and pulled Ember in with a stare. This was finally the true Maryse. Her eyes were hard and her aura frightening. It swirled around her like a storm cloud, and indeed, the sun had dipped below the horizon and clouds appeared throwing the ocean into chaos.

"No, it wouldn't," Ember admitted, but she was afraid Maryse knew what would. Maryse was a mirror of Ember. She could sense people. Read them. But though Ember did it for good, and maybe self-protection, Maryse did it for control.

"Show her," Maryse told Hugh. His expression grimaced as he turned and opened an armoire behind him to reveal what could only be described as a portal. It reflected the prison they'd put Shep, Paine and Hawk in. They were bound. Blindfolded. Somewhere a hellhound brayed.

Ember jumped to her feet. She would have jumped through the portal if she could. "Shep!" He was the closest. She reached the portal and almost got her hand through before Maryse snapped it closed again, but he'd heard her. She knew it. She rounded on Maryse. Blood thundered in her ears. Options. What were her options?

Not much. "What now?" she asked. She heard Hugh's low sigh behind her. Was he disappointed? Really?

"I will prepare the ceremony." Maryse could barely control her glee. She'd shed the business jacket she had on and replaced it with a rainbow shawl. Her gray hair flowed, and her light blue eyes flashed. It had gotten dark outside so quickly. Ember felt Shep's pain but not his fear. She felt his belief in her, though she didn't quite believe it herself. What was she supposed to do?

Maryse put a hand on her shoulder as she passed. "This all began much before you were born. We are part of a wheel, both of us. Not quite spokes. Nothing that important. But pieces, indeed. We shall set this wheel right." Ember pulled away before she could get any more life advice. No thanks.

"Just hurry up," she said. Maryse gave her an empty smile and went out the way they'd come.

"That was a mistake," Hugh said as soon as the door was closed. "But if we hurry, we can fix it."

She rounded on him. He looked like he came from one of her 80's rom-coms, with a crisp suit and not one of his brown hairs out of place. He could be calling stocks on wall street or leading a defense team in a trial, but it was his eyes. They were a color amber she'd never seen before. "What the hell was I supposed to do, Vamp?" she asked. "Tackle her?"

His face smiled, revealing one fanged tooth. "First of all, it's Hugh, not Vamp." He held out a hand in the most absurd gesture she couldn't help but shake it. "Secondly, no. But we have a chance now, albeit a small one, to save the city, and your friends both."

"How do you propose we do that, Hugh?" she asked. He tugged her toward him before he let go of her hand.

"I propose we wake everyone in this facility up?" he whispered, a twinkle in his eye. "I suspect they will not be happy with what happened to them, and Maryse will lose her power source."

She swallowed. "And Atlantis?" she asked, her eyes wide.

He shrugged. "We'll suss that out later, but you have to trust me."

He hadn't let go of her hand. This time she tugged him. "Why?" she asked. "Why ever should I trust you?"

It wasn't a magical cure. She knew that. Hugh wouldn't just take her and magically make Maryse disappear and everything okay. But nor would he screw her over. She sensed something true in his heart. Something authentic. Atlantis. She sensed Atlantis, and that was enough. It had to be.

He smiled before he let go of her hand. "Because you have no choice," he said, and indeed, he was right. But she did have a choice, just a bad one.

"Okay," she said. "How do we wake them up?"

Chapter 36

Hugh had magic as strong as Shep. Ember could feel it, but what she couldn't feel were his motives and it was driving her crazy. He opened the door and looked both ways. Magic could mess with the camera, but it couldn't stop anyone from walking down the hall.

"It's clear," he said, picking up pace toward the stairs. "We'll have to wake them before she starts her ceremony, or it will be too late."

"We'll have to wake them before she realizes we're not up there," Ember corrected. Through the glass, the sun had fully gone down, leaving only a purple streak in the sky that made her think of Draco. She wished she could reach out to her dragon.

"She won't return until the last minute," he said, continuing to the main floor. "The preparations are... messy."

When he stopped and reached for the door, Ember grabbed his arm, which was much more solid than it looked. "What's your deal?" she asked. "Are you going to sell me out or something?" She searched his eyes, the color amber she thought of as a desert storm, with flecks of gold.

He grinned, making no move to remove her hand. Indeed, he seemed like he liked it. She gripped it harder.

"You've not got time for my story," he told her. "But I'm as much of a prisoner as anyone in those rooms," he said. The grin left his face, leaving only a pale sadness behind. "Like you, she has taken someone I love, and I would do anything to wake her up." He forced a smile, pretending he could charm her, but this time she could see right through him. "I'm afraid that's all you have time for, little dragon. You'll have to make your choice based on trust. Me? Or the evil queen?"

There was always a choice. She could bolt. She could fight him off. She could go through with Maryse's weird ritual, what Hugh had called messy. But though she couldn't read him, not truly, there was something about vampire magic that damped her ability, all she could tell was what she saw in his eyes. Hope. Fear, perhaps? Entirely human emotions, and ones she'd not sensed in Maryse. Hope and fear could do terrible things, but in this case, she thought it could be the opposite.

"Okay." She reluctantly released his hand. "But first we get my friends." Though they hadn't looked ill-treated, their fate had been weighing on her. She folded her arms and pursed her lips, planting her feet on the steps.

"We don't have time." He tried to pull the door open, and she kicked it with a boot.

"Then we'll make time," she said.

"Ember," he pled, "she's going to be watching them. She'll know."

"I don't care."

"Please…" he began, but several floors above, a door opened, and a conversation carried down. "Fine," he hissed, "but you're risking this whole thing for an emotional decision."

This time, it was she that smiled. She'd risk the whole thing for an emotional decision, all right. Especially because it was the right thing. Instead of getting off at the main floor, he continued down further than she thought the building went. *Had they passed the anomaly*, she wondered? *Were prisoners kept even below that?*

"How do you know where they're held?" she asked, out of breath from chasing him. Not that she would admit it.

"I know everything," he said, not a hint of bluster in his voice. Nor tiredness. Maybe being a vampire had its advantages.

"She trusts you," Ember said, struggling to catch up.

He heard the pant in her voice and paused, looking her up and down. "Like you, she could not enchant me, so instead, she turned me. She finds those that do not bend to her magic fascinating. You're lucky she hasn't had time to experiment on you."

"I'm sorry," Ember breathed out. She knew the moral issues Shep faced, and she'd seen how Hawk had reacted. It wasn't right, and certainly not when forced on someone.

He shrugged. "There are worse fates," he said, turning back to the stairs, then looking over his shoulder, "and better ones, too."

"I hope there are better ones," she said, thinking of her books and the heroes journey and wondering if she were finally on the precipice of something great, of saving the world. Or maybe of dooming it. Life wasn't a book. Sometimes you lost.

"I believe if anyone is capable of finding that out, Ember Weathers, it's you." He opened a door, checked the hall, then motioned her through. She paused to look at him on the way by and for a brief moment, his guard was down enough she could see his heart. It wasn't fear she saw there, but admiration. Something greater than hope. Belief. Pure and utter belief in her, and in them.

"Why do you trust me so much?" she asked. She'd been so busy figuring out his angle she never stopped to wonder why he would even want her help. Couldn't he wake them on his own?

"You're more powerful than you know," he said, and when she frowned, he added. "It's not a prophecy or anything as silly. I feel it." He put his hand where his heart should have beat. "Here, but here too." He pointed to his temple. "I see it in you, Ember. See it in yourself."

She shook her head and walked past him to a dimly lit hallway. He kept pace with her. "More rooms," he whispered, waving a hand over a security camera. She felt a wave of his magic. He, too, was very powerful. "These are older. For those who don't have visitors. For those almost used up."

"Used up?" Ember swallowed. "Is that a thing?"

"I forget you haven't grown up in this world. It's not a thing, usually." He started to peek in the windows of the doors, wincing before keeping her away. "But magic requires a connection to source. Like you to your dragon." He stopped and frowned as he looked in the window of another door before moving them on. "This far below ground that connection is dampened. They can only give, not receive."

"Why disconnect them?" she asked.

He raised an eyebrow. His pale face was perfect, and she wondered how old he was really. "They begin to struggle against her binds," he says. "Such magic goes against the laws of the universe. It cannot last forever. We are just… helping it along to break that bind." He shrugged and continued down the hall. His well-polished shoes clicked on the floor. She avoided looking in the windows for fear of what she would see, and only followed.

"How did she get you?" she asked quietly.

He gave a mirthless laugh. "She preyed on my weakness," he responded, a tick in his voice. He turned and winked, adding: "one of the seven deadly sins." He looked at the closest door, which was the last in the hall that then branched to the left and right.

"How many are down here?" she asked.

"Hundreds," he responded. "Here they are."

Ember rushed next to him. The door had no knob. No visible way to open it. Hugh stood back and crossed his arms while Ember pressed her face to the pane. They were in there all right. Shep, to the left, his arms bound but his face free. She let out a breath that fogged the window. Wiping a circle, she saw Paine with a bruise forming on her cheek and Hawk sitting opposite. He was speaking, but she couldn't hear him. She banged on the door. "Shep!"

"They can't hear you." Hugh remained with his arms crossed. "Dampened, remember? That means our magic too. Lucky for you I'm resourceful." He pulled a small screwdriver out of his jacket pocket. Now it was her turn to raise an eyebrow. "They can't open with magic, but she forgets…" He put the end of the screwdriver between the door and wall and wedged it. "Not everything is magic."

The door gave enough to pop open, and Ember shouldered her way in, running to Shep and kneeling before him. "Are you all right?" she breathed, framing his face with her hands. His skin was cold and his face pale. He tried to lift his hands, but they were bound.

"I've been better," he attempted a smile, but he was weak. Even Paine and Hawk seemed drained. Ember took the bindings and pulled, but they only got hot.

"What has she done to them?" Ember asked. Shep's dark eyes refused to focus. He blinked, and his eyelids stayed closed. His breathing labored.

Hugh was playing around with a folded pair of scissors no bigger than his thumb. "Dampening field, remember? It's affecting more than their magic." She raised her eyebrows, and he twirled the scissors. "Fabric scissors." He smiled. "They'll cut through anything."

"Huh." She held up Shep's hands and Hugh made quick work of getting through the bindings, though Shep still had a hard time standing. She propped him up. Hawk was able to stand on his own, but Paine seemed worse than either.

"Now what?" she asked Hugh. He retreated to the door, popped his head out and then quickly in, pulling the door closed behind him.

"Now we hide," he said, propping Paine back on the door with her hands behind her to hide their non-bindings.

"You're kidding, right?" Ember struggled to hold up Shep's weight. She knelt so he wouldn't fall.

"I told you they'd be watching," he snapped. He took her arm and pulled her under the window to the door. "Hide," he said.

From their spot, they couldn't be seen from the window. Not unless they came in, and gods Ember hoped they didn't. Could just one thing go right?

"Do you think she noticed we're gone?" Ember asked, but Hugh only shushed her. She had her answer a moment later when the guards passed by, talking something about their missing prisoners. They paused at the door, seeming to take count. Shep gave them an offhand wave, winking at her. They waited long enough for the footsteps to pass.

"We have to hurry." Hugh lifted Paine, leaving Ember to somehow deal with both of the others, and they were heavy.

"Can you walk?" she asked Hawk.

"For a short while, yes." He slurred his words and braced himself on the wall. His cheeks were pink in a way she didn't like. She ducked and pulled Shep up. He touched her cheek.

"Thank you," he said, "for saving us."

"Don't be so sure," she muttered.

He leaned in and rested his forehead on hers. "You've already done that, Ember. The day I met you."

She touched him gently. "Don't get all emotional now," she said, but she was touched all the same. How far they'd come since that day in the bookstore. Maybe it was he that saved her?

"What now?" she whispered out in the hall. Hugh frowned.

"We have to get to your sister before Maryse does," he said. "We still have time."

Now it was Ember's turn to worry. "How much time?" she asked, shuffling them all down the hall.

"Not much," Hugh admitted.

231

Chapter 37

Shep gained strength as they climbed the stairs. Even Ember could feel the dampening field lift, though somewhere below them, the anomaly churned on. The one Maryse was planning to use to pull Atlantis down. Ember didn't even want to think what would happen after that. *Did Maryse want to destroy Atlantis? Would she stop there?* She shook her head.

"There is something…" Shep paused to take a breath, "… in the lower levels."

"I know." She squeezed his arm. "It's a long story. She has some kind of dark magic to draw Atlantis back. She wants to destroy it."

He pursed his lips and nodded once. "She is Zyah's wife?" he asked.

"Yes," Ember said, "and she's crazy."

Hugh looked back. "That's an understatement," he added.

Shep paused them at the door. "I know about this woman." He let go of Ember's arm and shook his head. "My thoughts are jumbled now, but there were stories of her…"

"Stories aren't helpful, mate," Hawk twisted the doorknob. They'd arrived at the main level.

"This one may be," Shep said. "Something about her past. A weakness."

Hugh looked out and around. "While you think about it, we have somewhere to be." The main floor was deserted. They made their way through familiar corridors, ones where Ember had once passed to visit her sister. She knew the way by heart, but Hugh took them around to a back staircase. Even the nurse's station was empty.

"Preparations," Hugh only said by way of explanation. Ember shivered.

She'd let go of Shep, who was walking on his own. Paine caught up with her. "Sorry they nabbed us so quick," her friend said, swiping an apple from the desk and taking a bite. Ember laughed at her friend. The color had returned to her cheeks.

"They nabbed me too," Ember admitted, "but it's not over yet."

Hugh knew his way around. He kept them from the well populated areas, the common rooms, the dining halls, but even those were empty of both patients and nurses.

"Where are they?" Paine whispered. Ember looked in a door with two messy beds and a wheelchair tipped on its side. Outside, the shore was foggy and dark.

"She is gathering them," Hugh said. "Come, we may still have time. She's yet to get those downstairs and they're the most powerful."

Ember swallowed. Her friends had been downstairs, but what could they do except keep a ship afloat? Except, perhaps, if they could keep a ship afloat maybe they could call one down too? And then what?

"The kitchen stairs." Hugh shouldered a door open. Ember raised an eyebrow.

"As if they won't be looking there?" she asked.

"They're busy," he said. "I promise you that."

"What is this ritual anyway?" Ember asked as they climbed. She noticed the cameras. Hugh had stopped visibly blocking them, but his magic was powerful. He hesitated a minute before he answered. The others hung back. They were still getting their strength back.

He looked at her as if sizing her up. She met his gaze, as steady as she could. She'd come this far. She could face another amber eyed vampire. "She needs blood," he admitted. "A lot of it." He turned to climb again. "She's not as powerful as she makes it seem. Weak, even, as far as magic. The anomaly can help her magic, but it demands a sacrifice. A big one."

The hair on Ember's arm stood. "I knew that thing was no good," she said, then reached out to touch his arm lightly. "How many?" she asked. There had to be hundreds in the rooms and downstairs.

"All of them," he answered. "And she won't stop there. When Atlantis is returned…"

"Wait." Shep grabbed her arm and put a finger to his lips. Outside the door, a security detail passed. They were on the main floor, and there were a lot of them.

"Now what?" she whispered.

Hugh turned to her. "It has to be you," he said. "You are the only one who can wake your sister. She can stop this." He exchanged looks with Shep.

"We can hold them off," Shep confirmed. He turned to Ember. "He's right. Go to her."

"I've tried to wake Sierra up for years," Ember argued. "How can I do it now?"

Shep put his hands on her cheeks. "With magic." He kissed her lips lightly. "Go into her dreams, Ember. Find her. Together the two of you are strong enough to fight back. Implode her plans."

Ember had teared up. "And what about Atlantis?" she asked. "What about your daughter?"

"There will be another day for Atlantis." He touched her forehead to his. "Not like this. Not now."

She felt the weight of his feelings, as she always did with everyone, but with Shep she never had to second guess. He was disappointed, yes. Worried. But he believed in her. In them. She kissed him gently on the lips.

"I'll call Draco to help," she said. Shep nodded once, the shadow of worry clouding his features, which were still pale and worn.

"Do you really think…" she started to ask.

"Go," he told her.

Hawk pulled the oldest trick in the book and broke the glass for the fire alarm, then pulled it. The box let out a shrill buzz. "Worth a try," he shrugged then smiled.

"The buildings might be magic, but they must be up to code," Hugh said. He turned to Ember. "Hurry."

Paine gave her a quick hug and the others were off plotting and making noise. She shared one last look with Shep. Separated, again. Would there ever be a time they were together?

She ducked behind the desk when a couple guards passed, but that was all she saw. She tried the camera trick and found it quite easy to project a picture of peace and calm. Too easy, almost. Was she walking into a trap?

The back elevator was for staff, but there was no staff around. She passed through the cafeteria, empty, and the kitchens smelling of meatloaf, but also empty. The windows behind spoke of a stormy night. She reached out to Draco in her mind.

If you can hear me, they need help. She wasn't sure though, that dampening field existed far further than just the dungeons, but she felt a rush back that was Draco dying to help. She felt a roar that started in her heart and burned its way through her. What the dragon could do, she wasn't sure. Stay away from the west turret, she hoped.

She paused for a moment watching the waves kick up in the ocean, wanting to pull Atlantis home but wanting to keep it safe. Was this what the king felt? No wonder he was under such pressure. The clouds swirled around in the wind, moving quickly from west to east, letting in only shafts of sunlight here and there. Was the world ready for such magic? Or would the same thing just happen again and again and again. It wasn't for her to decide, but she had to save the people here. The ancestors. The survivors. Perhaps even, people with magic that was all new.

The elevator was in the back. She pressed the button, looking cautiously around her and wondering about this ritual Maryse was going to undertake, and how someone's heart could turn so black to think it was all okay. The doors slid open, and she stepped on.

Sierra was only on the third floor, out of five, though now she knew there were more offices above. The elevator moved maddeningly slow. She looked at her reflection in the mirrors. Her face had sharper edges. Her dark hair was pulled back, the black growing out replaced with a dark brown. Where she once wore dark eyeliner, now only her amber eyes looked back, and for someone so used to reading people, she'd rarely checked in with herself. Her eyes shone a confidence she'd never known she possessed, and her lips were a color mauve that couldn't exist with coloring. There was fear, yes, but there was love.

The doors slid open. The hallway beyond was empty. This was a patient's floor. She passed them, most of the rooms were empty but not all. They'd not collected everyone yet. She had time. If Hugh was right, Sierra would be last.

A duo of patrol came to collect a patient in another room, and as Ember ducked into a patient's bathroom, she had a memory of she and Sierra playing hide and seek. It was one of the rare times they'd played with neighborhood kids, before the Weather's kids got "too weird" and Sierra had let Ember hide with her in the bathtub.

She remembered Sierra stifling a giggle as she lifted Ember and put her in, the bathmats sticking under her feet. The blue tile with grout. Sierra's blonde hair tied back, and her finger to her lips telling Ember to be quiet, but Ember was too young to know that.

"Why?" she'd asked.

Sierra bent down to her level. "Because they'll find us, silly." She tweaked Ember's nose. In the end it was Sierra's giggles who gave them away.

The memory faded. There were plenty of others. Sierra getting older, leaving Ember behind. Sierra meeting Brad, always sneaking off. Sierra moving off to college, telling Ember to take care of mom and dad. Some job she'd done at that.

"She wants them all by the quarter past the hour. Then the ones upstairs." The woman's voice echoed. She heaved as they pushed the patient out. The one behind her snored lightly. There were no life support machines here. No beeping. All were just under a deep sleep. Ember liked to think they slumbered peacefully, unaware. They would have quite the wake up if that were the case.

The hallway stilled, and Ember had precious moments to get to Sierra's room. She darted down the hall and to the left. Sierra was in a suite at the end. She paused at the window to see a purple blur in the sky and sent love to Draco. They both had jobs to do.

She opened Sierra's door and let out a huge exhale when she saw her sister sleeping in the bed. To her count, they had at least five more patients before they reached here. Not long. She braced a chair under a door. She'd seen that in a movie. It wouldn't stop them, nor slow them down. It just made her feel better.

"Okay." The bed gave as Ember sat down beside her sister. It didn't creak. Everything in the hospital was top notch. Even the windows were clear of any streaks. Ember pulled the curtain back a bit to see the dark sky. She didn't dare reach out to her friends. There was only one person to reach out to now.

She took Sierra's hand, as she'd done a million times both as kids and sitting next to this bed, reading her a book. There was still a poetry book on her bedstand, neatly marked with a bookmark. Sierra had been a nursing major, but Ember liked poetry. It wasn't like she was going to read her sister *Grey's Anatomy*. She scooted in.

"We don't have much time," she told Sierra, but then she remembered Shep's advice. Could she reach her sister the way she reached them? Did they have that kind of connection? She closed her eyes. It was difficult to settle in, but she tried.

Sierra, she said inside. *Where are you?*

She startled when she heard that little giggle. Her eyes flashed open. She looked to her sister. Still rosy cheeked and sleeping soundly. It worked. She settled in again, deeper this time.

Show me, she said, and felt herself pulled.

Chapter 38

Falling into Sierra's dream was the same sensation as falling through the portal in her folk's old house. It had been so long since they'd done that, since they'd escaped Maryse the first time. Then, she'd tensed up and almost ended up in the astral plane. This time, she let go.

Follow me, Sierra's voice said. Ember let go of her senses and floated. She heard them outside the door, presumably getting another patient. Coming closer and closer and closer. She let go and her body drifted through darkness and stars and space and planets. They seemed to come and go, as if time itself was bending for her. But was it time, space, or reality? There were the most beautiful colors and shapes and explosions of light. There was a chill in the air, but Ember didn't know how she felt it, unless it was in her very soul. Sierra laughed. Ember grasped on to that sound.

The darkness opened up, but it wasn't the scary kind of darkness like under the bed on a dark night. It was completion and emptiness, and within it floated a city. Like a beacon of light, calling her. The laughter got stronger.

Ember, come on!

She floated close to the towers of the white castle. The sun had come out and bathed the city in light. She flew through clouds. Their mist pooled in corners of the city, and magicians made shapes out of them to amuse the children, but there was something in their eyes that spoke of sadness. The streets were clean and stone lined. The stalls were fresh. Some sold fruit, others fabrics or jewels. Ember tried to reach out to one, but her hand went right through. The stall keeper, a tall woman of middle age, looked her way only briefly, as if a wind had blown across her cheek.

The smell of cooked meat and spices hung in the air. A child dragging one of the mist animals ran right through her. Her own body was as insignificant as a magic trick.

"Look now!" the little girl said. The mist had formed the shape of Ember. It smiled and broke apart.

"I wonder who that is?" A woman took the girl's hand and frowned.

"Ill luck," the shopkeeper responded, and spit on the ground.

"Or perhaps good," the woman said. She shifted her long robe and held the child closer to her. "Often luck is what we make of it."

The shopkeeper laughed. "Indeed so," she said. "Though lately there is no luck to be had either way."

Sierra's voice echoed again. Where was her sister? She was in Atlantis. Though if it were Atlantis now or only in a dream, Sierra didn't know. It felt real enough. Right down to the buzz of a bee by her ear.

"Good luck stinging me," she told it. The bee hovered by her face, then passed by to a patch of wildflowers by the stall. The shopkeeper looked through her again.

"Ill luck or good?" the woman wondered out loud. She took out a pipe and packed it, humming a vaguely familiar song. Ember studied the lines on her face. She'd been old already when Atlantis had been cursed. What must if feel like to be stuck like that? Never to be able to move on. She wanted so badly to reach out to her.

"It's good luck," the woman decided. But perhaps not today. The woman bent with a cough that racked her body. Ember moved on. She looked for the little girl in the market but could only see those blasted mist animals swerving between people's legs. One reached her, paused, then ran right through. How was all this possible, she wondered? She was here, but she wasn't.

Ember, hurry! Sierra's voice again. It was coming from the great white castle. It was just past the market, with grandiose houses beyond the stalls. Outside them, men sat playing cards, paying no note of her. She floated rather than walked, but she forced what she thought were her feet to move one after another. They were slow, as if they were underwater, and she left a trail of blue behind her. *Blue*, she wondered. *Ill tidings or good?*

"What I'd give to feel the rain again," an old man said. He was sitting on a chair in a small yard, a deck of ornate cards on the table between them. The other slapped down a card and laughed.

"It's not what you remember," he answered in a gravelly voice. "An annoyance, as I recall."

The first man pursed his lips. "Aah, but a most welcome one."

Just past their home was a town square, filled with more stalls and people milling about. A fountain sat in the middle, but its waters had run dry. Though there was magic, the people looked lost. Purposeless. *Lifeless.* Ahead of her was a great white staircase, and on the top step, Sierra waved.

Here! she called, but of course she would be at the center of town. Ember smiled despite herself, and for a fleeting moment she looked around. If this was heaven, or the afterlife, perhaps she'd spot her folks? But no, of course not. The hope was always there though, and especially now. If her father had been inclined to give her a sign, this sure was one.

She weaved through the crowd, avoiding the others though she could have just walked right through them. It wasn't a sensation she wanted to repeat. It chilled and disorientated her, and she was disorientated enough. Atlantis felt like walking upside down. She took the steps one by one, feeling, somehow, the smooth marble underneath. At the top, she turned and looked at her sister.

She looked the same as the day of her accident. Her long blonde hair pulled back in a ribbon. She was wearing the same outfit as she was in the hospital, a fitted pink sweater and jeans. The faintest blush was on her cheeks and her lips were tinted pink. Her eyes, though. Had they always been this bright blue?

"Sometimes the queen comes out," Sierra said. "I think she can feel me. She's the only one."

Ember felt a rush of emotion. She wasn't sure if she could cry, but she certainly would if she could. "Have you been here all this time?" she asked.

Sierra pursed her lips. "How long has it been?" she asked quietly. A laugh carried up from the crowd below them, but to those people, they were invisible.

"Three years." A lump formed in Ember's throat. She'd lost hope after all this time, and maybe even this was a dream.

"Three years…" Sierra stared off into space, which was only the blue sky and whisps of clouds that surrounded them. "I suppose Brad has moved on?"

"You could suppose a lot more than that," Ember answered.

"I'm sorry." She took Ember's hand and Ember could feel the warmth of it. "It's like a dream here, every day. One you can't wake up from. Mom and dad?"

That lump again. "They died in the accident."

A shadow crossed Sierra's features. It happened so rarely Ember couldn't even recognize it. Her sister was not born to be sad. "I'm so sorry." She squeezed Ember's hand. "It must have been so hard for you."

Ember only nodded. She pulled her hand back. "There's a lot more," she said. "Do you know the history of this place? Our place in it? Why you're here?"

Sierra blinked the sadness away like a passing cloud. It was a skill Ember greatly envied. "Only what I can gather, but I think there's something inside. This is as close as I can get to the castle. I'm barred from going in."

Together they watched the town gather on the square. *Was this a special day*, Ember wondered, *or was every day a market day?* Every day the same forced merriment over and over and over. And Sierra, stuck in a dream. She put an arm around her sister and rested her head on Sierra's shoulder. She still smelled of fresh flowers and pine, as if they'd just been playing. Her hair blew in the breeze, and yet no one could see it.

"I have an idea," she told Sierra.

Chapter 39

But first, she told her sister everything. She didn't know how time worked here. If they were as short on time in this plane as they were at home, they'd be in trouble indeed, but it couldn't be helped. They'd missed each other, and there were things to be sorted through, quickly. It helped that Sierra knew magic. After all, she'd been trapped in this place. She was most open to Ember's explanations.

"So, we have to wake up?" Sierra pursed her lips and stared into the distance. The corner of her lip turned up as she looked at Ember out of the corner of her eye. "I've been trying to do that since I got here."

Ember took her hand, threaded her fingers through her sister's slim fingers that used to play piano in their living room. "You didn't have me," she said, then added, "or all the information." She turned to look behind her. "What do you suppose the castle has to do with it?"

Sierra looked back over her shoulder, but she hesitated to answer. Below a child's laugh carried. A magician made a dragon out of mist. A juggler tossed three apples in the air and caught them. A grandfather took a child by the hand. "I don't remember any accident," Sierra admitted. "I just remember going to sleep and waking up here."

She stood and brushed off her sweater. In one of the top windows, a curtain fluttered. "Do you know one of the last things dad said to me? That I can remember anyway."

Ember smiled. Her dad had all kinds of sayings. "I couldn't possibly guess."

Sierra looked down and smiled. Her blue eyes misted. "That life was going to seem impossibly hard sometimes, but we have to do our best to find joy in it anyway."

Ember nodded. It was something he would say.

Sierra shook her head. "I'm going to miss them so much."

Ember stood and hugged her sister. "If we get out of here, you mean," she said, by way of lightening things up. It had the opposite effect, as if the clouds moved closer around her.

"We'll get out of here," Sierra promised. "But then what?"

Then what, indeed. Would they return Atlantis and change the world? Or be forever on the run? "Look," Ember pointed to a high window where a woman leaned out, staring at them.

"The queen!" Sierra waved. "Help! We need your help!" She turned to Ember. "She can see us. I'm sure of it. But she never speaks to me. Maybe you should try?"

Ember looked up and could feel the deep blue eyes of the queen even from a distance. There was magic involved, yes, but there was a deeper connection. A fate. She cupped her hands around her mouth. "I've come to take my sister home, and to return Atlantis!" she called. "But I need your help!"

She felt the queen's response rather than heard it. It was the same way the dragon communicated, directly to her. The queen's face remained passive, afraid. Her tone reflected that.

Quiet, child, lest the king hear you. I am not the only one with eyes in this castle. She turned, her long braid falling out the window. *Meet me in the stables, behind the garden, just after dinner. And be careful. There are those who do not wish Atlantis returned.*

She backed out of the window, all that was left of her was a whisp of blue curtain. Ember looked around the square. No one seemed to notice their interaction, though there was a guard on the far corner in a red cloak watching the window where the queen had disappeared. He had a gray beard, and a face too weathered for a man who'd been trapped in Atlantis for years. The look on his face was one of wistfulness. Love.

She turned back to Sierra. "Tell me about this queen," she said.

Sierra took her hand and pulled her down the steps of the castle. Ember looked for the guard but all she saw was the swish of his red cloak and he was gone.

"Okay," Sierra agreed. "But first I have to show you Atlantis."

Ember didn't know how long it was until dinner. Sierra explained that with the movement of the city through the clouds, you couldn't always trust sunrise and sunset to be at the same time. "Though they try to keep it regular, I gather," Sierra said. "Anyway, it's not like I need sleep. I just wander. They keep time by their meals."

They threaded their way through the crowd. Ember looked this way and that, taking note of the magic all around them. Magic that allowed them to grow the ripest of fruit, and to produce the lushest of fabrics and perfumes. The scent was like nothing she'd experienced. Intoxicating. Two young girls twirled in a circle by a shop, and two boys watched them shyly.

"They seem so happy," Ember said, wondering at their decision to return them. Perhaps they didn't want any help. Perhaps they were just happy as they were.

Sierra didn't break stride. "They're not," she said. She took a side route to a street that was filled with taverns. Here and there, men and women slept on the street, though occasionally someone would come and shuffle them off. One man woke reluctantly. For a brief moment, Ember saw the hope in his eyes as he woke, then it faded, replaced by the realization of where he was. He spat and waved the help away. "I'm going," he said.

Ember held tight to Sierra's hand. Indeed, she never wanted to let it go. *How close were they at home*, she wondered? *Would they be wretched from their dream, or worse?*

"Here." She stopped in front of a place with a cobbled together sign that read "Tavern."

"Original," Ember commented.

Sierra sighed. "Why bother with originality?" She walked right through the door in a way that turned Ember's stomach. "Everything's been done before," she raised her voice. "Come on. It's not so bad."

She was wrong. It was bad. It was bad in the way of traveling through the astral plane, but without the stars and wonder only a vague nothingness and questions about the nature of reality. "That was a trip," she commented as she squeezed through.

"That was nothing," Sierra said. "Come on there's an empty table."

Ember wondered if someone would come by and just sit with them, or on them or in them. It was all a lot to take in. She wondered how Sierra did it. Sierra squeezed them into a booth in the back. From what Ember could tell it had been midday when she arrived, but the tavern was full enough. Not with merriment and cheer, but with desperation. A group played cards in the corner, and it was getting loud and heated, but otherwise most of the patrons sat drinking alone.

"It almost makes me glad I can't taste anything," Sierra said sadly. "I'd become one of them. What else is there to do?"

"For a while I wondered that too," Ember admitted. The island had been its own kind of prison. What an irony. She'd not had a tavern or any way to blow off her steam. She'd cried, until she didn't. She'd just got on with it, but even then, she knew that wasn't living.

Sierra reached over the table and took Ember's hand. "Tell me what it was like," she said.

"After?" Ember swallowed. A major feat considering the fact she didn't have a corporeal body. Some habits die hard, like the fact she wanted to bounce her leg.

"Yes," Sierra said. "You can see what it's been like for me…"

"I'm sorry," Ember interrupted, "I didn't know…"

Sierra stopped her. "Of course you didn't. But now we have a chance to change things. Before we do, we have to clean up what went before."

"You mean understand it?" Ember asked.

"Understand *us*," Sierra corrected. "Our parts. Our responsibilities. Our potentials."

"That's all?" Ember laughed and raised an eyebrow, but she was right. How could you move forward until you could let go of the past. Somewhere, her father smiled. "It started when this guy walked into the bookstore…" she started.

She thought her story would be short and to the point, but Sierra had a way of listening. And for the first time Ember opened up, truly, about the pain and loneliness she'd felt when she lost them. About the burden she'd taken on by taking things over and taking over Sierra's care. Her sister's eyes misted over, but she didn't interrupt.

Then she told Sierra about Shep, and the way he breezed into the store. His story was his to tell. She left out some important details, and ones about Hawk too, but Sierra's thin lips formed an O when Ember told her about the flying ship, and Maryse, and the hellhounds.

"I've heard them in the distance." Sierra rubbed her arms. "But I don't think they can get here. One perk, anyway. What do you think they would make of me?"

"Let's hope we don't find out," Ember answered. "But as for Maryse, she'll never stop. She'd on some kind of mission. And she's nuts."

"Great combo." Sierra smiled. She watched the table next to them down their drinks and get into a loud argument about where they were. Sierra shook her head.

"The king is ill," she said, "though it's forbidden to talk about. He holed himself up in the castle. Word is he walks in circles mumbling to himself. The burden of cursing Atlantis was too much to bear. But the queen…" A fight broke out at the next table about whether they were in the east or west. The bartender just let them go on. Sierra didn't even wince.

"I believe the queen would be on our side. I believe she wants to return."

Ember sucked a breath in. "But Maryse?"

Sierra took her hand. "Maybe not this way, but somehow. Things are started now, Ember. I'm not going back to a dream and you're not going back to that bookstore." She stood and pulled Ember by the hand.

"Where are we going, then?" Ember asked.

"I wish I knew," Sierra replied. "Right now, to see the queen."

Chapter 40

Sierra gave Ember a quick tour of the city. It was much bigger than it seemed at first glance, with farms and shops and homes spread out all over the island.

"The children?" Ember asked as one ran by laughing, followed by another.

"They age," Sierra responded, "just slowly. That girl there. She was an infant when Atlantis was raised."

Ember studied her. The girl had a pink dress with bows in her hair. She ran trailing ribbons that the other girls were trying to chase. If Ember had to guess, she'd say the child was seven or eight. She had clear, milky skin and dark hair, the way she'd think Shep's would grow in. Could this be his daughter? She was reluctant to tell Sierra that part. It wasn't her secret to tell.

"What a burden on them," Ember commented. The girl turned the corner, but she left a ribbon behind. Ember bent to pick it up, but it just fell through her fingers.

"On the contrary." Sierra watched Ember sadly. This had been her life for so long. "I think they breathe life into this place. When they're grown…" She trailed off. "No new children have been born, though. It seems like part of the curse."

"How sad," Ember said. Perhaps the children breathed life. Children do. But without new blood, the place would wither away.

"For some." Sierra threaded her arm through Ember's. "Come on, I'll show you the stables. I sit out there sometimes."

For an island in the sky, the place was filled with greens of all kinds: gardens, flowers, greens of the kind Ember couldn't identify. They were used to make spells and poultices. For luck – good or ill. For food. Or just for decoration.

Sierra had always had the ability to change the subject quickly. To brush off the bad. Look only at the positive. Ember had thought it an annoying trait when they were younger, but now she saw her sister was trying to protect everyone. She hoped it wasn't at the cost of her own heart, though somehow, she'd ended up here.

"Do you really remember nothing?" Ember asked. They walked a cobblestone street between homes where the smell of cooking spices drifted out. It was largely quiet except for the bark of a dog or a soft cry. Not enough laughs, though. Not enough at all. On one stoop, an old woman hummed as she knit a purple sweater.

"Of the accident?" Sierra asked. She'd stopped to watch a black cat cross in front of them. The cat paused and meowed, then continued on his way.

"Yes." Ember knew it had been no accident at all. Maryse had tried to kill Sierra, and barring that, had siphoned her magic.

Sierra frowned. "No," she said, "nothing." She was lying. Ember knew enough to know her sister, too, had her own secrets, but she let her have them for the time being. The fields opened up before them. It was hard to tell time of day, but the sun was high and wispy clouds nowhere in sight. Ember marveled there was room for such fields here. Magic was certainly at work. The shadow of the castle's spires set long shadows over the tall grass. Sierra cut through.

"The queen takes the horses out here sometimes." Sierra looked back over her shoulder, but if they were watched, she couldn't tell. "It's one thing I'm jealous of." She turned forward where there was a gentle hill, over which Ember saw only sky. "The horses can sense me, though. It makes them nervous. I try to stay away."

Sierra stopped to run her hand over a yellow flower. Ember could feel how much her sister wanted to pluck it and feel something real between her fingers. Ember was already restless after such a short time.

"What's over the hill?" she asked.

A smile broke out on Sierra's face. "Fun," she answered, picking up her pace. "Come on!"

A horse whinnied as they passed the stables to the left. Ember had to scramble for purchase up the hill past them. It was covered with shrubs and pickers that blessedly didn't scrape or pinch but produced a slight tickle. Ember wasn't weathered or tired, but just nothing at all. She missed having a real body, at least until she reached the top of the hill.

"Whoa…" She wavered on her feet and took a step back. They'd reached the end of the island and looked out over a cliff that overlooked the ocean. Even the clouds were below them. The sun itself seemed closer.

"You can't fall." Sierra plunked down on a little ridge. She bent her knees and put her chin on them. "I've tried. I've tried everything I can to get out of this place."

Ember sat on shaky legs. "I'm sorry it took me so long to find you," she said, measuring her breath for anxiety's sake.

Sierra gave her a sad smile. "We're here now," she said, and Ember noticed a tear in her sister's eye. How much she'd give to reach out and touch her. "Dad would say something about forward being the only direction," she said.

Ember looked ahead and tried to make sense of the coastline under them. A line of smoke came up from the distance. Was that where her body lie? How much time did they have?

"I think of dad's sayings a lot," Ember admitted. "And mom's paintings. They led me here. They were a story, although the last one…" She thought back to when she was in their attic with Maryse and frowned. "The last one depicts a great battle."

"That's just perfect." Sierra managed to laugh. "And here I thought I was getting rescued."

"Maybe it's you that's rescuing me," Ember said. They had time before the dinner hour, and Ember and Sierra spent it watching them slowly circle a spot on the coast. They talked about the past and their parents. The things they did that made their parents crazy, and the things that made them laugh. Her mother's quirks. Her father's witticisms. How much they missed each other. What they didn't discuss, and Ember kicked herself later, was the accident. It would have led them down a road where Sierra knew a lot more than she was saying.

Instead, the sun set, and they let go of their connections back home, and as their dad would have advised, looked forward. Only sometimes you needed to look back, too, to make sure you were going in the right direction.

Chapter 41

The world spread out under Atlantis, vast and unknowing the magic that traveled above. The island didn't even leave a shadow. It was as if they didn't exist at all, a fact Ember found so sad. She'd felt that way at times. As if she were so insignificant, she didn't even leave a shadow. Her own hand was strangely translucent. She tried not to think about it.

Sierra tucked her knees under her chin. Her hair blew in the breeze. "There is talk the king has lost his mind," Sierra said. "That the burden of casting the city in the sky was too much for him. He's killed the advisors that try to tell him how to return." Sierra met Ember's gaze. "They disappear, anyway. He's afraid, I think. He's afraid of his brother."

"His brother is dead," Ember answered.

"But if you're correct, his widow is quite alive and willing to fight."

"More than willing." Ember frowned. Far below a flock of birds flew across the sky. It was still winter. They flew south, she guessed. Or maybe they just flew for fun.

"He is the key. We have to get the queen to let us see him."

"Tell me about the queen," Ember asked, but it wasn't what was on her mind. She wanted to know how her sister felt after all these years. How hard it was. How she'd survived being so invisible. And she wanted to say she was sorry, so very sorry, but perhaps such things were felt and not said.

"The queen is…" Sierra looked off over the land they drifted over. How many times, Ember wondered, had she looked up and not seen what was right there? "Sad," she finished. "She is the heart of this city. She holds court and sees people. She goes out, sometimes, in town, but alone. The rumors of the king's illness spread, but it's risky to talk of. They say he has spies…"

"He does have spies." A voice cut through the brush on their left. Ember scrambled up, but she wasn't sure why. It wasn't like anyone could see them. Except this person. Before them stood the queen. Her blonde hair was down, and she picked a leaf out. She wore a long, white dress with sleeves. Her smile was stretched thin and there was something sad about her eyes. "You should take caution," she said. "Although, I'm not sure how much more cautious you could be. Being invisible and all."

Ember let out a breath. Whatever threat she believed this queen carried, she disarmed them with a smile. It wasn't hard to tell, though, that beneath that smile there was sadness. Danger.

Sierra curtseyed. "Your Highness," she said. The queen laughed. She sat on the tall grass and looked over the world below.

"I think we're beyond such formalities, don't you?" She patted the ground next to her. "It's beyond time we spoke. I've seen you for so long." She eyed Sierra, "but my husband is, as you say, ill. He is terrified of returning Atlantis to the ground. To the point he has lost his mind. He has spies. He follows me. I do not know if he can see you, but I'd not risk it unless I had to."

Sierra swallowed. "I think he is the key."

The queen frowned. "Woe to us if he is," she said softly. She ran her hand over the grass. What Ember wouldn't give to feel the soft dew on her palm. "Tell me your story," she said. She turned to look over her shoulder. "But make it fast. I have dodged the guards, they think I am in the baths, but they will not leave me for long."

Sierra began. She told the story of an accident in her world that made Ember think she knew more than she let on. She told her how she woke up here, and Ember continued with the story of Maryse, and the curse, and how they planned to stop Maryse from killing all the patients in her hospital. "If she returns Atlantis now," Ember finished, "she's going to attack you, and hard."

"Just as my husband feared," the queen said. "He has run from a confrontation with his brother for centuries, and now his widow. After that, he will run from something else. No, I think the world may never be ready to welcome us home. To welcome magic. But we are who we are. We belong as much as they do. Perhaps we must fight for it. Perhaps, we just have to believe we belong."

She stood. "I thank you, and I am sorry for all those years you wandered Atlantis alone." She tipped her head to Sierra, who somehow managed to blush. "I think I was as afraid as the king, in my own ways.

I will connect you with him, but it will not be easy."

"Nothing has been easy," Ember gave a quick smile,

thinking of how long ago Shep had blown into her store. Shep. She prayed he was safe. The queen tipped her head and watched Ember, as if reading her mind.

"You have had great courage," she said. Now it was Ember's turn to blush if she had a body with which to do it. "I am sorry about your parents. We have asked such sacrifices for the cause of magic. And of the most innocent." She held her hand out to Ember's cheek, and somehow, she felt the woman's touch. It felt like her mother's – warm and caring. Behind them, the brush crackled, but the queen didn't appear startled, even when a guard showed up behind her. His breast plate caught the fading light, and a red cloak was draped behind him.

"They seek you, your Highness." He bowed his head, but before he did Ember caught a look of longing in his eye as he spoke to the queen.

"As expected," she responded. "You have laid the plans?"

"Indeed, they are done." He looked over the edge of the island warily, but he looked right past Ember and Sierra. The queen only smiled.

"I thought our time might be short, but not quite so short. I apologize. I have laid plans for the guards to go to the taverns. It should free up the castle to sneak in."

"Your Highness?" The guard raised an eyebrow. He had a weathered face and a long beard, but for all that his expression was soft.

She turned back and returned his gaze. "You will understand in time," she told him. "Right now, we must get to the king."

"The king!" He blanched and put a hand on the hilt of his sword. "It's too dangerous."

"It's time to trust in Atlantis, Javiar." She looked as if she were going to touch him the same way she'd touched Ember, but she dropped her hand. Ember felt a wave of fondness for the queen. She was everything Maryse was not. Warm and welcoming. Love incarnate. How had she survived being trapped?

Javiar grinned. "Trust is one thing, your Highness, but safety is another."

"Come with us, if you will," She pushed past him, but there was no malice in her voice.

"Us?" Javiar looked past Ember again, and the queen called from ahead where she'd already started walking.

"It will become clear," she said. "But we must hurry."

She wasn't kidding. She cut through the brush, taking them so precariously close to the edge Ember felt a wave of vertigo. Sierra only shrugged, placing one delicate foot in front of the other. Ember was not so delicate. She climbed and clawed, thankful the pickers couldn't get to her.   "Where are we going?" she asked in a loud whisper. It was impossible to tell where they even were on the island. The scenery below had chanced to clouds, and the sun dimmed as if they floated into twilight.

Sierra looked up. "The back of the castle abuts the edge. I didn't think there was a way there, but..." The queen had stopped. There was a gated drain that pooled water outside the walls of the castle. High walls. With no windows. If given a choice between a gated tunnel and a steep climb over slippery rocks, both were impossible. She would have said so, but the queen gave them no time.

"Help me," she said to Javiar. They'd clearly done this before. He helped her push the gate in. The bottom of her dress caught the water and made a mess, it would pull her down if it had the chance. They made enough room to just sneak by.

Sierra marveled. "I am not able to enter the castle," she told the queen. "Not by any other way."

"Take my hand," the queen said. She held the bars of the tunnel in one hand and Sierra's hand in the other and helped Sierra over the threshold. When she walked past, Sierra's form shivered, and Javiar gasped.

"You can see me?" Sierra asked, and indeed, she'd lost the otherworldly quality she had. Her hair was messed. Her skin wet.

Ember took the queen's hand and stepped in, feeling the same rush. "Sierra, we're real," she said. The first thing she did was pull her sister in for a hug. The tunnel smelled like mold and the light was low. But it didn't matter. Sierra was whole.

"It is a short walk past the prison cells. They are… unpleasant," the queen noted. Javiar had gone up ahead. He found a torch and lit it, but the torch produced precious little light. It was as if the tunnel sucked the light right out.

"Perhaps it is time to let the prisoners free?" Sierra said with a twinkle in her eye. She winked at Ember and for the first time, she thought they just might get out of there alive.

Chapter 42

The tunnel was dark and scary, and now Ember could feel things that she hadn't when her body was less real. Things like slime on the walls, or something squishy in the two inches of water they slogged through. She inhaled sharply, but it wouldn't help to ask what it was. No answer would have made her feel better.

How long, though, was a question on the tip of her tongue when she noticed they were walking on an incline and finally, blessedly out of the water. There were lights at the end. Javiar doused his torch.

"We'll have to be more careful here. They don't guard often, but if they do…" He trailed off. *If they do, they were screwed*, she thought. Sierra grabbed her elbow.

"An adventure, just like we pretended as kids," Sierra whispered. The cool stone walls seemed to hear her. If they wanted to mock her, they didn't dare. Sierra's voice had always held weight.

"Not exactly," Ember answered, but they'd pretended a lot in those days. Adventure. Pirates. Romance.

They'd lived out their mother's stories. Ember had missed them so much. She clung tighter to Sierra.

"Remember Captain Hottie?" Sierra giggled, and Ember had to suppress a laugh. She could always bring lightness in a situation. "Is he anything like your Captain Hawk?" she whispered.

Captain Hottie had been the fictional captain they'd fought over. Sierra, being oldest, usually ended up with him. Ember cocked her head. "Sort of," she teased. Javiar turned around and shushed her. Ember realized they were close to the cells.

If she'd thought it was bad at the facility, these were so much worse. The queen had stopped at one. The cell was built into the stone, with iron bars. Ember saw a tear on the corner of the queen's eye. The person in the cell lay flat on a stone floor in a puddle. He was breathing, but just. Wearing only a rag and in his own filth.

"They were his advisors," she explained. "When they say something he doesn't like, he turns on them." She turned her back to the cell. "The king is an evil man, fueled with fear. I have tried to temper him, but…" She exchanged a glance with Javiar. "I can only do so much." She turned back to the cell. "I am so very sorry, Ryland."

There was rustling in some of the other cells. Soft, as if the people inside them could barely move. No wonder they barely patrolled down there, it was a morgue and not a prison. "We should let them out," Sierra said. "Break their locks."

The queen shook her head. "And then what? We don't have the power to stand up to the king. Not yet. Balance must be restored."

Sierra approached her quietly. "But they should be given a chance. Please."

The queen let a tear slide down her cheek. "And if it is worse?"

"Can it be?" Sierra pressed. "We will simply have to convince him," she said. "If we return Atlantis first, it will stop Maryse's plan." She turned and grinned at Ember.

"*That's* your plan?" she asked. "Beat her to it?"

"It's a work in progress," Sierra answered. "The element of surprise."

Javiar cut in. He pressed his hands onto the walls so hard they turned white. The other hand held the hilt of his sword, though what he'd fight here she didn't know. Only the smell of despair and waste, and that was not something you could slay with a sword. "Only the guards have keys to these cells," he said. "It's impossible."

At this, Sierra smiled. "Is this not an island filled with magic?" she asked. Her eyes shone in a way that was impossible in such a place. They reflected hope. The prisoners in the closest cells stirred.

"Magic has been tried..." Javiar argued, but the queen held up a hand to silence him.

"Not ours." Sierra smiled as she looked at Ember. "You did say we were waking people up, right? Let's wake them up."

Ember felt the thrum of magic in her veins. It was just as thrilling as the first time she felt it back in the bookstore with Shep's guidance. She'd do this for him, for all of them. So she could return, so they all could return. She flexed her fingers. Made a fist. "How?" she asked, but the how was so easy. It always had been. Sierra laughed. She took both of her sister's hands and looked in her eyes.

"I have no idea," she smiled, "but I think you do."

Ember had never been a leader. She'd had teachers that had made half-hearted comments about her skill. She'd been called bossy, but knowing what to do and telling someone? She shied away from it. There was too much on the line to shy away from now. She felt the prison cells drift away so it was only her and her sister in a little bubble.

"You have to concentrate hard." She squeezed Sierra's hands. "It's easy to get out of control, and that?" She looked up and around. She'd not want a fire or tornado here. "That would be a disaster."

"Okay." Sierra blew a long bang out of her face. "Lesson one, control. Got it."

Ember closed her eyes and felt the magic build in her heart. "Feel it inside you. See it. Frame it. Picture the locks breaking. Picture Atlantis on the ground. You—home."

She'd said the last words before she could stop herself. This wasn't the magic she'd come here to do – not now, but it was too late. The magic had taken shape around them, swirling like dust and pixies. When she opened her eyes, they were in another place entirely. The cells were so far away, and it was just her and Sierra.

"We've done it!" Sierra said. They heard the sound of the locks breaking, the prisoners slowly leaving their cells, but the roar got louder and louder and louder, overpowering their senses as if magic had finally been released and taken over everything. She lost control again. She'd known it, but it had been building for a long time. She felt the spirit of Draco and Shep and all her friends. She released them.

"We've done something," she said. As the roar retreated, she saw what they'd done. The doors were blown off the cells. The prisoners who were able gaped at the doors. The queen herself had her hand on her heart and tears in her eyes. Dirt and smoke swirled in the air. And they were surrounded by the king's soldiers.

Sierra took her hand. She'd forgotten her sister was there. Ember herself was crying, and she didn't know why. Something was released. Something inside her, or something inside Atlantis. The ground under their feet shook.

"It was worth it," Sierra said. They were grabbed roughly by the guards.

"You're coming with us," one said briskly, but there was a note of admiration in his voice. The guard that held Ember was barely older than her, with the whisp of a mustache and the curl of a smile on his lips.

"What's happened?" Ember asked.

"Damned if I know," he said as the others rounded up her friends. They'd abandoned the doors. There was far too much damage to put them back into place. "But it's more excitement than we've seen here in some time. Is it true..." He searched Ember's eyes. She saw the familiar gold ring around his irises, which were gray-green. He swallowed. "Is it true you're going to bring us home?" His voice cracked.

"We're going to try," she promised, but she realized the only way to get herself home might be to go with the whole island.

Chapter 43

The castle was in chaos as a result of the magic they'd unleashed. Still, the guards moved them swiftly – their red cloaks a stark contrast to the dark levels they traversed. Without a torch, the whole place would have been in darkness. Ember shivered.

"How could he do this?" she asked. The parallels to the facility at home were stark, though at least that place was well taken care of.

The guard bit his bottom lip. "We had no choice, or we'd have ended up here too. And the spot for guards who defy the king is even worse than this."

Ember watched the back of the queen. She held her head high as she led them, but there was no doubt their group had become prisoners as well. The other guards weren't as kind as hers. The man in charge of Sierra, a heavyset older man, pulled her along and leered at her. He was threatened, perhaps, and why not? They'd just blown the doors off all the prisons. Magic that hadn't been seen here in a long time if the queen was to be believed.

As they walked up a stone staircase the area became lighter, and windows let in a breeze Ember drank up. She could see the darkening skies beyond, and in the cells, shouts of confusion.

"Hurry up," the closest guard called. At the end of the stairs there was a door closed and locked. Iron, she noted. Immune to Sierra's magic, or perhaps it hadn't reached this far. There was still so much she didn't know. She reached out to touch it, but her guard tapped her hand gently.

"I wouldn't," he said, eyeing the other guards. She let it rest. Past the door was the castle proper. They emerged into a dark, guarded room—the guards standing at attention at the sight of the queen—into a gathering hall with tables and the leftovers of food the likes of which Ember hadn't seen in some time. Her stomach rumbled, but she was in no mood to eat, though her guard did swipe an apple and put it in his cloak.

"For later." He winked at Ember, offering it to her. She shook her head, but thought she might have an ally in this boy, and she sorely needed allies.

They wound through the castle, chatter and questions following them, then up the turret farther than she thought they could go. The stairs were polished marble, the curtains rich reds and golds. Everything spoke of perfection and royalty, but under the surface Ember felt the currant of fear.

"How long has it been that the king has been shut in?" she asked. The guard blanched.

"We do not talk of such things," he answered carefully.

"We do now," she answered. She turned her eye on the broad door at the top of the stairs. The queen turned a handle. "I am not afraid."

The guard cleared his throat. "You should be," he whispered. "I have seen the king do things to those who don't agree. Terrible things."

She turned and saw her reflection in his eyes. Sadness and fear, but was there, indeed hope? "Someone you loved?" she asked.

"Someone I loved very much," he answered, looking away. She pulled from his grasp and patted his arm.

"Stay here. I will enter with the queen," she told him, but though the other guards hung back, he followed Ember and Sierra into a large, circular room. It was at the top of the turret, the feeling of height pressing. A round table took up most of the middle, with a perfect model of Atlantis on it, down to little people walking the streets. The castle even opened. A fire roared at the far end of the room, making it hot and stuffy. Ember pulled for breath. The curtains were drawn but the wind blew them like a breath that desperately wanted to get in.

"Your Highness?" The queen paused by the fireplace. Ember hadn't noticed him. His back was to them in a high-backed chair, and he was much smaller in stature than she'd imagined. He could be mistaken for a boy, even with the patchy brown and gray beard. When he tipped his head up, his eyes were red rimmed.

"What has happened to my city?" he asked. The queen knelt by his side.

"We have lingered too long in the heavens when we are needed below. It's time, Corin." Ember could hear the hesitancy in her breath. She wondered if they'd all be thrown down in those cells, but no. It was too late now. She could hear outside his window the sounds of the city waking up. Taking its first breaths. Celebrating.

"But my brother?"

The queen took his hand. It was a gentle gesture. "He is long dead, your Highness, but his widow lives. As for that, there will always be enemies. It is the time to stop running away and fight them."

He ran a hand over his face, a gesture that seemed to age him many years. How long he'd lived with this burden. Trying to protect his people but damning them at the same time. Ember would have had more empathy if it weren't for the cells she'd just seen.

"You can't just run away!" She tried not to yell but her voice wavered. "People are suffering!"

The king met her eyes. His reflected nothing but sadness. Not even the ring she'd come to associate with magic, and she realized the king's only magic was in the power he wielded. Interesting.

"It is easy to judge from there, I suppose." He said it without malice. "But when you are responsible for lives, the lines gray, child. Morality fades. You will do all you can to protect them."

At this, Sierra stepped forward. She seemed to carry her own light. Perhaps because she was insignificant here for so long. "They no longer need your protection," she said. Her voice carried weight, as if there were magic in the words themselves. She dipped her head and curtsied. Her hair caught the breeze and rustled off her shoulder. "Free them, your Highness."

"I don't know how," he admitted. Outside, the roar of a dragon caught the wind. Ember had felt his presence building. The walls around Atlantis were falling. She met Sierra's eyes and smiled.

"I think we can help you with that," Sierra said.

Ember leaned in. "Are you sure you know what you're doing?" she asked.

Sierra shook her head. "No," she answered with a smile. "You?"

"Not at all," she admitted, but she felt the pull of the land below. Whatever Maryse was doing, it was starting. The ground under them shook.

"Chairs, around the table," Sierra instructed. "We need your strongest magic. We're not going to block her magic, we're going to mirror it. It should reflect back and break the spell she has on everyone down below. Hurry now…" She dragged a high-backed chair to the table where they'd be looking over the miniature of Atlantis. A shadow had fallen over it.

"Sierra…" Ember started. Javier had begun pulling chairs, but there were only a few of them. The table was so big, they'd barely be able to see each other much less pool magic.

"I have an idea," Ember said. "I need you." She turned to the king. "We need everyone in the city. You'll need to address them."

He blanched. "I can't."

The queen touched his shoulder gently. "You have to. It's time." He fell into his chair.

"And say what?" he asked, looking up with red rimmed eyes. "That I've failed them, for so long? That I was so afraid of facing my brother I kept us in the sky though I knew lifetimes ago it was time. That I let magic and evil brew on the surface without our help and guidance. That I let my city… wither." His voice cracked on the last word and a tear fell down his cheek. Ember stepped forward. Her sister might know magic, but she knew empathy.

"You tell them that's all over." She knelt by the king's side. He'd done terrible things – she'd seen the result of them in the dungeon, but she did not yet think his heart was black. Whether it was worth saving, well, that was up to him. "You tell them we need their magic and their hope. You tell them to set their sights on home, and with all of us together…" She looked at Sierra, who nodded. "With all of us together, we can set things right. But you, your Highness, you must make that call. You must right the city. *You* must turn us around."

He met her eyes. His were light blue and cloudy as if he'd lived more years than anyone else here in Atlantis. As if this burden had aged him. As if he had regrets. "I have done terrible things," he said.

Ember closed her eyes and opened them. Forgiveness was not something she was good at, but perhaps they all had battles to fight before this was over. "I cannot offer you absolution," she said, "but I can offer you a way forward." She stood and offered her hand. The struggle played out on his face, and it was everything she could do to wait him out. She bounced on her heels, feeling Maryse's pull even now.

He stood, brushed the cloak off his shoulders. "I shall need my crown," he said. Javier offered it to him. "Assemble my people. I shall address them one last time." He made eye contact with Ember. She had guessed what he'd known. The return of Atlantis would demand a sacrifice, but what would it be?

Chapter 44

Ember bit her thumbnail down to the quick as the guards scrambled to assemble the city. The whole castle had been ready – holding their breath until the king got his shit together. They'd been holding their breath a long time.

"What do you think he meant, one last time?" Ember asked. She could feel Draco close by, but he couldn't breach the perimeter of the city.

"One time in the air before they return home?" Sierra guessed. She'd always loved her sister's persistent optimism, though at times it could be trying.

"Or?" she asked

"Or nothing, Ember. I understand why you worry for the worst but try to look at what could happen instead. Atlantis could return today!"

She held her sister's hand, felt its warmth. Good had already happened this day, she knew, but she worried about her friends on the ground. Her own self. Was she in two places at once? She asked the queen how that magic worked, and the queen only touched her face.

"Once you are real here, you're here," she answered in a cryptic way. Ember only hoped that meant her body wasn't being experimented on below. Or her friends.

"How long is this going to take?" she asked, but then a group of guards came in. They escorted the king, who'd cleaned up. In his crown and cloak, he looked like a leader. It was only when you looked at his eyes you saw the worry there. The questions. Ember thought her eyes probably looked the same, but she didn't have to address a whole city.

"Tell them it will be okay," she offered, a wholly unuseful suggestion.

"Tell them they're needed at home," Sierra offered, but it was the queen who silenced the room in her approach. They were in a waiting room. The curtains were pulled over the balcony, but they heard the expectant hum of the crowd. It spoke of both hope and fear. They needed their king.

"Tell them it is up to them to return Atlantis. If they so choose, they can direct their magic to break the bonds. We can amplify it..." Her gaze flitted to Ember. "But they've always had that power."

"They've always had that power? Are you kidding?" Ember asked, but the queen continued as if she hadn't spoken.

She took the king's hands and looked in his eyes. There was so much unspoken there. Resentment. Love. "Tell them it's time, and it has been for a long time. That there is fear and love and heartbreak in the world, and they need to be home as much as home needs them. Magic is again needed in the world. The magic of love." She kissed him gently on the cheek and he let out a sigh.

"I will try, my Queen, but so much has passed…"

"Let it pass," she said. "Water only flows downstream, not up. Leave the past as it is, my king. Take us home."

She had also dressed for the occasion, with a matching red cloak, a jeweled crown sitting on her braided hair. The red brought out shades of yellow Ember hadn't seen, but it was her poise and countenance that marked her as leader. Ember chewed on her fingernail. "We use magic to break the spell?" she asked Sierra. "And stop Maryse from draining everyone down there? Free them? Then what?" she asked. She hadn't thought much farther. It wasn't like she was returning to the bookstore. Maybe Hawk had a place on his ship for her?

"Then I'd like a steak and cheese," Sierra laughed. "I've been so hungry!"

She couldn't help smiling. Sierra had that power over people. To lighten their load. To make them a little happier than she left them. To look on the bright side. That was her real magic. And Ember grounded her. "Deal," she agreed.

The wave of guards parted. Javier had a cautiously expectant look on his face. How much had he seen of this king, she wondered. He'd sent people to the dungeon for just mentioning this – and worse. He'd lost their trust, and maybe their hearts. Could he get them back? Was there a way for the city to forgive? Could she?

Draco roared louder. The dragon wanted in, and she wanted to let him. "Not yet," she said silently, then added, "almost. Send us your magic Draco. Break the binds."

At the same moment the king and queen stepped through the curtains to the balcony. The guards followed, and Ember and Sierra snuck out. It was a beautiful sight –

all the Atlantians gathering under the late sun. Ember felt their apprehension. Their hope. Their fear. It was an overwhelming wave, and she stepped back into Sierra, who braced her. A low murmur grew. The king held up his hand to quiet it.

"It has been many years since I have addressed you," he admitted. He ran a hand over his beard. His voice echoed over the crowd. "Too many. For that, I am sorry. I am sorry for a lot of things, the length of which would take up most of the day. I have failed you, but it's not too late. We have the power within us to return Atlantis to the ground. Today." As the chatter grew, he turned and took the queen's hand.

Her eyes filled with tears, briming with the same mix of emotions: happy, sad, fearful, excited. "Now," she told him. The ground under them shook. He turned back to the crowd.

"The magic that holds us back is strong, but we are stronger. Unleash it now. Use your magic to send us back to the ground and we shall restore balance to the world. We shall return home."

The murmurs grew in intensity. The king fell back. Javier caught him under the arms, but the crowd didn't seem to notice. Their magic grew. Ember felt it just as much as their emotions. It was magic built on love. It would steer the island the right way, but the king had grown pale and ashen. Javier pulled him back into his sitting room.

"What's wrong with him?" Ember asked. They lay him across a couch. The queen knelt by his side. Javier leaned in.

"He's dying," he said.

"Dying?" Ember asked, but Sierra didn't look surprised. "You knew?"

"I suspected." They spoke in hushed tones. "The reason the king wanted to stay in the sky wasn't just fear. I felt it, but I didn't know why."

The queen got up from the king's side. His breathing was labored. "Give him a moment before you pool your magic," she asked. "You are the ones who will tip the scales and bring us home, just…" She turned to look at the king. "One more moment."

"He's been cursed," Ember guessed. The queen nodded.

"That he would never set foot on the ground again. He would die before he did. Here, in the skies, the king was safe. He thought it protected his people also, but it's complicated. He is willing to make this sacrifice now, but…" she wrung her hands.

"Go to him," Sierra nudged.

The queen nodded. They offered her space. The mix of sad and excitement in the air played in Ember's head. She felt Draco pushing. Her friends below pulling. And she – in the middle. Her magic itching to get out.

The king drew his last breath. He died with sadness. He died with regrets. They lay heavy in the air. But he died doing the right thing. He died forgiven for his sins.

The queen rose, wiped the tears from her face and took Javier's hand. "We should join the people," she said, her voice only slightly cracking. She'd loved him in her way, Ember guessed. Perhaps love was even more complicated than she thought.

Draco roared so close the city could hear, and they let out a cheer, but he was not close enough. For that, they'd need all of them. Instead of turning to the balcony, the queen crossed the room to the stairs. Ember, Sierra & Javier followed. She shed her crown. She shed her long cloak. She was only a woman in a white dress, but she was so much more than that. She was the one that held the city together. That carried the hope of all of them. When that hope was let loose – that's when they'd return. Ember wiped a tear off her cheek.

"It was never about us at all," she said, taking the turning staircase one by one following Sierra. Sierra looked back with a smile.

"Everything is so intertwined. Who's to say who caused anything? Just a flick of a butterfly's wings can change the course of history." She squeezed Ember's hand as they reached the landing. The great hall spread out before them, and outside its doors – Atlantis.

Ember had heard that before. The butterfly effect. How one tiny thing could change the path of the whole world. She'd doubted it until she realized all the little things that had gotten them there.

"What do you think dad would say?" she asked softly. The queen paused at the doors.

"He who hesitates is lost." Sierra smiled and walked past the queen to pull the doors open.

Magic, in Ember's experience, wasn't something you could see, but something you could feel. She'd felt it inside of her, from that first moment Shep had called it forth, and maybe even before. She felt it in her attachment to Draco. She felt it now, but so much more powerful, and she could see it. A swirling cloud of mist. Pure intentions. Love. It was enough to almost bring her to her knees.

"They want to go home," Javier said. His sword was sheathed beside him and all but forgotten. He placed a hand on the queen's back.

"Let us help them," she said, and raised her palms to the sky.

Ember remembered the feeling of calling forth magic from your very soul. It was the essence of the king that drove them on. She felt the love of Sierra. Of Shep. Of her friends on the ship. Even that of the people of Atlantis. It mingled and pulled, like an elevator slowly falling. Draco circled closer and closer, but Ember's eyes were closed. She felt with her heart. She reached for the ground. She held those around her in her heart. And she breathed. She breathed them right home.

Chapter 45

For a moment, Ember was in that in-between plane where she'd stepped through the portal. She didn't open her eyes, but she felt a cool breeze and the flickering of stars. Time and space spread out. She could choose any path she wanted. She sat on a bench outside her old store. It was real, and it wasn't. A figure sat next to her. Ember kept her eyes squeezed closed, afraid that seeing would ruin the dream. She felt an arm around her. Her dad's old cologne. Her mom put a hand on her knee on the other side. She projected that last painting, and Ember saw that she had closed the circle.

"Proud of you, kiddo," her dad said. She rested her head on her dad's shoulder as her mom patted her knee.

"I knew you could do it," her mom said.

Ember hiccupped as she laughed. She opened her eyes. The bench was there but the sky was the astral plane, darkness and stars and planets dancing in the sky, beckoning her back. She sighed and looked at each one.

"I'm sorry I wasn't there, I'm sorry…"

Her mom put a finger to her lips. "You did amazing," She tipped Ember's head down and kissed her forehead. "You have nothing to be sorry for. It was our time, but it's not yours. Go." She tipped Ember's head up, and Ember saw the amber of her mom's eyes. The curl of her lip as she smiled. Her dimple. Her parents had had magic too. The world might call it ordinary, but it was the most amazing thing in the universe. Love. She embraced her mother.

"Thank you," was all she could think of to say. Her father embraced them from behind, and they stayed there like a little cocoon for as long as time and space would allow, which wasn't long enough but was also forever.

"We'll see you again someday," her mom said.

"Yes," her dad added, "you won't believe the parties they have here," he laughed, and she felt herself pulled.

"I love you," she called, and they didn't reply but she felt it from ahead and she felt it from behind. For the first time in her life, Ember felt surrounded by it. She could let go if she wanted. Stay here. But her parents were right, it wasn't her time. "Enjoy the parties," she said with a smile, and she began her journey back home.

When she opened her eyes, they were almost home. Draco circled the square, landing in the opening in front of them. He'd grown, already. Ember felt awe, but no one there was afraid of him. Indeed, she felt more dragons in the distance. She dipped her head and felt Draco's fur as the queen looked on with wide eyes.

The city landed not with a jolt but with a soft sigh, as if the very world was embracing their return. Ember felt it not just in her body, but in her heart. She was home.

She met Sierra's eyes. "Go," Sierra said, but Ember pulled her along.

"Come with me." She laughed and they made their way through the crowd. There were cheers and jubilation, but there was also fear. What would happen now? Who would lead them?

Ember wound her way to where the front gates would be, and for once, they were open. A crowd had gathered there. Ember knew right away when she saw the ocean to her left, the island on the far shore. The facility her sister was in directly in her sight, and people. So many people. They'd just woken up, but they knew. They took slow steps toward the city.

"Is it true?" one said. Ember wondered if they'd all been sleepwalking like Sierra. Ember embraced the woman.

"It's true," she said, but she looked over her head. "What happened here?" she asked. Draco took flight and circled the facility.

The woman shook her head. "I just know we were in pain, and then we woke up." She looked back. "There is a fire." Ember saw the stream of smoke building in the distance. *Shep.*

She and Sierra began to run, pushing their way past an ever-growing crowd. How many had Maryse had? Hundreds. But none of them were her friends, and the smoke began to grow, picking up speed from the wind on the ocean.

Draco, do you see them? She asked, but the dragon only roared. The facility was so close but so far. She'd barely made it halfway when she saw three figures come out, and she stumbled. Sierra righted her.

"Is that your Shep?" she whispered. "He's cute."

Ember smiled. She could see from here, it was, indeed, her Shep, but he was carrying something. She rose and ran to them.

She met Paine first, dirt covered. The girl hugged her fiercely. "We fought her Ember, we fought her so hard. We bought you time, and you did it." Ember pulled back and saw the signs of strain on her friend's face.

"Thank you," was all she could manage.

Hawk reached them next, hugging Ember and then introducing himself to her sister. "I've heard so much about you." He raised her hand to his lips, and she giggled.

"Your pirate?" she asked. Ember nodded but she was already walking to Shep. He had bags under his eyes. They were red, and his skin pale. He carried the body of Maryse in his arms, weak and limp but still breathing. He placed her down.

"I could not let her burn," Shep said, "though it is what she deserved." He ran a hand over his chin. "All those people…" He focused back on her and a smile came across his tired features. "You've done it," he said.

"We," she corrected, finding herself in his arms. "Paine said you bought us time." Her voice was muffled in his shirt. His scent took over her senses.

"It was… difficult." He measured his words, held her tighter. "But it brought us here."

She looked over her shoulder at Maryse's body. Atlantis in the distance. The queen. Her dragon circling. So many people. In the distance helicopters began to arrive.

"What now?" Shep wondered. He kept his arm around her as they looked at the city, glistening and sparkling in the sunlight.

"I have no idea," she admitted, but her feet started taking her back to Atlantis. Already the people from the facility were being welcomed, but the people of the city itself? Well, she wondered about that. "They'll need help," she said.

He kissed the top of her head. "They will," he agreed. Sierra took her hand. "We'll help them," she said.

She wasn't sure how, but it would be another chapter, another adventure.

CHECK OUT THESE OTHER GREAT READS
FROM ROWAN PROSE:

Amy Cip is an author, blogger, people watcher, sci-fi junkie, website novice, eternal optimist, and introvert. She is the author of seven YA science fiction/fantasy/dystopian books. She resides in Massachusetts. www.amycip.com